Eva's Revenge

Fighting for Justice: Book 1
Joe Smith

Cover Art
suzukishinji
https://www.patreon.com/suzukishinji
https://suzukishinji.deviantart.com
http://www.comicgirlfights.com

Copyright 2017 Joe Smith

This book is licensed for your personal enjoyment only. This book may not be sold or given away to other people. If you would like to share this book with another person, please purchase an additional copy for each recipient. If you're reading this book and did not purchase it, or it was not purchased for your use only, then please return to your favourite book retailer and purchase your own copy. Thank you for respecting the hard work of this author.

Chapter 1 – The Free Minds

In 1967 Guenther Schmidt is working as an astrophysicist at NASA. As a thirty-five-year-old he has achieved a lot and is climbing the corporate ladder fast and as head of the research department he has a lot of responsibilities. America is behind in the space race and the pressure to overtake the Soviet Union and to be first to set foot on the moon weighs heavy on everybody at NASA, including Guenther. He is no longer enjoying his job, as he is not keen on taking part in office politics, but in a highly competitive world nobody can survive without playing politics. Guenther hates himself every time he has to use politics to get his way. He has decided he no longer wants to work for a large organisation like NASA. He still has to discuss this with his wife Heidi though. They are living the American dream. They are both second-generation immigrants from Germany and they have good jobs. Heidi is one of only a few female theoretical physicists in the country. They are both paid good salaries and they make a comfortable living together. They don't have children as they have diagnosed Heidi with the Kallmann syndrome. Both wanted children, but accepted their fate and made sure they enjoy their lives together. For this purpose they save as much money as possible and use some of it to go on regular holidays in America and abroad. On a trip to Ecuador a year ago they took a wrong bus and ended up in a small town named Aloag. They had nowhere to sleep, but the friendly community were quick to help them, despite the language barrier. They agreed that they want to retire to a community like this one day.

Heidi is a beautiful twenty-eight-year-old woman with blonde hair and blue eyes. She does not allow her beauty to hide her brains though as she studied hard. In her view, this gives her as much right to work at the University of Houston as any of her male colleagues. Her field of research is deep space travel. This is a new field as most other researchers involved in space travel are still spending time on researching travel to the moon and Mars. Her colleagues view her and her field of research as novelties. Most of them cannot wait for her to fall pregnant so she can do what women are supposed to do, raise the kids and do housework. It is not natural for a woman to still work in her late twenties, especially not as a theoretical physicist. It is a man's job after all. To make things worse, Heidi plays field hockey for the university's first ladies team. She is by far the oldest member of the team as the rest of the players are all students. Her colleagues are of the view that this is inappropriate for a woman of her age. Young women competing in men's sports is bad enough, but a woman of her age should know better. Heidi is very unhappy at the office, but she does not share this with Guenther as she is determined to show that women can offer more than just taking care of their husbands and children.

One night during dinner Guenther brings up his unhappiness at work and to establish whether Heidi is open to a total shift in their careers and lifestyle. 'Do you remember our holiday in Israel last year?'

'Yes, off course. How can I ever forget it?'

'What did you think of the kibbutz on which we worked while we were there?'

'You know I loved it. I found a community working together and sharing the spoils of their hard work very rewarding. It also appeals to me that women are equal to men and that everyone shares the work.'

'I researched the hippie communities in San Francisco and their aim is to operate similar to the way a kibbutz does. For the past few months I have been toying thinking of leaving my job, but I want to carry on with research in space travel. We have enough money saved up to support ourselves for at least a year and I think we should join one of the hippie communities for about six months. We will both be able to get a job again if it does not work out.'

'You will easily find a job, but I will not find a job in my field again. My colleagues are hoping and praying that I should go away and I don't think they will ever allow a woman to invade their sacred little club again.'

This surprises Guenther as he always believed Heidi was enjoying her job. 'Are you also unhappy at the office?'

'Yes, I love my job, but not the circumstances I work in. The men hate it that a mere woman can compete with them.'

'Let's do it then, we should take this chance while we are still young enough. We will contribute to the community with physical labour and research space travel together to contribute to the future of humankind.'

Heidi thinks for a while. She might just enjoy her job again if she does not have to feel guilty for being a woman in a man's world. 'I am in for six months and then we reconsider.'

They spend about a month at the first hippie community which they joined, but the poor work ethic of the community members disappoins them. Most of them party all night and sleep all day. The parties are a mix of orgies, alcohol and drugs. The community funds itself by trading in drugs and some women dance at strip clubs or work at brothels when they need money. It disappoints Heidi that men see women as property they can use whenever they want to. After they leave this community, they join a second hippie community, but find much of the same, except for a group spending their time on political quests. They put all their energy into protesting against whatever perceived issue they come up with. In their minds, the government is always out to abuse its citizens and they are always the crusaders on a quest to save the masses who cannot think for themselves. Guenther and Heidi spend even less time at this community and decide to give one more community a chance before they write this idea off as school fees paid. The third community also disappoints them, as there is also a lack of any purpose other than sex, drugs and political ideologies. However, a group of eight women stands out. They speak a strange language and keep to themselves. Unlike the rest of the community, they are hard working and do not use drugs or alcohol.

One morning, while on his morning jog in a nearby forest, Guenther hears some excited female voices in the distance. It sounds like they are cheering someone on. As he gets closer, he hears the sounds of fists connecting with flesh. He slows down and moves towards these sounds until he can see the eight women in a clearing in the forest. Six of them are standing in a circle and cheering the other two on while they fight each other in the nude and with bear fists. Guenther has never seen women fight before and he is both fascinated and aroused by the sight of two naked women engaged in a vicious brawl. One woman soon dominates the fight and knocks the other down. Instead of using this advantage to finish the other woman off, she steps back and waits for her to get back to her feet. She asks her something in their language and the other woman nods. They both lift their fists and the fight starts again, this time lasting only about twenty seconds before the same woman is knocked down again. Once again the other woman steps back and waits for her opponent to get back to her feet. This time the woman shakes her head, and it is clear she had enough. They move towards each other and hug each other and the winner whispers something into the loser's ear before she kisses her forehead and her cheek. As the two women dress, two others undress. Guenther cannot believe he saw two naked women fight each other and that he is about to see another fight between two naked women. He watches this fight with interest. The women are closely matched, and the fight lasts for about ten minutes before one of them gets knocked down. She stays down for a while and one of the other women kneels next to her and chats with her before she motions to her opponent that the fight is over. The winner also kneels next to the loser for a few moments before she and the other woman help the loser to her feet. Once again the two fighters hug each other before they dress. After they dress, the eight women make their way back to the camp and Guenther waits a while before he jogs back.

Heidi is still sleeping when he returns to their tent just before six o'clock. Normally he would leave her to sleep longer, but he cannot wait to share this experience with her. She looks at him with eyes still half closed and a pissed off expression on her face. She has never been a morning person, and he learned long ago not to wake her without a good reason, but this is a good reason.

'You will never guess what I witnessed on my run this morning.'

'What?'

'You know the eight women with the strange language?'

'Yes.'

'They were fighting each other in the forest this morning.'

'Why? Are they not getting along? They always seem so close to each other.'

'No, it's not like that. These looked like organised fights. Two fought and the other's cheered them on. Afterwards they hugged each other. Then two more stripped down and fought each other and also hugged each other afterwards. They seemed to enjoy themselves. It was very interesting to watch."

'Did this excite you?' She did not have to ask this as she can see from the bulge in his pants that just talking about the female fight he saw, excites Guenther.

'Sorry, but yes it was very sexy to watch.'

Heidi smiles at Guenther and pulls him closer. Men are all the same. She overheard her ex-colleagues sharing their fantasies about women wrestling or catfighting each other enough times to know men get aroused by women fighting with one another. She knows Guenther well enough to understand that he needs to have sex so she leans over and kisses him on the lips. He grabs her head between his hands and kisses her back. While they kiss he removes his clothes before he pulls the shirt she sleeps in over her head. He is glad he does not have to waste time on underwear as Heidi never sleeps with any underwear on. He rushes through foreplay as he cannot wait too long before mounting her. His penis is rock hard when he slides it into her vagina and his thrusts are quick, deep and urgent. He ejaculates quickly but carries on pumping, trying to get her to orgasm. She soon realises that he will not last long enough, and she fakes her excitement and builds it up to a fake orgasm. Like most men, it will hurt his ego if he cannot bring her to orgasm and she does not want to hurt him. He rarely fails to get her off. ‚But if he is this excited he sometimes cannot last long enough to bring her to orgasm, especially if he has not warmed her up with foreplay.

Later in the morning Heidi and Guenther are working in the garden which they have started hoping the rest of the community will get involved with planting vegetables and maintaining the garden. They soon gave up on this hope as they realised that they were doing all the work while the rest, except for the eight women, shared in the fruits of their labour. The eight women have their own garden and their vegetables seem to be twice as big as the ones grown by Guenther and Heidi. Heidi stops removing weeds and walks to where Guenther is busy working on an irrigation system he designed.

'We should go over to the women tonight.'

'Why?'

'I want to get to know them better and I think you should come clean about watching their fights this morning.'

'I don't think it's a good idea. They will probably not like it if they find out I was watching them.'

'That gives you even more of a reason to apologise to them. If you do, there may be a nice surprise for you.'

She knows Guenther will find it difficult to ignore this promise of future fun and that night they make their way to the women's camp. They introduce themselves and Guenther explains what happened in the morning and apologises to them. One woman tells him they prefer to keep their fighting contests private and asks him to respect this. He promises not to share this with anybody else and the woman asks Guenther and Heidi to join them for a braai, which they soon find out is the Afrikaans word for a barbeque. The women are all from South Africa and grew up in conservative Afrikaner homes. They are lesbians and their families had rejected all of them due to their sexual orientation. They met each other during a lesbian get together on a farm outside Pretoria. This get together was supposed to be secret, but police swooped down on the farm and arrested most of the women on the farm, including all eight of them, for taking part in and/or watching a mud wrestling competition. Female wrestling and boxing were against the law in South Africa and they were all found guilty of transgressing the Boxing and Wrestling Act of 1954 and were fined. They had enough of the constant attack on their rights and moved to America to join a hippie community. However, what happens in this community disappoints them and their hope that a hippie community would accept them as lesbians were soon crushed. They found that the men here have a sense of entitlement to all women and they do not take kindly to women who are not willing to sleep with them whenever they have the urge to do so. They tell Guenther and Heidi that they are looking for other options. Hearing this, Guenther and Heidi shares with them that they are also looking for a community where all contribute and where women have equal rights to men. Their friendship grows stronger over the next few weeks and the women even invite Guenther and Heidi to watch a few of their arranged fights. Heidi can see why this excited Guenther so much. The thrill of the fight, combined with the beauty of the female body, excites her as well and this new experience injects some spice into their sex life. They soon decide that the ten of them should start a new community, one where the dreams they had about hippy living can become a reality. After many more discussions Heidi proposes that they visit Aloag in Ecuador again to investigate whether settling their community there is viable. Guenther, Heidi and two of the lesbians, fly to Ecuador and spend a week in Aloag. On their return they decide to start a community on a farm a few kilometres from Aloag. Everyone will contribute to it according to their ability and share in it according to their needs and everyone will have the right to make choices about their own life. Two weeks later they buy the farm and they start their commune. They call the community the Free Minds Community and they are careful to invite only people who they believe will fit in with the spirit and values of the community. Guenther drives a campaign to convince scientists to join the community as one of the key plans of the community is to one day move to another planet. They soon build up a great relationship with the local community and their hard work and willingness to help the locals ensure that they found themselves a home for decades.

Chapter 2 – A New Beginning

In the year 2077 scientists of the Free Minds Community, also referred to as the New Age Hippies, complete years of research and development of their version of the Alcubierre drive. In the 1990's a Mexican theoretical physicist, Miguel Alcubierre suggested that travel faster than the speed of light may be achieved by contracting space in front of the spacecraft and expanding space behind it. Although this theory was widely criticised, Guenther and Heidi saw potential in it and together with the rest of the scientists at the commune they worked on developing this theory. After eighty years of development, the community was at last ready to travel into deep space, their target the Canis Major Dwarf Galaxy, was now within reach. It took another seven years of preparation before forty-two spacecraft left earth on 4 October 2084 for humankind's first inter-galactic colonisation mission. On board were 4 197 men, women and children, building materials, plants and animals chosen for their high nutritional value, scientific equipment and the most important, atmospheric water generators. As per their wishes, the ashes of Guenther and Heidi were also on board. The destination was twin planets discovered, and kept secret, by the Free Minds Community. The atmosphere and temperatures on both planets were like that of earth. Water was also plentiful on both planets. They named these planets after the twin brother and sister in Greek mythology, Apollo and Artemis. Apollo moved not only the sun across the sky daily, but he was also the god of light and the god of truth. He also gave man the science of medicine. Artemis was the goddess of chastity, virginity, the hunt, the moon and the natural environment. There were a few who wanted to replace Artemis with Athena as she was the goddess of reason, intelligent activity, arts and literature. The women of the community associated more with these qualities, but as these are twin planets, they named them after the twin children of Zeus and Leto.

They were determined to start a new life away from other humans. A life where everyone would be free to pursue their own ideas and live out their own fantasies and desires. The only rules would be that they should harm no humans without consent. They could only give consent from the age of eighteen for decisions which could cause harm. Where a decision may cause serious harm or death., the age of consent would be twenty-one. Although this may seem extreme, the Free Minds Community believed each human should have full control over his or her own life. This belief extended to his or her own death if they so desired. On 21 July 2127, they sent advanced parties of 30 people each to the planets. Their mission was to build basic shelters and test the living conditions on the planets. Both parties confirmed that the atmospheres on the two planets were like that of earth and that humans could breathe the air. However, after about two weeks, all men on Artemis and all women of Apollo became ill. Years of research identified the viruses causing the illness, but they never found a cure. Artemis became home to women only and Apollo to men only. Marriage became something impractical and sex tours became the norm for both men and women. Short visits to Artemis for the men and to Apollo for the woman had no effect on them and they generally limited these visits to seven days, with at least a month break before the next visit.

One of the sex tour companies introduced oil wrestling matches between women to establish who had first choice of the available males. They soon broadcasted this on television on both planets and it proved to be extremely popular. Other shows with boxing, MMA and catfights followed. Some fights were for choice of male companionship, some for other prizes and some to settle arguments or grudges. A show called 'Catfight' relaxed their rules. They allowed women to fight with minimal rules, or even no rules. Soon, they arranged a fight with baseball bats. More followed and soon resulted in the first fatality in the fighting ring on live television.

After various court cases, the constitutional court ruled that every citizen over the age of eighteen may decide whether she wants to take part in fights with basic safety rules. It further ruled that any citizen over the age of twenty-one may decide whether she wants to take part in any fight, even if the fight may cause serious injury or death. Duels were no longer against the law as long as both women were of legal age and both agreed to it. The court also ruled that nobody could interfere with a duel and that only a fighter who is clearly winning a duel may stop the contest before one fighter are dead. The court introduced this rule to make sure that a third party does not influence the outcome of the duel. If they did, they could charge them with murder. Some women fought duels the old fashioned way with pistols or rapiers, but most preferred to settle their differences like the gladiatrices of old, some fighting with bladed weapons, others preferring to fight unarmed. The owners of the "Catfight" show used the media attention on the court ruling as cheap publicity to launch a new show called 'Duel'. Live death matches on television were a reality. Despite some protests, this show proved to be even more popular than "Catfight". They used a combination of unarmed and armed combat between women who agreed to duel. Although there were a few exceptions, they held their fights in a metal cage and they fought the first ten minutes without weapons. If both women were still alive after ten minutes, they made the weapons chosen by the fighters available to them. The fights continued until one combatant died. On the rare occasion a woman would spare the life of her beaten opponent. However, as women who challenged each other to a duel generally hated each other and as the crowd was always baying for blood, it almost guaranteed the death of a fighter. Although doctors were always next to the ring to treat the winner, they could not save a wounded victor.

Chapter 3 – The Death of a Mother

Megan Hajnal is a beautiful woman who turns the heads of both men and woman. She is intelligent and hard working and is climbing the corporate ladder fast. She is thirty-three and has a very busy eleven year old daughter, Eva who is doing well at school and also at various sports events she participates in. Megan's sister is her best friend and they do everything together. Eva also loves her aunt and she is like a second mother to her. Megan tells everybody that she won Eva in a wrestling tournament. This is kind of true as she and her sister went on a sex tour when she was twenty-one and her sister nineteen. They both entered an oil wrestling tournament for the right to have first choice of a lover for the week they were on Apollo. She had her eye on a tall guy with a magic smile and she knew that many of the women, including her sister, were interested in him as well. She fought hard and managed to beat woman after woman until she reached the final of the tournament. Her opponent in the final was her sister. They often wrestled each other and their matches were always hard fought and close. Both sisters were exhausted from their previous fights and their match started slowly as they were feeling each other out, trying to ensure that they did not run out of energy too soon. The final was a one round wrestling match to pin or submission and both knew that it may take a while to pin or submit each other with their thong bikini clad bodies covered in oil. The intensity picked up as their holds, pushes and grabs started to hurt each other. Megan's sister has always been a dirty little bitch during their fights and she ripped Megan's top off and mauled her breast. This was against the rules, but nobody was going to interfere as the fight was picking up speed and this sparked something between the sisters. Megan screamed out in pain and she tore into her sister. The oil wrestling match soon included slaps, punches and plenty of clawing, hair pulling and mauling. When Megan eventually trapped her sister's head between her thighs for a head scissor hold combined with hair pulling, her sister had to submit. They glared at each other for a while, but could not stay mad at each other and they soon got up and hugged it out. Megan won her price with a lot of blood, sweat and tears and she made full use of him. They spend the week pretty much making love the whole time and the result was Eva.

Megan's life is pretty good and it is about to get better. The vice-president of the company she works for called her in yesterday and informed her that she got the job as new branch manager. The two of them had a few flings in the past and they went out celebrating last night. Megan ended up making love to the vice-president until the early morning hours. She is tired from the lack of sleep and their marathon lovemaking session, but she is filled with euphoria. Partly from the joys of sex and partly because the announcement of her promotion will be made to the rest of the employees in a few minutes. They are all gathered in the large meeting room. The vice-president is talking about the positive growth of the company and their recent successes with big contracts being won. When she announces Megan's promotion, the rest of the employees applaud her for this achievement. However, Emily Theron jumps up and she does not look happy.

'You know I deserve this promotion. I have been here longer than you and my results are better than yours. The only thing you do better than me is to sleep with the right people.'
There is a murmur in the meeting room and Megan is shocked. She has not anticipated this outburst and she does not know how to react. The vice-president starts to say something, but Emily talks over her.
'I will not stand for this unfairness. I challenge you to a duel. I will kill you and I will get the promotion I deserve.'
Megan is put on the spot and she knows that she will lose face and a lot of respect if she does not accept the challenge. 'I accept your challenge.'

For a few days she hears nothing further from Emily and she starts to think that Emily was just bluffing or that she has changed her mind. But then she receives a call from the television show 'Duel' to confirm whether she accepted the challenge. She almost puts down the phone, but her pride makes it almost impossible for her to back down from this challenge. Reluctantly, she confirms that she is willing to fight Emily in a duel. The woman from the show informs her that the fight will be in two weeks time. The first ten minutes will be an unarmed fight and after that each of them will receive their weapon of choice as well as the opponent's weapon of choice. Having a choice between three weapons, Megan chooses a baseball bat. Her choice is limited as she is not sure whether she will be able to use a knife or motorcycle chain effectively. Over the next two weeks she spends as much time as possible with Eva to prepare her for the possibility that she may not survive the fight. She is confident that she has a good chance of beating Emily as she is athletic and has wrestled a lot in her life. She even had a few catfights against her sister. Emily does not participate in any sport and Megan is sure that she has never been in any fights in her life. But in a fight to the death anything can happen and she wants to make sure Eva is mentally prepared for the possibility that she may die during the fight. She knows that her sister would be a very good mother to Eva, should this be required. Eva will get over the initial shock and sadness of losing her mothe. Her sister will ensure that she has a happy live and that opportunities will be made available to her.

Megan's sister wants to go with her on the night of the fight, but Megan asks her to be with Eva and to ensure that Eva is fine should something happen to her. She is alone in her change room and has already stripped down to her thong as this is the maximum amount of clothing allowed on the show. She warms up and tries to focus her mind on the fight itself and not on the potential consequences of fighting in a death match. Megan takes a deep breath when she hears a knock on the door. She gets up and follows the assistant to the cage. She barely hears to loud applause as the studio audience first see her beautiful body appear on set. Her heart beats fast and her hands are moist with sweat. She waits as a woman unlocks the cage door and motions her to enter. She suddenly feels very alone and the reality of what she is about to do sets in and the focus on the fight suddenly makes way to a fear of death. She forces this from her mind and starts to go through her game plan again. She will stay on her feet for a while to gauge Emily's skills and to try and hurt her as much as possible with punches and kicks. When she thinks that Emily is weak enough, she will take her down and choke her to death. She does not want to take a chance with the weapons, so she wants to kill Emily before the ten minute mark. If not, she wants to be in full control of the fight at this stage to ensure that weapons do not come into play. Her attention is brought back to the present when she hears the host talk again.

'Ladies and gentlemen there is a slight change in plans. We just received word that Emily Theron has fallen ill and cannot fight Megan Hajnal tonight. However, her best friend has agreed to fight in her place to ensure that this grudge is settled and that you still get a fight tonight.'

Megan cannot believe this and her first reaction is to leave the cage, but the crowd is chanting 'Fight! Fight! Fight!' When the host asks her whether she accepts the new challenge, the word 'Yes' escapes her lips before she is able to stop it. Her pride has gotten the best of her. The studio audience erupts at this and Megan knows that there is no way to change her mind now. Her new opponent is announced and the cage door is locked. When the women face each other alone in the cage, Megan sees the scars of previous battles on the woman's face and upper body. The woman is about her size, but she is more muscular and looks a lot tougher than Megan. Megan fights the urge to run away and readies herself for the fight. When the bell is rung the woman moves in quickly and corners Megan, rocking her head back with a stiff left jab, followed by a straight right. Megan swings back wildly, but the woman avoids her punches and rocks her again with a left right combination. The fight has just begun and Megan's nose is already bleeding. She tries to get out of the corner, but her opponent catches her with another hard right to the side of her jaw and Megan stumbles to the ground. She regains her senses quickly and kicks out as the woman rushes in, connecting with her left thigh. The woman steps back and allows Megan space to get up. However, as she starts getting to her feet, the woman steps in and lands a hard kick to Megan's side. She quickly follows it up with another hard punch to the side of her jaw and Megan goes down again. This time the woman is quick enough to dive on top of her before she has time to defend herself. Megan is trapped under her opponent's weight and from full mount, the woman rains down punches and elbows to her face. Megan tries to stop the punches by blocking with her arms, but she is unable to block all of them and some hard strikes connect with her head and face. Blood is soon streaming down her face and she can barely see the punches coming her way anymore. Then, to Megan's surprise, the woman stops punching her and instead tries to roll her over. Megan wraps her arms around the woman's upper body and pulls herself up so that her face is pressed against the woman's breasts. This move was meant to get her head away from more punishment and to stop her opponent from turning her onto her stomach. However, she makes use of the opportunity and bites down hard on the woman's left breast. The woman screams and immediately retaliates by pushing her left thumb into Megan's right eye. Megan is shocked by this and releases the grip with her teeth on her opponent's breast and turns her head away. The woman is furious with the wounds on her breast and grabs Megan's shoulders and slams her upper body back onto the floor. Megan's head hits the floor hard and she loses consciousness for a few seconds. When she regains consciousness, the woman is choking her from behind. Megan grabs at her arms and tries to pull them away from her throat, but she is unable to pry the women's fingers away from her throat. In a frantic attempt to break the hold, Megan scratches the woman's arms and hands. She hears the woman cursing at her for this, but she does not release her hold. Soon Megan's arms start to feel heavy and they drop to the floor. Before her world goes completely dark, she suddenly feels very calm and she can see her daughter's face clearly in her mind before everything is gone.

Chapter 4 – The Promise

Eva's aunt is crying when she enters the room in which Eva is supposed to be sleeping. However, Eva is still wide awake as she couldn't fall asleep without knowing that her mother is ok. When she sees her aunt's face, Eva breaks down and cries uncontrollably. Her aunt stays with her the whole night and only tells her that her mother was killed during the fight. Eva only finds out about the change in opponents on the day of her mother's funeral when one of her friends tells her about it. Her aunt tries to protect her by not telling her the full truth. However, she soon comes clean as she can see that Eva will not give it a rest before she knows the whole truth. Upon getting confirmation that Emily Theron was replaced by a skilled fighter, Eva makes a promise to her mother that she will revenge her murder.

A week after the funeral, Eva's aunt lays charges of murder against the company who owns the show 'Duel'. She also gets a lawyer to sue them for wrongful death of her sister. She became aware that Emily was not only replaced by another fighter, but that this fighter was not a friend of hers, but a professional fighter. The prosecuting office declines to take her case to court as Megan has agreed on live television to fight the new opponent. They therefore do not believe that they have any chance of success with criminal charges. However, the judge in the civil case finds that the host of the show put undue pressure on Megan and that her consent was given under duress. The company is ordered to pay Eva a huge amount of money, which her aunt has to invest for her until she reaches the age of eighteen.

Eva's whole life changes after the death of her mother. Her aunt loves her almost as much as her mother did and she makes sure that Eva concentrates on her school work and that she still participates in sport. However, Eva's focus is on one thing only, to revenge her mother's murder. She spends a lot of time researching death matches through the ages and specifically modern day duels. Her aim is to face Emily Theron in a death match and she wants to kill her with her own hands. To achieve this she needs to improve her fighting skills, so she includes fighting academies in her research. She will only be able to join an academy when she turns eighteen. This will give her three years to train for a death match with Emily Theron.

When her aunt learns about Eva's plans to challenge Emily Theron to a duel, she tries to talk her out of it. After realising that she will not be able to convince Eva to change her mind, she takes her to various psychologists. However, none of them are able to change her mind either. Out of other options, she decides to give Eva time and to talk her out of fighting Emily Theron over time. Eva made a promise to her mother to revenge her murder and nobody and nothing will stop her from keeping this promise.

Chapter 5 – Interview

On her eighteenth birthday Eva visits the Combat Sport Academy for an interview. She did her research and is convinced that this academy will provide her with the best preparation to challenge and kill Emily Theron. . She wanted to join earlier, but this academy, unlike some others, strictly applies the rules and only interviews new girls when they've reach the legal age of eighteen. Eva ignored the temptation to join another academy earlier, as the Combat Sport Academy had a track record of producing top fighters. Eva nervously sits in the reception area, waiting to be called for her interview. Less than five percent of applicants are accepted by the Combat Sport Academy, so she goes over her strategy for the umpteenth time. She will show her commitment by sharing her story and her goals with them. For the next three years she will do whatever they expect from her. She will give it her all, her live depends on it. After she revenged her mother's murder, she will stay with the Combat Sport Academy for at least another three years to pay them back for training her. The clincher, she hopes, will be the fact that they don't have to pay her a salary during the entire period. The academies do not charge fees to their students. Instead, they make money from fighting sports events in which their students participate. The students are paid a small fee based on their skills, the number of events they participate in and the success of the teams they are part of. She will even pay her own medical bills and anything else they want her to pay. The money awarded to her by the court will hopefully guarantee her acceptance into the most prestigious fighting academy. A hand on her shoulder startles Eva and she spins around raising her left arm in defence. She did not hear the other woman approach her and she needs a few moments to compose herself slightly as her eyes focus on a tall woman with a bemused smile on her face. The woman is wearing training shorts and a sports bra only. Her muscular body is glistening with fresh sweat. It's Helga Brand. She knew she was meeting with Helga today, but the sight of the best fighting trainer around still makes her nervous.

'Did I scare you?' Helga is still grinning. Her voice is soft, yet strong. A voice of someone who is at ease with herself, confident that she can hold her own, no matter what the circumstances are.

'No, just surprised that's all'. In contrast Eva's voice sounds nervous and devoid of confidence. Her mind is racing at a thousand miles a second. She shoots out a hand and grabs Helga's hand in an awkward manner. 'I am so please to meet you miss Brand. I really respect you. You are the best trainer and I really want to be trained by you.' Her mind is shouting at her to shut up, but she can't help herself, when she is nervous she talks a lot. 'I will do whatever, you tell me to. You will not regret it if you give me a chance.' Eva is relieved when Helga interrupts her.

'Why do you want to join us?'

Without hesitation and unfortunately without thinking Eva just spurts it out. 'Revenge, I want revenge.'

Helga stops her again. Her tone has changed to one of irritation. 'We don't train girls to take revenge here. The Combat Sport Academy is a respected academy. We do not get involved with underground fights or death matches. We do train girls who enjoy fighting sports and we do train them to be competitive and to win, but we do not train them to kill each other, whether or not they believe that revenge is justified. Thanks for coming in, your application is unfortunately not accepted.'

Eva cannot stop the tears from flowing. 'But you don't understand. She murdered my mother. I need to kill her as I promised my mother that I will revenge her death.'

Helga's voice is softer again. 'I read your application. I know who you are. What happened to your mother was awful and it must have been very difficult for you. I would also take revenge if I was in your shoes. However, we do not get involved with death matches and we cannot risk our reputation by training you to kill someone. I wish you all the best, but unfortunately we cannot accept your application.'

With that Helga turns around and walks back to the training grounds. Eva stands around for a moment, tears still rolling down her cheeks. How did this go so wrong? After a while she composes herself enough to walk to the bathrooms to clean up. As she washes her face, she hears the bathroom door open, but she does not turn around as she does not want anybody else to see her crying. She feels humiliated enough as it is.

'Hello Eva, I am sorry you had to go though that, it was brutal.' The voice lacks the empathy one would expect to accompany such a statement.

Eva looks up and sees Nancy O'Grady in the mirror. She did not expect to see the owner of Combat Sport Academy behind her. She slowly turns around. 'Hi miss O'Grady. I just wanted to join. Whatever I do after my three year contract should not make a difference.'

Nancy gives her a forced smile. 'Call me Nancy. Let's go talk in my office.'

Eva somehow feels uneasy, but the hint of a second chance quickly drowns that feeling.

Nancy has a large office with a view of the training grounds. A display case in one corner is filled with trophies and the walls are covered by photos of girls in action in all kinds of sports events. Nancy takes a seat behind a large, very tidy, desk and motions for Eva to take a seat on one of the two visitor chairs. Helga is busy training a few girls outside and for a moment it seems to Eva that she is looking straight at her. 'Don't worry, they cannot see us. I had one-way windows installed. I love to watch them, but I don't like it when they are watching me.' Eva turns her attention back to Nancy. 'Let me get straight to the point. How do you plan to convince Emily Theron to fight you? She did not pitch up for the fight against your mother, even though she was the one who challenged your mother.'

Eva has never really thought about this. She planned her revenge so many times, but never entertained the thought that Emily may not accept her challenge. 'I don't know yet.' she says sheepishly.

'I can help you with that, but you have to understand that I never overturn Helga's decisions. I will give you one chance. You accept my offer and I guarantee you a death match against Emily Theron. Alternatively, we shake hands and you leave and figure our all by yourself how you will convince Emily Theron to accept your challenge to a duel.'

Eva doesn't want to lose the opportunity again. 'I accept.'

Nancy raises her hand to stop Eva, 'Not so fast, you need to listen to my offer. I want you to be absolutely sure before you sign the agreement.' Eva nods in agreement. Nancy watches her intently for a few seconds before she carries on. 'We will train you for three years, during which you will compete for us in various competitions. When you turn twenty-one, you will fight three death matches for Combat Sport Academy. The third fight will be against Emily Theron.'

Eva can't stop herself. She half-shouts. 'No, I want to fight her as soon as I turn twenty-one. I will fight more death matches for you after that, but I want to fight her first'

She regrets the outburst immediately. Once again, there is a few seconds silence before Nancy calmly talks again. 'I understand, but my plan to get her to fight you will only work if we are patient. You will have to trust me on this.'

Eva nods her head, relieved that she did not ruin her last chance. 'I trust you, I agree to your stipulations.'

Nancy smiles again, this time a real smile. 'Great, one more thing though. You will not share your story, or our agreement, with any of the other girls.' Eva nods again.

After she signs the agreement, Eva waits in the reception area as instructed by Nancy. Helga walks into the reception area, clearly surprised to see Eva is still there, but she does not say anything to Eva before she enters Nancy's office. Eva can hear raised voices for a good couple of minutes. When Helga comes out of Nancy's office, her face is red and her eyes wild with rage. She starts towards Eva, thinks better of it, turns around and walks back to the training area. Eva nervously sits on the edge of her chair. She is not sure what to do next. Should she follow Helga? That does not seem like a good idea as Helga is obviously very upset with her. Should she go back to Nancy's office? She decides to rather wait a bit longer in the reception area.

Chapter 6 – Jana

About five minutes later, a girl of about her age walks into the reception area. She has a big grin on her face and walks straight to Eva. 'Ah, the infamous Eva I presume. You know how to make an entrance, don't you? Never seen Helga that upset before, I can't wait for tonight.' She gives Eva a cheeky wink. 'I am Jana by the way, your new roommate.'
Eva accepts her hand. 'What is happening tonight?'
Jana starts walking towards the exit leading to the training area. Eva follows her, still a bit confused. 'Don't worry about tonight, let's get you settled in. Where are your bags?'
Eva did not expect to move in today already. 'I will call my aunt to bring them later. I did not expect to move in today already.'

They walk over a large open air training area filled with sand. In the far corner, two girls, wearing only training shorts and MMA gloves, are slugging the daylight out of each other. Helga is giving them both pointers on defence and attack. She does not look at Eva and Jana, although they pass only a few metres from the brawl. Eva is enthralled by the intensity of the fight and almost trips over the edge of the training area, which is sunk a few inches into the ground. A few girls watching the action giggles as Eva almost stumbles over. One of them makes a comment, which Eva cannot clearly hear, but it causes the group to laugh hysterically. Eva is mad at herself for being so clumsy and focuses her attention on where she is going again. She follows Jana past the indoor training centre towards a cluster of townhouses. Jana opens the door to one and invites Eva in and they enter a comfortable living area. Jana shows Eva her room before she points out the kitchen and her own bedroom. 'My door is always open. You are welcome to come in for a cuddle if you feel lonely at night.' She says this with a huge grin on her face and she gives Eva an exaggerated wink. Eva smiles, glad that the tension she felt all day is broken. She knows that it was a joke, but she also suspects that she would probably not be turned away, should she make use of this open door policy.

After Jana has given Eva a full tour of the townhouse they both plop down on the couch in the living room. 'Who were those girls?' Eva cannot get the image of the two girls fighting each other out of her head.
'Just a bunch of cows, don't worry about them. They will try to rile you because you are the new girl. Ignore them and don't get into any fights with them, you are not ready yet.'
Eva nods as this information sinks in. 'No, not them, the two girls fighting.'
Jana has a big smile on her face again. 'Oh, I did not think you noticed those two. They are Janet and Margaret. Best friends, best enemies. They love each other, but they fight each other every few weeks. Sort out their issues and then they are back to being besties. Helga tried to stop their constant fighting by punishing them after each fight. She eventually gave up and now uses their fights as a training opportunity. They are our neighbours, I will introduce you later.'

Eva is keen to meet them. 'It will be nice to meet them. What happens tonight? You said earlier that you can't wait for tonight.'

Jana considers her answer for a few seconds. 'I am not supposed to tell you, but what the hell. New girl has to prove herself tonight.' She says this in a mocking tone and with a huge grin on her face. 'Don't worry about it. Helga will pair you with someone close to your skill level to ensure a fair fight. She will also not allow either of you to be seriously hurt. It's an opportunity for you to show the rest of us what you have, not only in fighting skills, but also in grit and determination. You can earn everyone's respect tonight. If not Ö well let's not go there now. Tell me more about yourself, why are you here?'

Eva has to think fast as she is not allowed to share her story with anyone. 'Not much to tell. My mom died in an accident when I was eleven, so my aunt raised me. I wanted to fight since I can remember, so I am here to try it out.' She thinks that her answer is vague enough.

'Why is Helga so upset with you then?'

Eva is not prepared for this question. 'I don't know. She and Nancy disagreed about whether I should be accepted.' She can see from the frown on Jana's face that her answer was not convincing.

'Nancy never gets involved with decisions relating to whether or not a girl's application to join the academy is accepted. Why did she get involved with yours?'

Eva does not know how to respond to this. 'I don't know, I really have to phone my aunt to bring my stuff.'

Jana decides to let it go for now. It is obvious that Eva has something to hide. She may push her on this again later. But then again, she has been hiding her true identity since she joined a year ago. Only Nancy knows who she really is and they both agreed to keep it a secret. Perhaps she should accept that Eva has a skeleton or two as well and perhaps she should allow her to keep them in the closet.

When Eva meets her aunt at reception, her aunt tries to talk her into going home with her. She does not push too hard though. They've had this argument so many times and she knows that she will not change her niece's mind on this. She told her so many times that revenge just causes a vicious circle of hate and violence and that it stops her from living her own life, but this seemed to fall on death ears. They say their goodbyes and Eva promises to call often. The tears in her aunt's eyes saddens her, but she has no choice, she has to do this.

Back in the flat Jana helps Eva unpack and settle in. Their conversation soon turns to Eva's fight that night. Jana assures her again that she will be fine and that all girls at the academy were initiated this way. Jana knows that girls who do not show some guts during the fight are soon asked to leave the academy. Helga does not give many of them a second chance. She does not share this with Eva as she does not want to make her more nervous than she already is.

Chapter 7 – Duel

Jana switches on the screen in their living room and selects one of the recordings saved in it. 'I want you to watch this fight with me, but before we do, I want you to understand the background and the motivation for the fight. I want you to notice how this influences the outcome of the fight and I want you to learn the most important lesson of fighting, which we will discuss after the fight.'

Jana gives Eva a slight nod to establish whether she understands. Eva nods back. She feels slightly uneasy, until now Jana was mostly lots of fun. However, she was a bit serious earlier when she interrogated Eva about her admission to the academy. Now Jana shows a very serious, almost businesslike side of herself. Being satisfied that she has Eva's full attention, Jana carries on. 'The fight is a death match on Duel. The challenger was twenty-seven at the time of the fight and her opponent was thirty-two. The challenger, the brunette fighter, accused her opponent, the blonde fighter, of destroying her relationship with her mother, before her mother died. Her mother was in a relationship with her opponent and she believed that her already bad relationship was made worse by this woman telling her mother lies about her. When her mother suddenly died in an accident, she also found out that her mother left all her belongings to this her lover and nothing to her. She blames her opponent for the fact that she was never able to mend her relationship with her mother before her death and she wants revenge.'

Jana presses play and the video starts with the challenger being introduced. Her name is Monica and she has short brown hair and an athletic body. As customary in Duel, she is already stripped down to only a small red g-string. Her skin glistens with thin layer of sweat. It is clear that she has been warming up for the fight. She enters the cage and continues warming up in the red corner. Next, her opponent, a slightly heavier woman with long blonde hair is introduced as Ellen who is also stripped down to a black g-string. She enters the cage and goes to the blue corner.   In contrast with Monica, Ellen just stands there, glaring at her opponent. Monica is clearly unsettled by this and stops warming up. She glares back at Ellen before she points at her while shouting at her how she will make her suffer before she kills her. The announcer confirms the rules with the women. It is a fight to the death. The first ten minutes will be without any weapons, after that a baseball bat and a knife with a one inch blade will be dropped in each of their corners. The announcer asks each woman whether she accepts the rules and whether she is ready. Both confirm. She then gives them each a chance to change their minds and when neither uses this last opportunity to avoid being in a fight to the death, she leaves the cage and locks the gate.

A bell is rung and the fight is on. Monica charges at Ellen and tries to tackle her to the floor, but Ellen manages to turn her body slightly and lands on top op Monica as they tumble down. She lands two elbows to Monica's face before Monica is able to dislodge her. They scramble back to their feet and face off with each other again. Monica kicks out and catches

Ellen on her thigh. She follows this up with a straight right to her face which causes Ellen to stumble back slightly. Monica jumps forward and grabs her around the neck. She forces Ellen's head down and locks it under her left arm, grabbing her own left forearm with her right hand to tighten the grip and squeezes as hard as she can. All Ellen can do is to flay wildly with her arms. She catches Monica with a few punches, but nothing with any real power or effect. After a while, Monica releases the grip slightly, still maintaining control though. She starts striking Ellen with her right knee. The first two strikes land cleanly on Ellen's midriff, forcing Ellen to use her arms to block the strikes. The next few strikes are ineffective, so Monica stops the knee strikes and starts to tighten her hold around Ellen's neck again. As soon as Ellen starts flaying with her arms again, Monica strikes with her right knee, catching Ellen in her unprotected ribs. Ellen's knees buckle and she grabs her side while screaming in pain. Monica realises that she broke Ellen's ribs and releases her grip, allowing Ellen to fall to her hand and knees. She jumps on Ellen's back and locks her left arm around Ellen's throat. With Ellen at her mercy, Monica starts squeezing and Ellen's face quickly turns red from the lack of oxygen. It seems that the fight is over. However, as Ellen starts to go limp, Monica releases her grip slightly, allowing Ellen to breathe again. She shouts at Ellen that she won't let her get off that easily and that she will make her suffer before the kills her. Tears run down Ellen's face and her eyes are full of fear. It is clear that she has no hope left. Monica repeats the tightening and releasing of her grip a few more times until the weapons are dropped in the corners. She releases Ellen and runs back to her corner, grabbing the baseball bat and using the string of her g-string to store the knife at her side. She walks back to where Ellen is scrambling back to her own corner and hits Ellen across her back with the baseball bat, causing Ellen to instantly fall flat on her stomach. Monica is in full control of the fight and she kicks Ellen in her already broken ribs to cause Ellen pain. She screams out and desperately tries to crawl away from Monica, but Monica grabs Ellen's left arm and rolls her over on her back. She pins Ellen's arms with the knees and start slapping her in the face, hell bent on humiliating her. Ellen manages to get her right arm free and she grabs at Monica's side and then starts to punch Monica's left arm and side. Blood starts to flow down Monica's side. Only then does Eva realise that Ellen grabbed the knife and that she is actually stabbing Monica. She manages about ten stabs before Monica regains control over her arm. Monica is still in control of the fight but she is losing a lot of blood. Her left arm also hangs limp. With Ellen's arms trapped again, Monica grabs Ellen's throat with her right hand and starts to squeeze, but she struggles to get a firm enough grip though. She releases the grip and sinks her forearm into Ellen's throat and leans forward to increase the pressure. With a huge effort Ellen bucks her lower body and manages to dislodge Monica. Both scramble to their feet, but Monica is faster. She grabs Ellen from behind and manages to get her forearm around Ellen's throat again, squeezing with all she has. Ellen grabs at het arm, but cannot loosen the grip, so she starts clawing at Monica's face, drawing blood with her nails. Monica is still bleeding freely, but she maintains her grip until Ellen's whole body goes limp. She maintains the grip for a while after this before she slumps forward on top of Ellen. The cage gate is opened and a doctor is allowed inside to establish whether either one of the girls is dead. Nobody is allowed to interfere in any way until one woman has been killed. She confirms that Ellen is dead and medics rush in to help her in trying to save Monica's life. Jana switches the screen off. 'They managed to save her. What did you learn from this?'

Eva thinks for a while. 'Her hatred for the other woman distracted her and she almost lost her life because of that.'

Jana nods her head. 'Yes, fighting is a combination of applying skills and adapting to circumstances. There is no place for emotions. They distract you and make you lose your focus. Never be emotional during a fight, focus on your job and win it as quickly as you can. Do not feel sorry for your opponent and definitely do not try to punish or humiliate her. It may cost you the match or even your life.'

They both jump a little with surprise as they hear a chuckle behind them. One of the two girls who brawled earlier is standing in the door. Her left eye is swollen closed and her bottom lip is split. She has a grin on her face. 'Fighting 101 by Jana Smith. Didn't help your previous roomy much, did it?

Jana smiles slightly. 'Eva, please meet Margaret, one of the bitches from next door.' This brings a big smile to Margaret's face. 'Howzit Eva. Careful Jana, my blood is still hot from fighting Janet. I can go a few more rounds and I am not sure whether you have what it takes to face an enraged bitch like me.'

Jana takes a stance used by the old prize fighters. 'Any time babe, any time. You look like Janet got the better of you this time, how is she doing? Are you guys friends again?'

Margaret walks in, sits down on the couch next to Eva and gives her a hug. 'Sorry that you got this old spoil sport for a roomy. Just tell me if I have to come beat her up for you.'

Eva smiles and nods her head. 'Hi Margaret. I will beat her up myself if need be.'

All three of them laugh at this. 'Good for you girl. Janet is fine, but I obviously won. Yeah, we are friends again. You know us, we cannot stay mad at each other. We just need a punch-up every now and then. Are you guys coming over for dinner tonight after the festivities?'

Jana makes eye contact with Eva and then says to Margaret. 'Sure, Eva saw a bit of your fight earlier, she is a big fan. I am sure she will enjoy getting to know the two of you better.'

Eva nods her head in agreement. Margaret stands up and walks towards the door, but she turns around just before going through the door. 'See you later then. You never know, we may just give you a bit of a show tonight, depending on whether Eva deserves it or not.' She smiles at Eva and disappears through the door.

Chapter 8 – Initiation Fight

Jana tells Eva that she does not want to spoil the show for her and that she needs to wait for it. She tells her that it is always very special and that the neighbours only perform the show for people they trust and respect. Eva is exited by the anticipation of the show she might see tonight, but she is also worried about her initiation fight. Jana sees the stress in her face and tells her to have a snooze as she needs to be rested for her fight. Eva goes to her room, but cannot sleep. She wonders what the show is about. She wonders what happened to Jana's previous roommate. She wonders who she will fight tonight, what the rules will be and whether she is ready for it. Eva does not want to embarrass herself and she wants to win Helga's respect. She definitely wants to win Margaret and Janet's respect as well as she really wants to see their show. If it is anything close to their fight earlier, she needs to see it. She is still deep in thought when Helga walks into her room without knocking first, still looking upset with Eva. 'Come with me.' She says this without any emotion and turns around and walks out without ensuring that Eva follows her. Eva rushes to catch up with her and follows her to the indoor practice area. In the middle of the training area is a blue mat with two white lines about three feet apart and each about three feet long. The mat itself is about fifteen foot by fifteen foot. Two stools are placed on opposite sides of the mat. Quite a few girls are already sitting on the stands placed around the mat. The stands are only about three feet away from the mat, giving the fighting area the feel of a cage. Helga shows Eva to a locker room. 'You fight in fifteen minutes, put on the outfit inside'.

Eva wants to say something, but Helga turns around and walks away. Inside, Eva finds a blue layered skirt and blue MMA style gloves. She puts these on and starts to warm up. It is obvious to her that it will be a fistfight and that they will fight topless. This will be a first for her. She has never been topless in front of an audience before. She should be fine though. There will only be girls in the audience and she is sure they have all fought topless before. Anyway, she thinks her 34B boobs suits her athletic body fine. She notices that her nipples are already rock hard in anticipation of the fight and this makes her a bit self conscious, but she convinces herself that this is natural and that nobody will probably notice and if they do, that they are probably used to erect nipples during a fight. There is a knock on the door and Jana walks in. 'I am your second, how are you doing.' Jana's eyes linger on Eva's boobs just long enough to make Eva slightly uncomfortable.

'I am doing fine, it is just a bit new to me to fight topless'.

Jana's eyes goes down to Eva's boobs again. 'Don't be embarrassed, you have awesome boobs, I can't help but to stare at them.'

Eva smiles and feels her face turn red in embarrassment. 'Thanks.' She doesn't know what else to say.

Jana manages to tear her eyes away from Eva's boobs. 'You will be in a prize fight tonight. The rules are simple, you are allowed to strike your opponent with fists and elbows and headbutts are allowed. No kicking and no wrestling moves. Each round carries on until one of you goes down. The girl who went down has fifteen seconds to make it back to the

scratch.' Jana can see from the confusion in Eva's face that she does not know what this means. 'The scratch is the white lines in the middle of the mat. You have to take a fighting stance behind your white line if you go down. If you do not do this within fifteen seconds, the fight is over. If you do make it, there will be a thirty second break before the next round. The fight continues until one girl cannot make it back to her scratch within fifteen seconds. Do you understand the rules?' Eva nods. 'Pace yourself, this can be a long fight and be careful, headbutts really hurt and they can do a lot of damage.'
They sit in silence for a few seconds. 'Who am I fighting?' Eva does not know many girls here and a name will probably not help her much, but she feels that having a name will settle her nerves a bit.
'I don't know. Helga did not want to tell me, but it will be someone with little experience as well. She will not feed you to the lions.'

There is a knock on the door and Eva follows Jana to the mat. By now the stands are packed and there is a buss of excitement in the air. Although these girls fight often and see many fights, the new girl initiation fights always draw big crowds. Jana leads Eva to the blue stool and starts to massage her shoulders as soon as Eva sits down. A few seconds later, another door opens and her opponent makes her way to the mat. It is the girl who made the remark when Eva stumbled earlier today. She has big boobs with big areolas. Her nipples are barely noticeable. It is obvious to Eva that her nipples are the only ones erect. She is surprised with herself that she looked at the other girls boobs. Hell she even focussed on her nipples. She is sure that it is as a result of being self conscious about her own naked boobs and her still hard nipples. She sees the concern on Jana's face. 'What? Is she good?'
Jana tries to smile, but does not have a lot of success with that. 'Her name is Amelia. She is good, but you will be ok. Just stay out of range of her head. She is a dirty fighter and will headbutt you every chance she gets.'
Jana makes sure that Eva's mouth guard is in. A petite girl, wearing a black and white striped skirt only, walks into the ring. Eva also remembers her from this afternoon. She was one of the girls watching the fight between Margaret and Janet earlier. The girl calls the fighters to the middle of the mat. 'Take your fighting stances. Are you ready?' Both fighters nod. 'Fight!'

Eva blocks a right hook, but does not see the straight left following it. Her lights go out for a split second and she finds herself sitting on her bum. She hears a lot of laughter and even a fee jeers. Her mind clears again and she quickly gets up. She hears Jana shouting at her to get to the scratch. It all comes back to her and she quickly takes her fighting stance behind the white line. Jana runs in and leads her back to her stool. 'Don't worry about that, she caught you with a lucky punch, it happens.'

The thirty seconds fly by and the fighters square off for the second round. This time Eva is more alert and she manages to block most of the punches coming her way. Some get through her defences though. Her bottom lip is soon cut and blood trickles down her chin. It takes a good thirty seconds before Eva manages to land her first punch. It is not a strong punch by any stretch of the imagination, but it got through and landed in her opponent's face. Eva gains some confidence from this and moves in for another attack. She jabs with her left and lets fly with a straight right. The next moment she sits on her bum again. Eva's punch missed its mark and Amelia landed an elbow in her face. The cut on her lip is bigger now and she sees blood dripping down on the mat. Eva gets to her feet, takes her fighting stance behind the white line and goes back to her stool where Jana manages to stop the bleeding with petroleum jelly.

All too soon the third round starts. They trade jabs for a few seconds before Amelia feints a right hook to Eva's temple. Eva raises her guard to block this and leaves her body open. A hard left hook drives into her right boob, causing extreme pain and Eva can't help but to scream out. She has never been punched in her boobs before. The pain is excruciating and she instinctively grabs her right boob with both hands. Eva is open to attack and Amelia lands three punches in Eva's face before she manages to grab Amelia around her waste. Eva hears Jana screaming something, but before it registers Amelia slams her forehead into Eva's face. Eva stumbles back but manages to stay on her feet. Her nose is bleeding freely and she is sure it is broken. She has tears in her eyes and she struggles to focus. Amelia follows her and lands two hard punches to Eva's face before she goes down again. This time a takes a few seconds before Eva manages to get up. She stumbles to her scratch before Jana helps her back to her stool. Jana manages to stop the nose bleed and tries to also stop Eva's bottom lip from bleeding. 'Do not get up again, she is hurting you. If you want, I will stop this now.'
Eva stares at Amelia for a second. 'No, I am fine.'

Eva manages to stay away from Amelia for a while at the start of the fourth round. The crowd starts jeering, but she ignores them as she needs time to clear her head. She knows that tying Amelia up is too dangerous, so running is the only answer she has for now. This tactic works for a while and Eva can see that Amelia does not like to move around a lot. Eva is quicker than Amelia and she manages to land a few jabs and gets out of range every time before Amelia can retaliate. She moves in again trying to land another jab, but she is surprised by a hard kick to her side. Eva looks at the referee, but only receives a grin in return. Just as she thought, the referee is not here to protect her against dirty tactics. The moment's lapse of focus costs her dearly. Amelia moves in and lands a hard punch to Eva's face and a knee to Eva's unprotected tummy. Eva doubles over and another knee to her face drops her again. Jana is screaming at her to stay down, but she struggles to her feet and makes it to the scratch at the count of thirteen. Jana is pleading with Eva not to carry on while she is working on the bleeding. She turns to Helga. 'Stop this.'
Helga shakes her head. 'She can stop it when she had enough.'
Jana is in tears now. 'She is too stupid to stop it herself. It is your job to make sure she does not get seriously injured.'
Helga turns to a girl sitting next to her and whispers something to her.

Eva tries to keep her distance at the start of the fifth round, but Amelia manages to catch her

more frequently now. The punishment she took in previous rounds has slowed Eva down, which means that she has lost her only advantage. Eva's eyes are swollen from her broken nose and she struggles to see the punches coming. Amelia is playing with her like a cat plays with a mouse and is punching her in the face at will, but not hard enough to put Eva down. Eva tries to strike back, but there is no power in her punches anymore. She tries to block a punch, but instead of punching, Amelia grabs her around her upper body, forcing Eva's arms up. Amelia uses her Muay Thai skills to land knee after knee to Eva's ribs. After about twelve knee strikes, Amelia releases her grip around Eva's body and Eva drops to the mat. Against all odds, Eva crawls to the scratch and manages to get to her feet just before the count of fifteen. She expects Jana to help her back to her stool, but when she turns around, there is nobody in her corner. Luckily for her, Margaret jumps up from where she is sitting and helps Eva to her stool, but just as Eva sits down on her stool, the bell rings for the next round. Eva is in bad shape and she struggles to breath. She starts to move back to the mat, but Margaret pulls her back. 'You had enough. You are going nowhere. You are done.'
Eva starts to walk again and once again Margaret gently pulls her back. The referee comes over and tells Margaret to let her go, but Margaret refuses to. Two girls come from behind Margaret and grab her arms and the referee leads Eva back to the middle of the mat. Eva hears a commotion behind her, but tries to focus on Amelia. She was later told that the commotion was Janet who came to the defence of Margaret. The two of them soon overpowered the other two girls. Eva lifts her fists, ready to fight, ready to prove that she has what it takes. Just as the referee is about to instruct them to fight, Helga steps onto the mat and tells Amelia to go shower. Margaret and Janet help Eva to lie down on the mat until the medics arrive to take her to the academy's clinic. She is kept in the clinic for two weeks with a broken nose, three broken ribs and various cuts and bruises.

Her first visitor the next morning is Helga. 'Do you think I was hard on you, unfair to you?'
Eva thinks a bit before she answers. 'Yes, you knew I had no chance against her. You allowed her to do this to me. Why?
Helga's response is measured. 'You could stop at any time. You also knew you had no chance, yet you carried on. I do not want to train girls for death matches, but I am forced to train you. I needed to give you a taste of what you wish for and I needed to see what I have to work with. I can teach you skills, but I cannot give you fighting spirit. I needed to see if you have the spirit and guts required for surviving a death match. I will train you when you recover, but only if you promise to give me the opportunity to talk you out of wasting your life on death matches.'
Eva nods in agreement. Deep down she knows that no one will be able to talk her out of this, but she will give Helga a fair go at it. Eva feels peaceful after Helga's visit. She has been accepted by Helga.

Jana visits Eva for the first time two days later as the doctor ordered that she could not have visitors for a few days, Helga being the exception. It has been eating at Eva for the last two days that Jana left when she really needed her. They talk for as long as the nurses allow them. Jana tells her how Helga had her removed during the final round. She was restrained by three girls, she fought against them but they were too many and she was unable to get away from them. Eva is glad that her friend did not desert her. Jana also lectures Eva on the mistakes she made during the fight. During her stay in the clinic, Jana visits her every opportunity she gets. There friendship grows stronger with each visit. Eva is growing fond of Jana and she really needs a good friend to rely on.

Margaret and Janet also visit her often. They promise her the best show ever as soon as she gets out of the clinic. She asks them a few times, but they refuse to share what the nature of the show will be. Although she does not wish any harm to their friendship, she secretly hopes that they will fight each other again. The bit of their fight she saw stirred something inside of her. She is not sure what it was exactly, but she liked the feeling and she wants to experience it again. Many other girls come to visit her as she gained their respect and she knows that most of the girls here have accepted her as one of their own.

Chapter 9 – Recovering

The morning after Eva's fight Jana goes to Nancy's office hoping to find out the truth about Eva. She considered ignoring her instincts about her new friend and to accept that everybody is allowed a few secrets. However, she has never seen Helga treat a girl like she treated Eva last night. Helga has been like a mother to all of them, always caring about the welfare of her girls. Last night she was the cause of serious injuries to Eva. She paired Eva with a much better fighter in a dangerous type of fight. She had many opportunities to stop the match, but she allowed Eva to stupidly carry on fighting. Jana needs to know what's going on so that she can protect Eva from herself. Nancy keeps Jana waiting for about half an hour before she calls her into her office. 'What can I do for you?' Nancy is a bit irritated and she does not try to hide this from Jana. She does not like to deal with the girls. They are old enough to sort out their own issues and if they can't, its Helga's job to make sure that they don't bother her.
'I want to know what the deal is with Eva. She is clearly here against Helga's wishes and she almost got killed because of that last night.'
Nancy considers her answer for a few seconds. 'You of all people should know that I do not share confidential information. There is nothing going on. Eva was nervous during her interview and Helga did not see the potential in her. I did and I think I was proven right last night. From the report I received, she will do well here. I have a busy day and you need to report to Helga for punishment. I understand you disobeyed orders last night.'

As Jana leaves her office, Nancy wonders whether her gamble will pay off. It was a risky move to put Eva and Jana together in a townhouse, but she needs them to be close to each other for her plan to come to fruition. She shrugs her shoulders. If this does not work, she may lose a few girls, but there are plenty girls out there who will give their left arms to join her academy. She has planned to launch her own television show for a while now and these two girls play an integral role in the drama and intrigue she has planned. When Jana joined the academy six months ago, she started laying plans for the future, but she still needed something to really make the launch unforgettable. She could not belief her luck when Eva's file landed on her desk. At first she hoped that Helga would accept the application, but in hindsight, things could not have worked out better. Eva was desperate to join and needed her help getting in. She now feels that she has full control over Eva. She just needs to make sure the girls do not share their true identities with each other. But she wants them to become friends. She needs raw emotions when the day comes when they will face each other in the Pit of Death. She came up with this name for her future show a while ago and it still brings a smile to her face. She believes that the name alone will guarantee good viewership. The concept will surely make a killing. She smiles again at her own clever pun.

When Jana reports to Helga she expects a harsh punishment. Instead, Helga takes her to a quiet spot where they can have a conversation without being disrupted. 'I am sorry I put you in an impossible situation last night. I was sure Eva does not belong here. I wanted to get rid of her, but instead she proved to me that I was wrong.'

Jana decides to get straight to the point. 'You almost killed her. What is the situation? Why were you so determined to get rid of her that you put her safety on the line?'

Helga hates lying to the girls, but she has been given strict instructions not to discuss Eva's history with any of the girls. Anyway, sharing the fact that she will train a girl for a death match will not do any good and will most probably affect the morale of the other girls negatively. 'I was just upset that Nancy ignored my judgement. I concede that I allowed it to go further than planned last night. I went to see Eva earlier. She will be fine. You will be allowed to go see her in a few days. For now she needs some rest.' She puts a hand on Jana's shoulder. 'I appreciate that you are looking out for her, she needs a friend.'

Jana leaves the meeting relieved that the Helga she knows and trusts is back. She knows that Helga is hiding something, but she also knows that pushing her will not yield any positive results.

Eva enjoys the attention she receives in the clinic. Her friendship with Jana becomes stronger by the day. They share a lot with each other, though both are careful not to give away their true identities. Jana decides not to push Eva on this subject again. She will be there for Eva and after witnessing how brave Eva was in her fight, she is sure that Eva will stick with her through thick and thin as well.

The doctor releases Eva after two weeks with the condition that she takes it easy and that she is not allowed to take part in any physical training for at least another four weeks. She also needs to go back for a checkup before the doctor will clear her to fight again. Helga uses these four weeks to discuss techniques with Eva. She explains to her what she did well during her fight, but they also spend a lot of time discussing the many mistakes she made. Helga tells her that she will include her in the novice bruchenball team as soon as she is ready to train. Novices compete in the sport of bruchenball. It teaches them teamwork and hones their fighting skills. When girls prove themselves in the bruchenball tournament, they advance to other fighting sports. Eva is a quick study and she uses the time available to her, while the other girls are training, to study the rules and tactics of bruchenball. She is determined to make her mark and to advance to other fighting sports as soon as possible.

Bruchenball is played by two teams of five girls each. The playing field is a large rectangular area filled with sand or mud. A leather sandbag, too heavy for one or even two girls to carry, is placed in the centre of the playing field. At the start of every half and after each goal, teams line up behind their goal lines. On the signal of the referee, both teams rush in and attempt to drag the leather sandbag over their own goal line. Girls are allowed to stop the opposing team from reaching their goal line in any way. Wrestling, punching and kicking opponents are not only allowed, but expected. The game is played over two halves of fifteen minutes each and the team with the most goals wins. Draws are not allowed and sudden death overtime is played should neither team be able to win the game during normal time. Each team is allowed two substitutes and rolling substitutions are allowed. However, substitutions may only be made after a goal is scored, during halftime, or before extra time.

Chapter 10 – The Greatest Show

On the Saturday after Eva is released from the clinic, their neighbours invite her and Jana over for dinner. Janet jokes that the last time they invited Eva for dinner she ended up in the clinic. Margaret, who is the cook of the two, gives her an exasperated look. 'You know well that my cooking had nothing to do with her visit to the medics. She never even made it to dinner.'
'Perhaps she lost the match on purpose to avoid your cooking.'
'The two of us are quickly heading for an appointment in the sand pit again.' Margaret says this with a cheeky smile.
Eva can't help but to replay the image in her head of these two fighting each other in the sanded practice area on the day she joined. This stirs something in her and she can't hide her excitement. 'I'll be the ref.'
Janet laughs at Eva. 'Look at New Girl trying to egg us on to fight each other.'
Eva blushes. 'No, not trying to make you guys fight. Just saying that I'll be more than willing to officiate next time you guys have a go at each other.'
Janet is still smiling. 'Well Margaret, I think we have ourselves a fan. Maybe we should start selling tickets for our next brawl.'
Margaret pops her head out of the kitchen. 'Maybe I will fight Eva next time. I would love some real competition for once.'
The girls continue with their friendly banter over dinner. Eva is thoroughly enjoying herself and wishes that this night could go on forever. Little does she know that the real entertainment is yet to start.

After dinner Eva and Jana are invited to their neighbours' gym. Margaret gives them each a glass of wine and tells them to relax as the show will start in a few minutes. Janet and Margaret leave the gym and when they return, they are both wearing small g-strings only. Eva's excitement levels rises. Are they going to fight each other again? She watches intently as her two friends face each other from opposite sides of a wrestling mat. They both start to apply baby oil to their bodies and soon both their beautiful athletic bodies are glistening under the dim lights of their private gym. Eva looks at Jana. She has a huge grin on her face. It is obvious that she knows what is about to happen. She turns her attention back to the two beautiful glistening bodies on the mat. They are now sitting on their knees facing each other. They move closer to each other until their bodies are only inches apart and start to fondle each other's breasts while their lips lock in a passionate kiss. Eva did not expect this, she was hoping for a fist fight, but started to think that they may oil wrestle each other. She did not expect them to kiss though. After a few seconds of kissing and fondling, as if they received instruction from an invisible referee, the two girls break their kiss and grab each other and start to grapple for position. Their slippery bodies make it difficult to properly apply any wrestling holds, but they both try their best to dominate the other. The match has changed from a soft and sensual few moments shared in each other's arms to an energetic and competitive wrestling match. Janet hooks her left foot behind Margaret and manages to force her onto her back. She wraps her arms around Margaret's neck and tries to get into a full mount position. However, her right leg is trapped between Margaret's legs and she is unable to gain this position. Janet gives up on the mount position and starts moving her right leg slightly forward and back, rubbing it against Margaret's crotch. Margaret turns her body slightly to avoid direct contact between her clit and Janet's leg. At the same time she grabs Janet's left breast with her right hand and squeezes it as hard as she can. This draws a yelp from Janet, who instinctively moves her body away from the attack and releases her hold around Margaret's neck before she grabs Margaret's hand to dislodge her tight grip on her boob. Margaret forces her left elbow between their bodies and pushes upwards while turning her own body to the right. Janet slips off of Margaret and Margaret gets back to her knees and ends up behind Janet. She wraps her arms around Janet's upper body pressing her C cups flat against het breast bone. Her own perky B cups are pressed into Janet's back. Janet reaches back and loosens the strings of Margaret's g-string. The small garment falls to the mat, leaving her clean shaven pussy on display. Margaret immediately retaliates. While maintaining her hold with her left arm, she reaches down with her right and loosens the right string of Janet's g-string. She reaches over to undo the left string, allowing Janet to grab her right arm while twisting her own body to the left and to toss Margaret over her right shoulder. Margaret rolls away and gets back to her knees, facing each other a few feet apart. Janet loosens the other string of her g-string and tosses it aside. She is also clean shaven. The two opponents slowly start moving towards each other on their knees and they lock their lips in a passionate kiss again. This time their hands go down to each other's pussies and they start to rub each other's clits. They both start moaning softly and their lower bodies start to gyrate slowly in response to the attention to their clits. Then suddenly the fight is on again. Janet manages to get Margaret down again and obtains side control. She traps Margaret's right arm between her thighs, with her chest on top of Margaret's chest and her left hand controlling Margaret's left arm. With her right hand she starts rubbing Margaret's clit again. Margaret crosses her legs to try and stop the sexual attack on her pussy, but Janet forces her hand further between Margaret's oil covered thighs and start finger fucking her, while she rubs her clit with her thumb. All Margaret can do is to kiss and lick Janet's left nipple. She considers biting Janet's left boob, but that may take dirty tactics they use during these fights a bit too far. Anyway, she is thoroughly enjoying herself at the moment and she does not really want Janet to stop now. She will concede the first fall and get her own back in the next round. She uncrosses her legs, spreading them slightly to give Janet better access to the pussy. Margaret's moans become faster and more intense. She bucks her hips up and down as Janet jabs her finger in and out faster and faster. Janet feels Margaret's pussy tightens around her finger, her abdominal muscles tighten and she screams out in ecstasy. Janet starts moving her finger around in small circles inside Margaret's pussy, rubbing against her g-spot while still rubbing her clit with her thumb, causing Margaret's body to shudder in a serious of orgasms. Margaret's lower body finally slumps to the mat in exhaustion. Janet releases her hold on Margaret and passionately kisses her on her lips. She helps Margaret to her feet and they both grab a bottle of water before sitting down on a bench across from where Jana and Eva are sitting. Their naked bodies are on full display and it does not seem to bother them at all. Eva is mesmerised by the show and she can't help but to stare at the two shiny naked bodies sitting a few feet away from her. She notices how stiff their nipples are and also eagerly takes in the sight of their swollen clits. She can feel that her own nipples are rock hard as well and that her pussy is moist. She is as horny as hell and she glances at Jana and sees het proud nipples straining against the fabric of her shirt. Obviously she is not the only one turned on by the fight so far. Margaret smiles at Eva. 'You like?'

All Eva manages to say is 'Wow!' This draws laughs from all three other girls.

'Well this was only the first contest, two more to come. Janet got the better of me, but she will beg me to stop in the last two competitions.' She gives Eva a wink. 'You better watch closely and learn quickly. Next time we may just challenge the two of you to a team contest.'

The thought of this excites Eva she gets even hornier than she already was. She desperately needs a sexual release and she hopes that Jana will be willing to help her out after the show.

On the mat Janet and Margaret have taken their positions for the next contest. They both lean back on their arms, left legs flat on the mat and right legs lifted over each other's left legs. Their pussies are pressed together and they start tribbing, rubbing their pussies and clits against each other. It doesn't take long for both girls to start moaning with pleasure. Their eyes are closed most of the time, only occasionally opening to assess the opponent or if they are both opened at the same time to lustfully stare into each other's eyes. Both their mouths are slightly open, moans escaping their lips as the excitement intensifies. Janet uses her left hand to fondle her own boobs and to gently tuck at her own nipples. The grinding intensifies as both girls near the point of no return. It is Margaret who once again explodes in an intense orgasm. She falls back still writhing with pleasure. Janet is too horny to resist an orgasm and she finishes herself off by rubbing her own clit. She has won the competition two to nil and she feels that she may as well celebrate properly. After Janet orgasms, both girls remain lying down on the mat. Janet slides over and they start kissing passionately while they cuddle each other.

Chapter 11 – Friends with Benefits

Eva is so transfixed by the action on the mat and she gets startled when Jana touches her shoulder. 'Come, we should leave.'
Eva looks at Jana with a frown on her face. 'Why? What about the third contest?'
Jana gives her a sympathetic smile. She knows that Eva wants to see more action. 'Does it seem to you like they care about another contest? They need some privacy.' Eva does not really understand why they would need privacy after what she just witnessed, but she does not argue and follows Jana back to their own townhouse. Jana senses her confusion. 'There is a difference between a sexual contest and being intimate with each other.'
This makes sense to Eva and she feels a bit foolish for wanting to stay longer. They enter their townhouse and Jana immediately grabs Eva and kisses her passionately. Eva does not resist at all and returns the kiss. When they break the kiss, she asks. 'Have you? I mean have you done sexual contest before?'
Jana gives her another kiss before she answers. 'Yes, but tonight I want to be intimate with you. We can challenge each other for a sexual contest another time.'
Eva had sex with other girls before, but she has never been this horny. She grabs Jana's shirt and yanks it over her head. She fumbles a bit with Jana's bra, but soon manages to discard it as well. At the same time Jana has started removing Eva's top as well. Eva reaches back and undoes her own bra. She stares at Jana's beautiful boobs. They are similar in size to Eva's boobs, with dark hard nipples adorning them. Both nipples are pierced and the current piercings are little silver bars, with silver balls on each side and a short silver chain hanging from each bar. The chains just reach the bottom of her areolas. Eva is fascinated by this and decides that she needs to get nipple piercings as well. She starts kissing Jana's breasts, taking time to lick and suck her nipples. She also traps the chains between her teeth, gently pulling on them. Jana moans softly while she fondles Eva's breasts with her hands while she kisses Eva's neck and shoulders. After a while they change positions and Jana's mouth explores Eva's breasts and nipples, while Eva kisses her neck and fondles her breasts. Eva loves her nipples being suck and her level of arousal goes through the roof. She starts to tuck on Jana's skirt and they both quickly remove their skirts and panties. Like Janet and Margaret, Eva is also clean shaven. Jana sports a landing strip and her clit is also pierced. A small silver ring hangs from it. Once again Eva is intrigued, but she is not sure whether she is up for a clit piercing. They explore each other's pussies with their hands, rubbing and probing until they are both completely aroused and ready to explode. Jana gently removes Eva's hand from her pussy and starts grinding it against Eva's thigh. Eva follows suit and both girls continue slugging on each other's thighs. Eva can feel her first orgasm building and she can hear from Jana's moans that she is close as well. Moments later Eva's body shudders and her knees buckle as the orgasm seems to consume her whole body. Jana screams out in pleasure a few seconds later. They sink to their knees and kiss each other's lips and faces tenderly while they cuddle each other. A few minutes later Jana leads Eva to her bedroom where she gently pushes Eva onto her bed. Eva lies on her back and opens her

legs as Jana climbs on top of her. Jana positions herself on her knees so that their crotches touch each other. She starts to gyrate her hips, grinding her pussy against Eva's, ensuring that their clits rub against each other. They both shudder with their second orgasm soon. The girls change position a few times and after a few more orgasms they fall asleep in each other's arms.

Early the next morning, Eva is awoken by Jana kissing and licking her pussy. She is pleasantly surprised by this and can't help but to let out a deep groan. Jana looks up for a second. She smiles at Eva before she gets back to the job at hand. She expertly uses her mouth and tongue to kiss, suck, lick and probe Eva's slit and clit. Most of her attention is on Eva's clit, but she also forces her tongue into Eva's pussy a few times. Eva is in ecstasy, she has never experienced a muff dive before and she makes a mental note that this is something she wants to experience as often as possible. She is soon screaming as her body convulse with a huge orgasm. Jana slowly moves her body upwards until she straddles Eva's face. She presses her pussy against Eva's mouth. Eva has never done this before, but she learnt from what Jana just did to her. She licks the length of Jana's slit. When her tongue reaches Jana's clit, she starts flicking her tongue up and down against it. She alternates this with gently sucking on Jana's clit tucking on the clit ring with her teeth. After a while she moves her mouth down and starts to probe her tongue in and out of Jana's pussy. Jana is in her own world at this stage and is gently pulling Eva's hair with her one hand while she softly slaps Eva in the face with the other. The pulling and slapping increases in intensity as Jana gets more exited. It never reaches a level where Eva feels the need to stop it, but she is not sure what to make of this. She feels some level of excitement by the little bit of pain she feels while she uses her mouth to get Jana off, but she is not sure whether she wants this to be a regular theme in their lovemaking sessions Jana eventually slumps down on top of Eva after she orgasms. She lasted a lot longer than Eva and Eva is not sure whether she has done it wrong. But judging by Jana's state of exhaustion and the satisfied smile on her face, she decides that Jana just have more control over her orgasms than herself.

Eva and Jana both decide that they do not want to be in a relationship. They both like men and neither of them want to be distracted by a relationship. However, they are both in agreement that they should be friends with benefits. They enjoy each other's company and the definitely enjoy each other's bodies, so this arrangement suits both to a T.

Nancy notices the close relationship between Eva and Jana and is very pleased with this. Her plans for her own death match show are gaining momentum and she already had discussions with a potential partner, Kelly Yates. Kelly is the owner of a production company producing mainly adult movies. She is looking for a new venture to take her company to the next level and Nancy, in turn, is looking for somebody who is able to produce quality live television episodes of her death matches. She has the concept planned out. She has the infrastructure to train women and the facilities to host the fights. She also has the perfect matches planned to start off the new show, Pit of Death. She just needs a proper production company to go into partnership with.

There are a few problems though. Kelly does not really want to wait three years to launch Pit of Death. She needs something sooner to develop her business. Nancy may have a solution to this problem though, but her solution does not involve death matches. She is adamant that the Pit of Death will only be launched when both Eva and Jana is of legal age to participate in death matches. She will organise exhibition fights between her girls and even between her girls and some of their rivals from other academies. These fights will be similar to MMA fights, but with a few adjustments to enhance the entertainment value. She will sell this to Helga and the girls as an opportunity for her girls to promote themselves by fighting live on a television programme. The fights will be safe enough and the girls will fight for prizes, but more importantly, for fame. Many of her girls want to make a career out of fighting after their time at the academy. Making a name for themselves now, will assist the girls to launch their fighting careers one day. She will also use this show as a method to raise interest in Eva and Jana. She will manage their appearances on the show in a way that will make them both household names by the time they face each other in the Pit of Death.

Her second problem is that Helga will not agree to train women for death matches. She knows that Helga accepted the fact that Eva may compete in a death match one day, but she will never get involved with training women only to a point where they have enough skills not to embarrass themselves and the academy during a death match. She will try to convince Helga to still train the amateur portion of her business, but she is not sure whether Helga will stay if a portion of her business gets involved with death matches. She is also sure that Helga will be very upset if she learns who Nancy plans to bring in as the coach for the Pit of Death. Few people know that Helga has a twin sister Olga. They used to be close and worked together as coaches at a professional fighting club. Between them, they produced various quality MMA fighters, including a few champions. Helga also coached a few amateur girls on the side. These girls did not compete in competitions and only wanted training for self-defence purposes. Helga fell in love with one of these girls and Olga felt that this infatuation distracted Helga and that it was bad for business. An opportunity presented itself when a previous business partner of Helga's love interest challenged her to a death match on Duel. Helga convinced her lover not to accept the challenge. However, Olga then told her that she would regret it for the rest of her life if she does not accept the challenge. She convinced her that people, and especially Helga, will not respect her if she refuses to fight. Olga hoped that Helga would never learn about her involvement in the woman's decision to accept the challenge. However, after the woman was killed on Duel, Helga received a letter which she wrote in case she would lose the match. In this letter she explained her reasons for accepting the challenge. Helga attacked Olga and they were both seriously injured in the fight before police managed to separate them. They have not seen each other, or spoken to each other since. Olga is Nancy's preferred coach for the Pit of Death.

Her third problem is still the risk that Eva and Jana discover each other's true identities before her plan reaches the stage where this will be revealed to them. She does not want to split them at this stage, so it's a risk she just has to live with.

Chapter 12 - Bruchenball

Eva recovers quickly from her injuries and she starts to push the doctor to allow her to start training. However, the doctor keeps her on the light duty list and only allows her to start with contact training when she is sure that Eva has healed physically and mentally. When she is eventually comfortable that Eva is ready to start with training, she instructs Eva to come see her if she feels any discomfort in the area where her ribs were broken.

Helga includes Eva in her light weight novice bruchenball team. She has attended tactical lectures with the team and she quickly fits in with the rest of the girls. Training consists of semi-competitive matches against the middle weight novice team and full contact fights against each other. In the semi-competitive matches, all wrestling holds are allowed, but punches and kicks are only allowed to the body. Slaps are still allowed to the face, but no headbutts are allowed. In the full contact fights, the girls are paired off for short ten seconds fights. After each ten second period, the pairs change and the odd girl out replaces one of the other's who then sits out that round. Helga also holds longer bouts, where only two girls fight each other for one minute. The other five have to watch the match and have to comment on each combatant's attack and defence. This forces the girls to think about fighting techniques. She also holds free for all fights at the end of every week. Six girls fight until one is knocked down. One girl starts on the bench while the others fight. The girl knocked down is then tagged by the girl on the bench and the fight continues. Should the girl on the bench refuse to tag, she is out of the contest and the girl knocked down has a choice to continue fighting, or to also exit the contest. If she exits the contest, the girl who knocked her down then moves to the bench. This carries on until only two girls remain in the contest. The winner of the contest is the one who first knocks down the other. Eva enjoys the training, but especially these free for all fights. She ends up in the final fight in almost each contest. Helga is pleased with this and starts using Eva in the point position. This is a pivotal position in bruchenball as the point defends the two carriers when they are attacked. As a result, the point often faces two attackers at the same time and it is crucial that she is willing to get up every time she is knocked down.

The day of Eva's first tournament finally arrives. She is both excited and nervous and she can't wait to test her skills in a competitive match, but she is afraid that she may let the team and Helga down. Jana calms her down, pointing out that she always gives her best and that nobody will expect anything more than that from her. She further points out that Eva's fighting skills has improved a lot and that she is probably the best fighter on the team. Her third point makes Eva smile. Jana tries to convince her that she looks so cute in her fighting outfit that no other girl would want to hurt her. She has to confess, the outfits are very cute and sexy at the same time. They will compete in female lederhosen. The leather pants are form fitting and covers little more than their bums. The leather straps going over their shoulders are not really needed to hold the pants up and are there more for historical accuracy. As such, the straps are very thin and do not cover any part of their upper bodies. The straps are held in place by an oval leather piece which connects the two straps. This piece is situated between the boobs and the naval and contains the academy's name and logo on the top half of the oval and the name of the girl on the bottom half of the oval. The outfits are black with the logo and words embroidered in a bright green.

They arrive at the indoor arena of the City Central Academy where today's tournament is held about an hour before their match. They will compete against the hosts today, but other academies will also compete against each other here. The light weight novice match between Combat Sport Academy and City Central Academy will be the first of the morning. There are already lost of spectators when they arrive and by the time their match starts the arena will be packed by about five thousand spectators. The field is about forty metres by twenty metres and is filled with mud. Helga takes the light weight novice team directly to the changing rooms on arrival. She goes through the tactics with the team again while they warm up for the match. She announces that the starting line-up will be Emma and Joanne as carriers, Eva as point, Chrissie and Marcy as attackers and Erin and Becky will start on the bench. Chrissie is the captain and Eva vice captain. The butterflies flutters in Eva's stomach as there is a knock on the door, signifying that the match is about to start. Helga opens the door and her team lines up in the corridor. Their opponents from the City Central Academy line up next to them. They are dressed in similar outfits. Theirs are made of bright red leather with black embroidery. The referee leads the teams down the corridor and into the arena to loud applause from the spectators. The two substitutes of each team remain on the side of the playing field while the other five members line up behind the goal lines on opposite sides of the playing field. The scoreboard displays the names of the two academies and the count down timer is set to fifteen minutes.

Eva tries to ignore the butterflies in her tummy by focusing her mind on the task at hand. When the referee blows her whistle, Eva's body reacts almost before she computes that the game is on. She follows Emma and Joanne closely trying to identify the opponents who may interfere with them. It is important that your carriers make it to the leather sandbag as fast as possible in order to obtain control over it. Chrissie is slightly ahead of everyone else and she makes contact with an opponent first. Both of them run straight into each other without slowing down. Eva and her two carriers rush past this collision and both carriers reach the leather sandbag without any interference. Emma and Joanne grab the leather sandbag moments before their opponents and manage to drag it about a metre before the opponent's carriers also grab onto the bag. Eva keeps her position just behind her carriers to protect them against any attack. Marcy manages to tackle one of the opponents' carriers to the ground and they are grappling with each other in the mud. This allows Emma and Joanne to drag the bag and the opponent still holding on to it back towards their goal line. Eva realises that only two of the opponents' players are in front of her and that Chrissie must be fighting three girls on her own. She looks behind her and sees Chrissie on her back, one girl is pinning her down and two are landing kick after kick to Chrissie's body. Eva rushes back and dive-tackles the girl pinning Chrissie down. She knocks the wind out of this girl and she stays down. Eva scrambles back to her feet and tackles one of the other girls. They fall into the mud and grapple with each other, with Eva in control, but the other girl manages to trap her arms and she is unable to get away from her to help Chrissie again. She looks at Chrissie to see whether she got up. Chrissie is on her knees locked in a hold with an opponent. The girl who Eva tackled first is back on her feet again and she grabs Chrissie from behind, wrestling her to the ground. The other girl starts kicking Chrissie again, this time some kicks find their way through to her head and face as well. Eva struggles to escape from her opponent's hold, but she is hanging on to Eva with all she has. Then Eva sees the opportunity she needed. She has never used a headbutt on anybody, but she remembers how much it hurt her and how disorientated she was when Amelia used this tactic on her. She moves her head forward as hard as she can and hits the other girl on the bridge of her nose. The girl screams in pain and Eva headbutts her again, this time catching her on her left cheek as the girl is turning her head to the right. The opponent lets go of Eva's arms and protects her face from another attack. Eva uses this opportunity to get to her feet and rushes over to help Chrissie. The girl kicking Chrissie sees her coming this time and turns to face her. They start trading punches, both landing to the other's face. Eva can see that the girl on top of Chrissie is landing punches and elbows in Chrissie's face. Chrissie tries to block, but she has taken a lot of punishment and is too weak to protect herself. Eva pushes her opponent aside and rushes past her taking a hard punch in her face for her troubles. She dives on top of the girl pinning Chrissie, knocking her off of Chrissie. As she wrestles with her new opponent, she sees the other opponent diving on top of Chrissie. She starts to punch Chrissie in the face again. Eva tries to disengage from her opponent, but once again she hangs on to Eva. All Eva can do is to kick out at Chrissie's attacker. She catches her on her side, but not hard enough to knock her off of Chrissie. Then the whistle blows and the referee assistants rush in to break up all remaining fights. Eva looks up to see that her team has dragged the leather sandbag over their goal line. Combat Sport Academy is leading 1 to 0. However, Chrissie is still down and it does not look like she will be able to get up on her own. Eva scrambles over to her. Chrissie's eyes are both swollen shut and it looks like her nose is broken. She is assisted of the field by the medics and the doctor rules that she is in no condition to continue with the match. Combat Sports Academy is down to six players. The doctor also rules that the girl who Eva head butted is unable to continue. Her nose is also broken, so City Central Academy is also down to six players.

The teams line up behind their goal lines again. Erin takes Chrissie's place as attacker. Helga sent instructions with her that Eva is captain now in the absence of Chrissie. Helga also instructs that they should ensure that no girl is isolated again. They cannot afford to lose another player. Eva looks up at the scoreboard. There are six minutes left in the first half. She only has a few second to talk before the leather sandbag is placed on the centre spot again. 'I want us all to make sure that all fights for the next six minutes are one-on-one. If any of us manage to neutralise an opponent, we can go for a second goal. If anyone gets into trouble, shout so that the rest of us can assist. I do not want anymore injuries.'
With that the whistle goes and they all rush the centre area again. Emma and Joanne reach the leather sandbag first again. Once again they manage to drag it about a metre before the

opponent's carriers latch onto it. This time Marcy and Erin hang back with Eva until they each identifies an opponent. Instead of attacking the opponent's carriers, they each engage an attacker. Eva waits till she is satisfied that all the other fights are one-on-one before she steps around the leather sandbag and attacks the opponent's point, who replaced the girl who Eva head butted earlier . The girl is shorter than Eva, but more muscular. She pushes Eva away from her and lands a hard straight right to Eva's face. The punch stuns Eva and she stumbles backwards and falls over one of the opponent's carriers. The carrier loses her grip on the leather sandbag and Eva reacts before she thinks about it. She grabs the girl around her waist, dragging her down to the mud. This allows Emma and Joanne to start dragging the leather sandbag and their one remaining opponent towards their goal line. The opponents' point has a decision to make. Either she helps her carrier who is being dragged with the leather sandbag towards Combat Sport Academy's goal line, or she attacks Eva. She decides to attack Eva, thereby creating a two-on-one situation. Eva realises that she has put herself in a difficult position. She can let go of the opponent's carrier, but then both may attack her. At least she has control over the carrier for now. The opponent's point jumps on her back and drags Eva away from her carrier and down into the mud. She has one arm around Eva's upper body and the other around her neck. The carrier gets to her feet and comes rushing over to attack Eva. All Eva can do is to kick out at her. The kick connects flush with the carrier's crotch and she goes down like a sack of potatoes. Eva did not plan that and immediately apologises. However, she realises that she is still in trouble and she focuses her efforts on her immediate opponent. She pushes back with her feet and at the same time she moves her upper body into her opponent. The unexpected movement surprises her opponent just enough so that Eva manages to force her right arm between her opponent's arm and her own throat. She is still trapped, but at least her opponent cannot choke her out. She knows that the carrier, who is still rolling around holding her crotch, is just stunned and in pain. However, she will recover soon enough, leaving Eva in a very dangerous position. Once the carrier is able to attack her she will be able to do very little to protect herself. She decides to call for help as soon as the other girl gets to her feet. This never becomes necessary though. Emma attacked the one remaining carrier of City Central Academy and Joanne was free to drag the leather sandbag over the goal line. Combat Sport Academy leads 2 to 0 with two minutes left in the first half.

Eva apologises to the rest of her team for not following the tactics she wanted all to follow. Helga sends Becky down with a message that Eva should take a break. Eva walks back to the bench, disappointed that she got pulled by the coach. Helga, however, assures her that she has done very well and that the only reason she was substituted was to give her a proper rest before the second half. The two minutes goes by without any major talking points. At half time Helga congratulates the team on their two goal lead. She wants them to keep the game tight and to ensure that no one gets isolated again. Eva is back as captain and point and Becky replaces Joanne to give her a rest. Chrissie is still in the medical centre, but Helga assures the team that she is fine.

The second half starts much like the first half. Emma and Becky reach the leather sandbag first and start to drag it towards their goal line. The opponent's carriers catch up soon though and a stalemate ensues. Eva, Marcy and Erin engage with their direct opponents, trying to slow the game down. Eva does not want to walk into the straight right that almost knocked her down again. She uses jabs to keep her opponent at bay. After about a minute of trading jabs, her opponent rushes in and takes Eva down. They both struggle for control in the mud before Eva's opponent obtains half mount and immediately starts raining down punches to Eva's face and upper body. Eva is able to block most, but a few land in her face and one flattens her right boob against her ribcage, causing intense pain. Eva tries to buck her opponent off, but her balance is good and she maintains her mount. All Eva can do is to block as many punches as possible. In the distance Eva can hear Helga screaming something at her. She reacts to this and sinks her fingers into the two ample breasts hanging bobbing in front of her face. She squeezes with all she has and she gets an instant reaction. The girl pulls back and Eva is able to buck her off by rolling her own body to the right. She scrambles to her knees and they face each other in the sticky mud. Eva can clearly see her handiwork. The girl's upper body is covered by mud, except for five clear lines on each breast. Eva can also see scratch marks where her nails cut her opponent's skin as she pulled away. For a second Eva feels bad, but the ferocity in her opponent's eyes makes it clear to Eva that revenge is coming her way fast. The girl does not waste time, her first punch is a right uppercut to Eva's left breast. The punch forces Eva's breast upwards before it slams down to its normal position again. Eva instinctively grabs hold of her breast as the pain is excruciating. She does not have any defences for a second, but the girl does not take full advantage, she is dead set on hurting Eva's breasts. She grabs Eva's right breast and sinks her nails into it. Eva screams in pain and quickly slaps her opponent's hand away. The girl immediately grabs hold of Eva's breasts again, sinking her nails into both of them. Although the pain is more than Eva can handle and although her instincts screams at her to protect her breasts, Eva sees an opening to end this fight. She pulls her head back slightly and headbutts her opponent with all she has. Blood streams from her opponent's nose immediately. Eva has broken another opponent's nose. The girl grabs her own face and before she has time to think, Eva is on her feet and a hard knee catches the girl on her chin. Another knee glances past the girl's forehead as she is dropping to the mud. Eva is yanked away by one of the assistant referees. She has deemed the situation to be too dangerous for Eva's opponent. The medics remove the girl while Eva scans the field. She sees four other fights, with no one on the leather sandbag. She could grab it and go score another goal, but she decides to rather go for total surrender. In three of the four fights, her teammates are either in control or in a position where their opponent cannot inflict serious harm. However, Erin's opponent is in full mount and is raining punches to Erin's head. Eva rushes over and grabs the girl from behind. She applies a full nelson hold and pulls the girl off of Erin. She forces the girl down to her knees and kneels behind her, maintaining the full nelson hold. The girl surprises her by jerking her head back. The blow catches Eva on her right eye and it starts to swell immediately, but Eva manages to maintain her hold. She presses her head against the girls shoulder, making her following headbutts ineffective. Erin has recovered from the mauling she took and comes over. She starts landing punch after punch to the girl's face. Eva screams at her to use her knees and when the second knee lands, an assistant referee breaks up the fight. Another opponent is out of the match. Eva and Erin rushes over to the nearest fight. Marcy and her opponent are both on their knees. Their hands are sunk into each other's hair, each landing the occasional punch to her opponent's body. Eva grabs the girl from behind and applies a full nelson again. This time she immediately presses her head against her shoulder to avoid another headbutt to the face. Erin immediately starts with knee strikes to the face and an assistant referee quickly breaks up the fight. A third opponent is out of the match. Before Eva and Erin can get to the next fight, the referee blows the whistle. Eva is confused at first as there are still seven minutes on the clock. She then realises that the Mid City Academy's coach has forfeited the match, sparing her last two remaining players a beating. Eva throws her arms in the air in elation before she hugs Erin. She hears the loud applause from the audience and she thoroughly enjoys it. Soon the other four girls rush in for a group hug of muddy half naked female bodies. Only Chrissie does not join in as she is still in the medical centre.

They eventually break up the group hug and form a line behind Eva and they move towards the opponents, who are also lined up. Each girl hugs each of the opponents. They were all in a hard fought match and the opponents earned their respect. As Eva reaches the opponent's point, they can both see the job they have done on each other's boobs. Her opponent gently touches her own boobs. 'I will get you back for this.'
Eva touches her own boobs. 'I think you already did, but I look forward competing with you again. It was one hell of a fight.' They hug each other. 'I am Eva by the way.'
The girl smiles at her. 'Lea here, now I know what to call my punching bag.'
Eva laughs at this and moves on to the next girl. When the formalities are done, Helga leads them back to the changing room. After showering, Eva checks out her war scars. Her right eye is completely swollen shut and dark-purplish in colour. The rest of her face is mostly unscathed, except for a small cut to her top lip. Her boobs are a mess though. They are dotted with bruises from Lea's breast mauling. Lea's uppercut also caused a big bruise on the underside of Eva's left boob. There are deep scratches on both boobs as well from Lea digging her nails in and these scratch marks burn like hell. She also has bruises on her ribs, her upper arms and her thighs. She looks at her teammates. All of them have bruises on their bodies and it is clear that all have been in decent brawls, yet none of them are nearly as badly marked as Eva. Helga hands her a cream to apply to the scratch marks which immediately sooths the pain.

After a quick debrief, Helga tells them that the bus will leave in a few minutes, but that anyone is welcome to stay behind with her. She came in her own vehicle and she will make sure Chrissie is fine. She also has to prepare the middle weight novice team for their match which will start in about two hours from now. All the girls, except for Eva decide to go home. They are all tired from their match and they want to go tend to their bruised bodies. Eva's excitement levels are too high to go rest now. Anyway, she can't wait to watch a few of the matches. Helga sits next to Eva for a while, asking Eva what the thinks about tactics used by the teams competing and about individual match ups. Eva learns a lot from this discussion with Helga and she is very glad she stayed behind. Helga later leaves her on her own to check up on Chrissie and to prepare the middle weight novice team for their match. Eva enjoys watching the matches. She finds the sight of half naked, muddy female bodies locked in combat very sexy and she is very turned on by this. 'Jana does not know what is coming her way tonight', She thinks to herself. This makes her smile. She is jerked back to reality when something very cold is pressed against her neck. She swings her neck around to see Lea with a huge grin on her face. She hands Eva the very cold fizzy drink. 'Mind if I join you?'

Eva has a flutter in her stomach, similar to the feeling she had when she saw the fight between Margaret and Janet. She did not expect to see Lea so soon again and she over eagerly says. 'No, please join me.' She recovers a bit before she says. 'I am very sorry about your boobs and your nose.'

Lea's nose is covered by a plaster and her eyes are both swollen. 'Please don't be. We were in a fight. Next time I may break your nose and may even do more damage. We can't feel sorry for each other. I have a feeling that we will do lots of damage to each other in future.'

Eva smiles, she knows that Lea is right. 'I know, but I am still sorry. I used dirty tactics when I scratched your breasts.'

Lea gently touches her boobs again. 'Yes you did. How are your tits by the way?'

Eva softly touches her own boobs. 'They burned like hell, but my coach gave me some cream to apply. They are feeling a lot better now.'

'Do you still have any of the cream left? My tits still burn like hell.'

'Yes.'

Eva gets the cream from her bag and hands it to Lea. She takes some and applies it to her boobs. Eva finds it very easy to chat to Lea and she thoroughly enjoys their conversation. They talk about fighting, guys, girls and their future fights against each other. They agree to be friends of the field but that this will not stop them from brawling on it.

When the middle weight novice team's match is done, Helga calls Eva. Eva and Lea hug each other before Eva joins Helga. Helga asks Eva to get Chrissie from the medical centre and to meet her at her car. She needs to go debrief the middle weight novice team who will travel back in the bus, which returned from dropping off Eva's teammates. Eva feels bad that she has not visited Chrissie yet, but she enjoyed her conversation with Lea so much that she did not even think about Chrissie.

Chrissie tries to smile when Eva enters her room, but her face is so cut, bruised and swollen that it is difficult to distinguish her smiling face from her crying face. Eva is genuinely concerned about het teammate and captain. 'Are you ok? I cannot belief the referees did not break up your fight, those girls were really punishing you.'

'Helga says she is going to lay a complaint. She also told me that if it wasn't for you, it would have been a lot worse. Thank you.'

Eva feels bad for not helping Chrissie earlier and for not visiting her earlier. She can't stop the tears from rolling down her cheeks. She helps Chrissie to Helga's car where Helga is already waiting. Back at the academy Eva and Helga helps Chrissie to the clinic. Eva promises her that she will visit often, a promise she diligently keeps. She also makes sure

that the rest of their teammates visit at least once a day for the five days Chrissie spends in the clinic. After they leave the clinic, Helga takes her to a quiet spot where she generally has private discussions with the girls. 'You have done very well today. You showed leadership and lots of guts. You also showed that you are able to adjust tactics when the situation changes. You have to be careful not to take on too much on your own though. Use your teammates to help you instead.' Helga pauses to establish whether Eva understands her points. 'Be very careful not to get too close to opponents. You will have to hurt each other again in future. It is sometimes not that easy to hurt a friend. Some girls find it easy to do that, being friends off the field and enemies on it, but I am not sure whether you will be able to. You are caring. I saw how Chrissie's injuries affected you and I know that you will look after her. I am scared that when the time comes for you to really hurt your new friend, you will hold back.'
Eva is a bit taken aback by this. 'I like her, but I will not hold back against her in a match.'
Helga gives her a soft sympathetic smile. 'I hope you are right. I will test this in the near future.'
Back in their townhouse, Eva shows off her war scars to Jana. Jana promises to kiss it better. However, her kisses soon moves to areas not bruised or scratched at all. They make passionate love to each other and Eva falls asleep in Jana's arms as a very happy girl.

Chapter 13 – Farewell Party

Eva competes in two more bruchenball matches. The light weight novice team learned a lot of lessons during their first match and they manage to get through the next two matches without any serious injuries. Chrissie is back as captain and Eva as her vice captain. The two of them work together well and the rest of the team follows their instructions without hesitation. After the third match Helga promotes Eva to the lightweight calcio storico team. Her teammates are all happy for her, but sad that they are losing one of their best players and their vice captain. She will miss them, but she has a lot to learn and want to move on as fast as she can.

A week later there is a knock on the door at about eight o'clock in the evening. Eva looks at Jana who only shrugs her shoulders. It is Saturday night and they have nothing planned. Well not entirely nothing, Jana took Eva to get her nipples pierced a few days ago and the plan was to try on different nipple rings tonight. Eva bought a whole bunch and she wanted her roommate to help her choose the sexiest ones. She also knows that this planned nipple ring fitting will surely lead to sex. It is clear to Eva that Jana is not going to open the door. She is lying on the sofa watching television. Eva gets up with a sigh to let Jana know that she is not happy with her laziness. They've had a few arguments the last couple of weeks. Eva suspects that Jana may be jealous of Lea. Eva brought her new friendship up during a discussion about her first bruchenball match. Although they are supposed to be friends with benefits only, she thinks that Jana is jealous of Lea. She told Jana that she has no sexual interest in Lea and that they are just friends. However, this did not change the situation. They still have many good times together, but they also irritate each other often. She discussed this with Margaret. Her advice was that Eva should take Jana to the sandpit so that they can punch some sense into each other. Who knows, maybe it will come to that. She opens the door and finds her former bruchenball teammates outside. They push past her with arms full of alcohol and snacks. Chrissie grabs her by the arm and drags her in. 'Come, it's your farewell party.'
As Eva is about to close the door, Jana pushes past her. 'Are you not staying?'
Jana hesitates. 'No, you nerds have fun. I've made other plans.'
Eva wrestles her arm away from Chrissie and goes outside with Jana. 'I don't know what's going on, but I do not want to lose your friendship. You mean a lot to me, you surely know that? I will do whatever it takes to make sure we stay friends. Margaret says that we should punch some sense into each other. If that is what it takes I will fight you right here right now!'
Jana smiles at her. 'Go enjoy your party, we will chat tomorrow. I love you too and you will always be my friend. I just have a few issues to sort out.' She hugs Eva and gives her a long kiss on the lips. 'We will chat tomorrow and if you still want to, we can fight then. I don't want to ruin your face before your party.'
She gives Eva that cheeky grin Eva fell in love with, turns around and goes to Margaret and

Janet's place. Eva composes herself and enters the house with a big smile on her face. They party to the early hours.

When Jana returns at nine o'clock the next morning, she finds girls still sleeping all over the place. Eva is in Jana's bed, cuddling one of Jana's shirts. Jana feels terrible for hurting her friend. That was never her plan. She is dealing with big issues in her life and it was just easier to lash out at Eva than to deal with her own demons. She is unable to discuss the current issue with anybody and she is not sure how to deal with it by herself. The only person she can discuss this with is Nancy and she is the last person she wants to discuss personal issues with. Jana left her home when she was sixteen, crashing at a few friend's houses. When she was out of options for a place to stay, she joined an underground fighting club and made a living fighting for prize money. By the time she was eighteen, she had some money saved up and she used it to enter a tournament in which sixteen girls fought in an elimination tournament. Each girl, or her sponsor, had to pay five thousand credits to enter and the full pot went to the winner. Jana was desperate to win the tournament, but she was knocked out in the semi-finals. She lost all her savings and was sure she would have to go back to fighting in the underground fighting clubs. However, a woman from the audience asked to speak to her. She introduced herself as Nancy and asked whether Jana would want to try out for her academy. She was always looking for fresh talent and she was impressed with Jana's skills and fighting spirit. Nancy asked her to tell her more about herself and especially how she started fighting and why she fights. Jana foolishly told her how her mother was supposed to fight in a death match, but decided to rather send a professional fighter in her place. How all her fellow pupils and even some teachers kept reminding her of what a lowlife her mother was. How she tried to talk to her mother about this, but that her mother started to drink heavily after news break of her deceit and that she never wanted to talk about it. How her mother lost her job and how their relationship became so bad that Jana left her home at sixteen and joined an underground fighting club. She could see a change in Nancy's whole demeanour after she shared this information with her. Nancy was now eager to sign Jana for her academy. She helped her with the application and even helped her pick another surname so that people would not realise who she was. This suited Jana and she promised Nancy that she will never share her true identity with anybody. Two weeks ago, her mother made contact with her. She told her that she has been sober for six months and that she found a job again. She wanted Jana back in her life so that she can make amends for all the harm she caused her. Jana does not know what to do. Deep down she misses her mother and she wants her back in her life, but she has been hurt so deeply that she is not sure whether she can trust her mother again. She knows she will not recover if her mother disappoints her again.

Jana gives Eva a soft kiss on her forehead. Eva opens her eyes and smiles at Jana. 'Morning.' Her smile quickly turns into a frown. 'Do you have something for a headache? I have a terrible hangover.'
Jana smiles at this. This is the first time she has seen Eva with a hangover. It must have been a good party. She goes to the kitchen and mixes ginger with brown sugar and tangerine

extract in a glass of water. This is the same cure she made for her mother so many times and keeps the ingredients for the occasions when she has a few drinks. Eva eagerly downs the glass and a few minutes later she feels well enough to get up. She is too lazy to walk all the way to her own bathroom and decides to shower in Jana's bathroom. She gets in the shower and takes a deep breath as the hot water massages her tense shoulders. A few seconds later she feels hands on her shoulders. These hands start to massage her shoulders, gently pressing down on her muscles at first and then intensifying the pressure, the thumbs really working on the knots underneath her skin. Eva gives a deep sigh and she lets her body relax. She does not have to turn around to know it is Jana. Her friend gives the best shoulder massages. She feels Jana's hard nipples brush against her back and her own nipples are soon rock hard as well. Jana's hands start to move lower down Eva's back. She massages the muscles all the way down to Eva's the small of Eva's back. Her left hand slides down and gives Eva's bum a gentle squeeze. At the same time her right hand explores around Eva's side until it strokes her tummy just above her vagina. Eva's breathing slows down and becomes heavier in anticipation of her clit being stroked. However, Jana's right hand slowly starts to move upwards and is joined by her left hand. They make their way slowly upwards until both hands cup her boobs. Jana starts to gently massage Eva's boobs, occasionally trapping a nipple between two fingers and tugging softly on the erect breast adornments. She kisses Eva's neck and shoulders while she fondles her boobs. Eva reaches back as far as she can and squeezes Jana's butt cheeks. She slowly turns around to face Jana. They look deep into each other's eyes and no words are required. Eva is sure that she has her friend and lover back. Their lips lock and they kiss each other for a long time. Their boobs squash together and their pierced nipples are jousting with each other as the occasionally brush against each other. Jana starts grinding her crotch against Eva's thigh and Eva soon follows suit. Both girls are soon panting with excitement. They ignore the fact that six other girls are sleeping a few metres away in the lounge area and that only a thin wall separates them from these sleeping beauties. Their moans and squeals grow louder by the second and crescendos into loud screams as both girls shudder with intense orgasms. This was more than making love. They shared a deep and true love for each other.

When they eventually appear from Jana's room, Eva's teammates are all awake. Most of them are sipping on strong black coffee to try and fix their hangovers. All of them have huge grins on their faces causing Eva to blush 'What?'
Chrissie laughs at her friend's embarrassment. 'Thanks for the show.'
Eva's cheeks turn even brighter red than before. Jana, however, seems to be less than bothered that their lovemaking session woke up the other girls. 'So this is the infamous lightweight bruchenball team. Careful, I may just smack all your skinny asses.'
There are a few 'oohs' and 'aahs' from the girls. 'So which one of you little bitches are going to slap us up some breakfast? You little drunkards look like you need some greasy bacon to recover from your hangovers.'
These mock insults are taken in the right spirit and Eva and a few of the girls make themselves handy in the kitchen. Half an hour later everybody are quietly munching on bacon and egg sandwiches. After breakfast the girls excuse themselves giving Eva and Jana

a chance to discuss the weirdness between them the last couple of weeks. Jana ensures Eva that she still loves her and that their friendship is very important to her. She has a few personal issues which she has to solve by herself and unfortunately she cannot discuss these with Eva. She promises to try her best not to take her own stress out on Eva. Eva apologises for being bitchy with Jana as well. She promises to be there for Jana whenever she needs a shoulder to cry on. The girls hug it out and give each other a passionate kiss which leads to another lovemaking session.

Nancy arrives back home content with the progress report she just received from a private investigator. She employed the investigator when Jana joined her academy. She wanted to keep tabs on Jana's mother to make sure that she does not interfere with her plans for Jana. The investigator found her in a halfway house. She just completed a session in a religious rehab centre and was in the process of getting her life together. She still did not have a job, but the church was looking after her, helping her to find odd jobs. When Eva joined the academy, Nancy's plan changed. Nancy wanted Jana and her mother to have a relationship again. This was crucial to her plan to convince Jana to fight Eva in the Pit of Death. She instructed the private investigator to plant a woman in the same halfway house. She needed someone to befriend Jana's mother, Emily Theron. This woman will be used to give them regular reports and to steer Emily in the direction Nancy wants her to go. She soon received feedback that Emily is desperately trying to find her daughter. Nancy arranged a job for her, all done through the woman she has planted. They soon got a flat together and Nancy had full insight into Emily's life. She was also able to control her without her even suspecting anything. Emily's new friend informed her that she saw a girl, who looks a lot like the photos Emily had of Jana. She said she was walking past the Combat Sport Academy when the girl came out of the front door. They bumped into each other and she had a good look at the girl. She convinced Emily not to rush over to the academy as this may damage any chance she has of mending her relationship with Jana. She instead helped Emily to pen a letter, which she promised to drop off at the academy. Nancy called Jana in and handed her the letter. She told her that she had no idea how her mother managed to find her and that it was up to Jana whether she wanted to make contact with her mother, but that she suggests that any meeting should be in a neutral venue and that she would be willing to accompany Jana should she choose to meet her mother. She could see the pain and confusion the news caused Jana. She knew that she would have to manage the situation carefully to ensure that she does not lose Jana to her mother. But she needed them to get close enough to each other so that Jana will be willing to fight Eva in order to save her mother's life when the time comes.

Chapter 14 – MMA at a Biker Bar

One Wednesday after practice Helga pulls Eva aside. 'Bring your MMA shorts, gloves and mouth guard. It is time for you to prove to me that you are willing to hurt a friend in a match.' Eva still remembers their conversation after her first bruchenball match, but she was not expecting to fight tonight. She wonders who this friend will be. She looks for Jana in their townhouse to share this with her, but Jana is nowhere to be seen. Will she have to fight Jana? This thought has crossed her mind before. She would love to fight Jana one day, but she is not sure whether she is ready to hurt her best friend and lover. She grabs her MMA fighting gear and meets up with Helga. They get in Helga's vehicle and drive to a seedy part of town. There isn't much conversation during the drive as Eva is caught up in her own thoughts and Helga prefers not to discuss the fight before they get to the venue. Helga stops in front of a biker bar. 'They have a MMA octagon here. It is available for any women wanting to fight each other.'

With that she leads Eva into the club. The club is dimly lit and Eva has to adjust her eyes to see properly. She sees the octagon towards the back of the room. She also sees a lot of bikers. Most of them are sitting around the bar area, drinking beer and chatting with each other and a few are around the pool tables, shooting pool. Helga tells Eva to wait for her and goes to the bar counter. The bar lady's face lights up when she sees Helga. They grab each others right hands and embrace. Eva watches the as Helga motions to the octagon and the bar lady nods her head. Helga has a broad smile on her face when she calls Eva over. 'This is my friend Spitfire. She says you can use her octagon as long as you give her a good show.'

Spitfire gives Eva a big smile. 'Have a good fight girly.'

Helga shows Eva to a small room at the back of the pub and tells her to dress and warm up. A few minutes later the door opens and Lea walks in. The girls are surprised, but happy to see each other. They give each other a big hug before Eva asks the obvious question. 'Are we fighting each other?'

'I think so. My coach told me that, if I want to be friends with you, I have to prove to her that I am willing to hurt you in a fight. I thought she was talking about a fight during a sport event though. Are you up for this?'

'You better believe it. I have been looking forward to fight you again.'

'Well you better take those off or I will rip them off during the fight.'

Eva quickly removes her nipple piercings. She remembers what they have done to each other's breasts in the bruchenball fight and she does not want to give Lea and opportunity to rip her nipples as she is sure that Lea will not hesitate to do it during a fight. They both smile at each other while Eva removes the nipple piercings, both knowing that they are in for a tough fight, and both eager to get it on. They warm up together until Lea's coach comes in and tells them that its time for the fight. As they exit the bar erupts in a mixture of catcalls and suggestions on how to rip each other apart. Eva is used to fighting topless by now and the lewd remarks about their half naked bodies do not bother her too much. The suggestion that Lea should rip her tits off concerns her a little though. Lea surely does not need more encouragement in this regard.

Helga acts as referee and she quickly explains the rules to the girls. There will be unlimited three minute rounds until one of them is knocked out or submits. In the first round, only punching and kicking are allowed and any kind of striking is allowed from the second round. Both these rounds will be fought on their feet only. If a girl goes down, her opponent has to let her up before she can punch her again. Grappling and wrestling rules are allowed from the third round. Both girls nod, confirming that they understand these rules. Helga steps back and the bell is rung. The two friends start to circle each other and both land with stiff jabs. Eva knows that Lea has the ability to hurt her with her fists and she keeps Lea at bay with a few kicks to her body. Lea seems to be more comfortable punching than kicking and Eva uses this to her advantage. She dances in and out of range, landing a quick punch or two before she moves out. She uses her legs to punish Lea every time she tries to close the distance. At the end of the first round Lea's ribs are already turning red from Eva's kicks and Eva is chuffed with herself.

Lea is much more aggressive in round two. She rushes forward, takes a kick to her ribs, but lands a straight right to Eva's face. She follows this up with a left and another right. Eva manages to grab hold of Lea and moves her head to the side just in time to avoid a headbutt to her nose. Lea's head still connects with her left cheekbone and Eva stumbles backward. As soon as she hits the floor, Lea is on top of her. She lands two punches to Eva's face before Helga is able to pull her off. Helga warns Lea not to break the rules again and asks Eva if she is fine. Eva nods and gets back on her feet and Lea rushes her again. This time Eva is ready and she jumps towards Lea, landing an elbow to Lea's face. Lea rocks back, but keeps her feet. Eva follows up with a left hook, but Lea manages to avoid this. She gives Eva a grin before she launches her next attack. It is obvious that she is revelling in the thrill of the fight. Lea lands another right to Eva's face, drawing blood from Eva's bottom lip. Eva barely notices the cut as she launches her own attack. She lands a hard kick to Lea's ribs, which clearly hurts Lea. So Eva feints another kick to Lea's ribs and land a straight left to Lea's face as Lea moves to protect her ribs. She grabs Lea around her neck and lands two quick knees to Lea's stomach. Lea pushes her away and attacks with a flurry of punches, catching Eva in the face with three or four of them. Eva lifts her arms to protect herself and Lea does not wait for a second invitation. She lands two vicious punches to Eva's boobs, drawing loud applause from the spectators. Eva fights the urge to grab her boobs as they both sting like hell. She moves out of range and keeps Lea away from her with effective kicks to Lea's body. The bell sounds and both girls are glad for a break after a hard fought round. Eva nurses her boobs which brings a huge grin to Lea's face. She has struck first this time. Although this is a serious fight, they both know that their boobs will be targeted tonight.

The third round starts and Lea goes for the takedown immediately. They go down together and scramble for control. Lea's upper body is stronger than Eva's and she forces Eva on her back. She wastes no time to go on the offensive and lands measured punches to Eva's face. Eva struggles to break the hold, twisting her body and pushing up with her lower body. Lea loses her balance for a split second, but is quickly back in control. She lands two elbows to Eva's right cheekbone and blood starts to stream from Eva's face as a cut opens just under her right eye. This does not slow Lea down at all and she lands two more punches to Eva's face before Eva is able to tie her up. Eva holds on to Lea's arms with all she has. Lea leans back a little and rips her left arm from Eva's grip and starts swinging again, forcing Eva to protect her face. Once again Eva leaves her upper body unprotected and Lea punches Eva's right tit with full force. As Eva lowers her right hand to protect her breast, Lea swings to her face again. Eva is forced to let go of Lea's right arm to protect both her face and breasts. Eva is in trouble and she needs to find a way out. She lifts her upper body as far as she can and locks her hands behind Lea's back, pulling her head into Lea's chest. Lea is unable to land any decent punches, so she reaches behind her back to break Eva's hold. Eva twists her body again and this time she is able to roll Lea off of her. She tries to gain control, but Lea pushes her away and gets to her feet. Eva is a bit too slow and eats a hard kick to her side as she scrambles to her feet. This stuns her and she takes a few steps back to get away from Lea. However, Lea is relentless and she jumps forward and lands three punches to Eva's face rocking Eva's head back and only the side of the octagon stops her from going down again. She leans against the side of the octagon and waits for Lea to get closer before she grabs Lea around the waist to tie her up, trying to buy some time to recover. Lea leans back and tosses Eva over her hip with a lot of force. The fall winds Eva and she tries to roll away from a stalking Lea, but Lea jumps on her back and starts to choke her. Eva manages to force a few fingers between her throat and Lea's arm, but she is still in trouble. As the world around her starts to blank out, she hears the bell ring. Lea reluctantly lets go and Eva slumps down to the floor. Helga helps her to her corner and works on stopping the bleeding. 'I have seen enough. You don't have to carry on in order to convince me that the two of you are capable of being friends and rivals. She is kicking your butt, do you want me to stop the fight.'

Eva shakes her head. 'No, I want to hurt the bitch and I don't care whether she hurts me as well. I just want to make sure she knows tomorrow that she has been in a fight tonight.'

Helga smiles at her. 'Ok then, she dominates on the floor. Stay away from her and land some kicks. Her defence against your kicks is weak.'

The bell rings and Lea rushes Eva. Eva lifts her right leg and catches Lea in the chest flattening her left breast, making Lea yell out in pain and frustration. Eva follows up with a kick to Lea's side, which forces Lea on the back foot. She presses her advantage with a flurry of punches and another kick to Lea's side. This time Lea is the one putting distance between them to give herself time to recover. Eva does not want to allow Lea any time to recover and she runs after her eager to punish Lea some more. Suddenly Lea stops, plants her feet and unleashes a right hook, catching Eva flush on the jaw. Eva goes down like a sack of potatoes. She is out cold before she hits the floor. Lea jumps on her, but Helga pulls her away before she lands any punches. When Eva regains her consciousness, Helga helps her back to her corner and sits her down on a chair. It takes Eva about a minute before her

head clears enough for her to be able to get up from the chair. Lea is standing about a metre away, her face full of concern. Eva extents her arms and the two hug each other for a long time. 'Lucky punch.' Says Eva dryly.
Lea smiles at her friend for making this cheeky comment. 'Which one? I caught you with so many, but after that last punch you probably only remember one.'
Eva laughs and hugs Lea again. Her friend well and truly kicked her butt tonight and she can't wait to turn the tables in their next fight. She wants to fight her friend again as soon as possible. She has never felt so alive as she did during this fight.

After the girls showered, Helga thanks Spitfire and tells her that she will see her soon. However, Spitfire is not having this. 'Where do you think you are going?'
Helga sighs. She is not up for a late night. 'The girls need to get to bed. They have a full day of training tomorrow.'
Spitfire throws her arms in the air in an exasperated gesture. 'You must be joking. First of all, these are not girls, they are fearless warriors. This was the best fight we've seen here in years. They made my day. It is only right that I reward them with some hospitality. They are young and their blood is hot with fight lust. They both need to relax and enjoy themselves for a while.'
Helga knows that it will be futile to argue with Spitfire. They have been friends for a long time and she knows that her friend will look after the girls and it is also probably fair that they get to spend some time together. They have earned their friendship tonight. She looks at Lea's coach. 'I am willing to give Eva the day off tomorrow. I think the girls deserve a break after their brawl tonight. Spitfire here will look after them and she will drop them off later. I promise you that they are safer here than at our academies.'
Lea's coach nods her head and look at Lea. 'Enjoy yourself, but not too much alcohol and be safe. Oh, and no more fighting. Are the two of you ok with each other?'
Both girls give her a big smile and they hug each other again.

Eva has never laughed as much in her life. The bikers share stories of their adventures and Eva is sure that most of these are exaggerated, but she is in awe of what these ladies get up to in order to get some kicks from life. Spitfire makes sure that their glasses are never empty and before long both girls are more than a little tipsy. They chat and laugh and truly enjoy each other's company. Around two o'clock, one of the bikers slaps Eva on the back. 'I bet you can take her if the two of you were to fight again right now.'
Spitfire was right, Eva's blood is still boiling with fight lust and the alcohol totally impairs her judgement. 'You are right, come Lea, I want to kick your butt.'
Lea stumbles a bit as she gets up. She lifts her fists and is ready to fight, but Spitfire quickly gets between them and forces both to sit down. 'You've done enough fighting for one night my brave warriors.' She gives the biker a dirty look. 'Roadkill, stop filling their heads with stupid ideas.'
Both girls giggle again at Roadkill's name and the story of how she got it and then as if nothing happened, they continue with their conversation. Just after four o'clock in the morning Spitfire locks the door behind her and helps the two drunken girls to her car. When

she drops Lea of, both girls get out and almost stumble over each other. They loudly laugh at their own clumsiness and Eva gives Lea a playful punch to the chin. 'Next time I will knock your teeth out.'

They both loudly laugh at this. After a clumsy hug, Lea enters her academy and Eva gets back in the car.

Chapter 15 – Slap in the Face

Back at the academy Eva tries to enter the townhouse quietly, but she knocks down a small table and a glass left on top of it shatters on the floor. Jana's light goes on and she appears in her door. Even in her state, Eva can see that Jana has been crying. 'What's wrong?'
Jana clears the larger pieces of glass from the floor before she sweeps the floor to get rid of any small pieces of glass. 'I am ok, just had a bad dream. Let's get you to bed.'
Jana helps Eva to her own bed and watches her friend for a while after she falls asleep. She has seen her mother last night and her emotions are all over the place. Deep down she still loves her mother, but this is all a bit too much for her to handle at the moment. She told her mother that she needs time to think and that she will contact her again when she is ready. She is not sure whether she should contact her again though. Her life was under control until her mother suddenly came back into it. She wants to discuss this with Eva, but she made a promise to Nancy and she also does not want to share this part of her life with anybody right now.

The next day Eva stays in bed till late in the morning. When she eventually gets up, she studies the rules of calcio storico. Her training has been going well and she should be in the light weight side for their match in two weeks time, but first she has to pass a test on the rules and tactics tomorrow. The rules are the same as rules used around six hundred years ago in Italy. Two teams of twenty-seven players compete on a rectangular, sandy field. Their aim is to force a ball into their opponent's net and the team with the most goals after fifty minutes wins. The rules of the game allows for full contact fights between players. However, only one-on-one fights are allowed. No attacks from behind or headbutts to a player who was knocked down is allowed. Fights continue until a referee breaks them up and the loser has to leave the field and is not allowed to return. Any players breaking the rules during a fight are also send from the field and are not allowed to return. The teams are made up of four goalkeepers, three defenders, five midfielders and fifteen forwards. As no substitutes are allowed, most games do not last the full fifty minutes as teams often run out of players long before full time.

Eva remembers that Jana was crying when she arrived home this morning, so she decides to prepare a nice meal before Jana gets home from training. When Jana arrives home, Eva hands her a glass of wine, while she runs a hot bath for her. She checks on the food and then joins Jana in the bathroom. She sits down and starts washing Jana's back. 'I am sorry I wasn't here for you last night. What is going on? Why are you so sad?'
There is a long silence before Jana eventually answers her. 'It is just an issue from my past which I cannot really discuss with you. I am ok. I just need to figure it out. Anyway, should I dare ask how your night was? I saw the end product this morning and it was not pretty.'
Eva laughs. 'To sum it up, had a fight, my ass got kicked, met some bikers and had some fun. No scrap that, had lots of fun.' They both laugh and Eva hugs her friend around the

neck and kisses her on the cheek. 'You know I love you and that you can share anything with me.'
'I know and I love you too. We both have our secrets and for now at least, I cannot share mine with you.'

A few days later during fight practice, Eva is paired up with Reka, the girl who refereed her initiation fight against Amelia. Eva remembers how she turned a blind eye to Emily's dirty tactics. The rules of the practice match allow for grappling and slaps to the body only. Eva does not outweigh a lot of girls at the academy, but she is at least five pounds heavier than Reka, but she soon finds out that Reka is strong for her size. It takes a lot of effort before Eva is able to pin Reka down. While Helga's back is turned on their scrap, Eva unleashes a stinging slap to Reka's face. She feels instant gratification, but also feels a bit guilty about the cheap shot. After practice, Eva and Jana are relaxing at their townhouse when there is a knock on the door. Eva opens the door and, to her surprise, finds Reka outside. 'Come, the two of us need to go to the sandpit to chat about what you did to me earlier.'
Eva did not expect Reka to call her out about the slap and her respect for this tiny girl instantly goes up a few notches. She shrugs at Jana. 'I will be back a bit later.'
'Do you want me to come with?'
'No, this is a private chat. I will be back soon.'

Nancy is working late when she sees three girls hiding behind the corner of one of the buildings next to the sandpit. She can see that something is up and her interest is piqued. She thinks of calling Helga to go sort this out, but decides to wait and see what they are up to. She then sees Eva and Reka walking towards the sandpit. They stop in the sandpit and face off to each other. Words are said and Reka pokes Eva in her chest. Nancy watches as the other three girls sneaks up on Eva from behind. The big girl grabs Eva from behind, trapping her arms behind her back, while the other two grab hold of her legs. Reka steps up and slaps Eva through the face. She says something again and then lands a flurry of slaps before she steps back to admire her handiwork. A trickle of blood is dripping from Eva's lip. Reka then jumps forward and lands five or six knee strikes to Eva's unprotected stomach, following these up with a few elbows to Eva's face. This opens the recently healed cut on Eva's cheekbone and blood starts to stream down her face. Reka slaps her one more time before she turns around and walks away. The girls behind her let go of her and the big girl hits her with a right hook from behind, catching her on the side of her jaw. Eva goes down and slowly struggles back to her feet and by the time she composes herself, all four girls are around the corner of the building and she is all on her own in the sandpit, bleeding, confused and pissed off. Nancy makes some notes. It is always good to identify rivalries. This may come in handy in future.

Eva opens the door and Jana's jaw almost drops to the floor. 'Wow, that tiny little thing really fucked you up. I never knew she packed such a punch.'
Eva is still too mad to answer. She walks to her bathroom to clean up. She will get all four these girls back. She started the issue between her and Reka today and she was prepared to

face the consequences, but you just don't gang up on someone. She will get them all back. When she tells Jana what happened, Jana wants to go confront Emily and her gang immediately. She is taken aback by Eva's response. 'Butt out, this is my fight.' Eva feels bad immediately. 'Sorry, but I want to handle this myself. You cannot fight my fights for me.'

Jana respects this, but is still a little hurt by Eva's blunt refusal to accept her help.

Nancy is a bit frustrated by the fact that Jana is not spending more time with her mother, but decides that for now she will not push the issue. There is still plenty time and she will manipulate the situation if it does not naturally work out the way she wants it to. She has signed an agreement with her new business partner, Kelly Yates. The partnership will officially start producing live programmes in three months time when she will launch her new MMA style competition, 'Grudge Fights'. The plan is to allow her academy's girls to settle their grudges, whether real or made up. She will also allow other women to settle their issues in the ring, but only after some training. She signed Olga as trainer for these women, with the understanding that she will be her head trainer for Pit of Death when it starts and she knows that she will have to share this news with Helga soon.

Chapter 16 – The Greatest Show Part II

On Saturday morning, a week before her first calcio storico match, Eva walks into their sitting room still groggy from sleep. Jana is already up and is sipping on a hot cup of coffee. She holds up a piece of paper between her index and middle finger. 'Look what the Easter bunny brought us last night. Eva takes the piece of paper and opens it. In a neat handwriting it reads.

> **'The Greatest Show Part II – The Challenge!**
> *If you accept, come face us at 20h00 tonight.*
> *Bring your favourite toy.'*

Eva is suddenly wide awake. Jana shakes her head. 'Get that stupid grin off your face. I don't think you truly realise what we are in for. A sexual contest is much different than making love. Those two are experts and we may bite off much more than we can chew if we accept.'
Eva totally ignores this warning. 'We have to do this. Well, I am doing it with or without you.'
Jana shakes her head again. 'Ok, we will go, but don't look for a shoulder to cry on if they screw your brains out tonight.'
Eva blushes. 'I don't have a, erm a favourite toy.'
Jana can't help herself. 'You mean you like them all?'
Eva punches her in the arm. 'No, you know what I mean. I do not have toys.'
'Well you are in luck. You are talking to a toy expert and I know just where to take you. We will go toy shopping after breakfast.'

They catch a taxi to town and Eva looks around nervously to make sure nobody who knows her sees her entering the adult shop. However, Jana walks in as if the place belongs to her and Eva quickly follows her into the shop. She is gobsmacked by the variety of toys in the shop. She did not know that vibrators and dildos come in so many shapes and sizes. Jana plays the role of the expert guide and explains how a few of her favourite toys work. When she shows Eva the Sybian and explains to her how it works, Eva fascination by this toy is clear to see. A sales lady picks up on this and floats closer. 'Would you care to try it, we have a demo model in the back. Don't worry though as we use new attachments every time we demo it. Al we ask is that you pay for the attachment.

Jana answers for her. 'Yes, she wants to try it and I will sponsor the attachment. It is a small price to pay in order to watch her taking on the Sybian for the first time'

Jana picks an attachment with a medium sized dildo and Eva protests a little bit, but just enough to save a bit of dignity. She really wants to try this thing. The saleslady attaches the attachment and shows them how to operate the controls before she leaves the room with a huge grin on her face. Five minutes later Eva is screaming with a tremendous orgasm. When she gets off the Sybian, her legs buckle and she needs to hang on to Jana for a while.

'I need one of these.'

Jana gives her a kiss on the forehead. 'Oh honey, we all do, but it is way too expensive and way to big to smuggle into the academy.'

After spending some more time browsing through the store, Eva settles on a magic wand as her favourite toy.

The day drags by and Eva tries anything to make time go faster. She is sure that Jana must be anxious for the fun to start as well, but Jana seems to be totally relaxed. Eva hates her for a second. How can she stay so calm? Eva's guts are in knots in anticipation of what is to come tonight. 'Let's do something.'

Jana gives her a lazy look. 'Like what?'

Eva shrugs her shoulders. 'I don't know. I just can't wait for the time to pass anymore.'

They decide to try out some of their collection of nipple rings. For the rest of the afternoon they model different nipple rings for each other and when the time comes to go face their neighbours, they are both properly worked-up and horny.

Shortly after they arrive at their neighbours' townhouse, Janet explains the rules for tonight's challenge. The first contest will be between Jana and Eva with Janet and Margaret deciding the type of contest and the rules. The second contest will be between Janet and Margaret, with Eva and Jana deciding the type of contest and the rules. The third contest will be between the two losers. This time the two winners will decide the type of contest and the rules. The loser of this contest will be sexually punished for half an hour by the other three. The butterflies in Eva's stomach flutters all over the place. She and Jana have regular sex, but they have never sexually competed against each other before. She knows how to make Jana cum and she is confident that she can beat her, but she also knows that Jana knows how to make her cum and there is also a good chance that Jana may beat her. Margaret clears her throat in a dramatic way. 'So ladies, rumour has it that the two of you are boasting that your nipples are tougher than everybody else's. They are so tough that you even poked holes in them. The question is, who of the two of you have the toughest nipples. The rules are simple. You will fight each other over three rounds. The two of you will sit on chairs facing each other. For the first and second rounds we will connect opposite nipple rings with a chain and you will have a single nipple pulling contest. In the third round we will connect right nipple to right nipple and left to left. You will have a crossed chain double nipple pulling contest. Because we love and adore you, we don't want you to rip each other's nipples open, so you will sit with your backs pressed against the back of the chairs. We will slowly ad weights to the chain and the first one whose back does not make contact with the top of her chair's back loses the round. Do you understand?'

Eva nods her head. Jana shakes hers slowly. 'Wow, you bitches really though about this one.'

She has seen a nipple tug-of-war contests go wrong in her days in the underground fighting clubs. It was not a pretty sight and it is not something she wishes on herself or her friend. At least the rules sound a lot safer than the rules in these underground clubs. The girls were allowed to pull back and jerking movements often led to serious nipple damage. 'Eva, do you know what you are in for?'

Eva just nods her head and Jana can see that she is very nervous. Margaret carries on as if she is oblivious to the tension both Eva and Jana are feeling. 'Ok then ladies, take your tops off and get your nipples nice and stiff for us.' She gives a soft whistle as both girls reveal their rock hard nipples. 'Now look at that Janet. These two have obviously been warming up for tonight. I have never seen so many stiff nipples in one room.' With this she rips her own top off, revealing her own stiff nipples. She gives Janet a wink. 'This is a topless party Honey, get your tits out.'

Janet smiles and complies with this order. They have been drinking wine the whole afternoon and she knows how jovial Margaret gets when she is tipsy. Margaret's attention is back on the two combatants. She gets them to sit down on their chairs and then attaches a thin chain to the nipple rings. For the first round Eva's right nipple will tug against Jana's left. Margaret starts to hang small weights on the chain. She waits about ten seconds between every weight she hangs. At first Eva quite enjoys the feeling of her nipple being gently tugged, but as the weight on the chain increases, the pleasure gives way to pain. Her nipple is tugged forwards and downwards at the same time and she looks at Jana to see whether she also has pain, but Jana's face is emotionless. When the eighth weight is hung on the chain, the pain is too much for Eva. She moves forward and forfeits the round. Margaret removes the chain and uses another chain to link Eva's left nipple to Jana's right. Eva braces herself for the pain and does not even enjoy the first few weights. She is tense and is only able to last till the seventh weight this time. Jana's face still does not show any pain and Eva is suddenly very annoyed by this. 'What the hell is wrong with you? Are those real or do you have rubber implants.'

Jana gives her a grin. 'Nipple tug-of-war is not for softies.'

The other girls laugh, but Eva is not amused. Her nipples burn like hell and Jana seems to be unaffected and now Jana tries to belittle her. Jana can see the fury in her eyes and tries to defuse the situation. 'Just joking, my nipples feel like red hot coals at the moment.'

Eva gives her a fake smile and Jana decides not to push it any further. 'What are the rules? Is a third round necessary?'

Janet also realises that Eva is not enjoying this contest. 'No, you won. What do you have in mind for us?'

Before Jana can think she blurts out. 'Double dildo.' She feels guilty for not including Eva in the decision. 'Sorry Eva, do you have any other suggestions.' Eva shakes her head. She feels a bit silly for losing her cool, but the pain was unbearable and she felt a bit sorry for herself. 'Ok then, double dildo fucking until one of you cums.' Margaret is clearly excited by this and she skips to her room, returning with a rather thick double dildo and a tube of lube. Without further instruction needed, Janet and Margaret strips down lube the dildo and themselves and slides the dildo into their pussies. They lie back resting their upper bodies on their elbows and start to move their hips in rhythm with each other. Eva is sure this is nothing new to them. She strokes Jana's back and gives her a kiss on the cheek. 'Sorry, I was a cow just now. I think I just realised that I hate losing to you.'

Jana kisses her back. 'No worries. I am very competitive with you too.'

They are both relieved that any tension between them is broken and they focus their attention on the sexy show again. Their friends are grinding harder and faster. Both are moaning with pleasure, eyes closed and mouths slightly open and soon they are both breathing heavily and their bodies are glistening with a thin layer of perspiration. After about ten minutes Margaret's body tenses and she lets out a serious of high pitched squeals. She bites her bottom lip before her body trembles with an orgasm. Janet does not stop grinding until she reaches an orgasm as well. They are both exhausted and lie back with the dildo still connecting their vaginas.

Eva grins at Jana. 'Don't tell me that we have to leave again.'

Jana smiles at her. 'And miss out on you and Margaret fucking each other's brains out? Not even an outside chance.'

Janet recovers enough to get up, She pulls the dildo from her pussy, but leaves the end inside Margaret's pussy. 'Maybe we should break for half an hour. That cow is fucked dry.'

They all get drinks and relax for a while. Then Margaret gets up, grabs Eva by the hair and gently pulls her up. Although she does not pull hard, it still stings Eva's scalp. She plays along and follows Margaret to the fighting mat. 'So what will it be then?'

Margaret is swaying her hips and is rearing to go. While the two winners discuss the match, Margaret starts stripping Eva's skirt and panties off. While she does that she kisses Eva's belly button and slowly moves her tongue down until it brushes her clit. She then suddenly gets up pushes Eva away. 'Don't get greedy bitch, you will soon be begging me to stop.'

Janet and Jana join them on the mat and Eva realises that Jana is also completely naked. This confuses her for a moment until Janet shares the rules with them. 'The two of you will have a muff dive race. Margaret will dive Jana and Eva will dive me. Whoever of us cums first and her roommate are the losers. The losers will be bound together with the magic wand pressed between their clits for half an hour or until one can no longer take it.'

Eva and Margaret are made to lie on their backs next to each other. Janet lowers her pussy on Eva's face and Jana does the same to Margaret. The girls at the bottom start to lick, nibble and suck. Eva concentrates on Janet's clit, occasionally exploring the rest of her pussy. Janet is slowly grinding her pussy on Eva's face. She leans over and gives Jana a deep kiss. They start fondling each other's boobs while they continue kissing each other. Both girls are getting close to reaching orgasm and they try to excite the other in order to gain an advantage. The rhythm of Janet's grinding on Eva's face becomes erratic and Eva knows that she is very close to an orgasm, so she increases the movement of her tongue against Janet's clit and this soon pays off. Janet grabs her hair and forces her face against her pussy while she cums. After a while she releases Eva's head and rolls off. Eva checks to her right and is glad to see that Jana is still grinding on Margaret's face. Jana has always been able to last a lot longer than Eva does when they go down on each other and Eva is pretty sure that it was Jana who came up with this challenge.

The next thirty minutes are epic. The magic wand buzzes relentlessly against their clits and both Margaret and Janet cum multiple times, but neither of them are willing to surrender before the thirty minute mark is reached. Jana leans over to Eva. 'Shall we leave them like this? It looks like they are both willing to carry on forever.'

Eva laughs. 'No, I like them and I don't want to start looking for new sexfight challengers.' She reaches over and switches of the power. They untie their friends and the four naked girls lie on the mat chatting for hours. They all agree that this will not be the last challenge and Janet and Margaret promises their friends that they will be on the losing side next time. Eva is still horny and is looking forward to get off at some stage tonight, but she is enjoying the conversation so much that she is willing to wait. Margaret suddenly gets serious. 'So how are we getting Amelia and her sluts back for ganging up on Eva?'

Eva is immediately upset. 'That is my fight. Stay out of it.'

Jana just rolls her eyes at Margaret, but Margaret does not let Eva's outburst deter her at all. 'You are my friend. Your fight is my fight. I respect you too much to get involved if another girl kicks your ass in a one-on-one fight, but when you get jumped by a group of girls, you better believe that I will get involved.'

Eva is quiet. She is still embarrassed by what happened to her and she still feels like handling this herself, but she understands Margaret point. She also knows that she will fight any group of girls who attack one of her friends.

'Let's fight them in a wall-on-wall contest.'

Janet's suggestion finds instant approval from Margaret and Jana, but Eva is not sure what it means. Janet explains that it was a popular sport in Russia where two groups of woman fought each other in a field without any rules, except that girls who surrendered were off limits and were removed from the field. The fight continued until all the girls of one team surrendered. Eva likes this idea and it is decided that Janet will approach Helga to arrange the fight. Helga tries to stop the girls from fighting each other, but she is always open to a sporting event. Anyway, she has given up on Janet and Margaret and does not even ask why they are fighting anymore. She can at least make sure their fights do not get out of hand if they come to her to arrange the fights. Janet winks at Margaret. 'After this fight I want you to piss me off again. We haven't had a fight in a long time.

It is time I put you in your place again.'

All the girls laugh at this, but Eva hopes that this will materialise sooner rather than later. She touches Jana's thigh and gives Jana her best come-hither look. Jana gets the hint and they soon excuse themselves. They make love for hours before they fall asleep in each other's arms.

Helga is happy to arrange the wall-on-wall challenge, but only if Amelia and her friends agree to it. She will also only allow it after the calcio storico season is done. Combat Sport Academy has three more games left in the season and she does not want any of her players getting injured now. Eva challenges Emily and her gang in front of the other girls after practice and they have no choice but to accept.

Chapter 17 – Calcio Storico

Eva's training for calcio storico goes well and she is included as a midfielder in the lightweight team. She is not sure whether Helga and Lea's coach planned this, but she is exited to learn that Lea has also made the Central City Academy's lightweight team. She will get a chance to compete against her friend again.

Jana does not have a match on the Saturday of Eva's first calcio storico match and she decides to accompany the team as a spectator. As luck would have it, Reka has no other place to sit on the bus and has to sit next to Eva. Eva does not like the tension and, as they are teammates, she decides to extend the olive branch. 'Listen, we will sort out our differences in the wall-on-wall match, but I don't want the tension between us to make it difficult for us to be teammates.' She offers her hand to Reka who gives Eva a relieved smile and takes her hand. 'I agree.' They manage to have a civil conversation on the ride to Central City Academy and Eva learns that Reka has been bullied as a youngster and decided to join the academy to learn how to look after herself. The irony does not escape Eva. The little bullied girl ganged up with others to bully her. Then again, maybe the slap to the face she gave Reka was her bullying Reka. Jana just shakes her head when they get off the bus. 'You are too forgiving. I prefer to slap the snot out of my enemies.'
Eva smiles at her, if only Jana knew about her grudge against Emily Theron. And how she plan to deal with her greatest enemy

Eva is nervous as the two teams line up on opposite sides of the field. Her role is to tackle any ball carrier who makes it past her forwards and Helga told her not to get tied down by a fight and that she should tackle, take the ball and distribute it to her forwards. She is disappointed that she is not allowed to fight and especially that she will not get a chance to fight Lea. Anyway, Lea is a goalkeeper and there is very little chance that they will meet up on the field. Eva adjusts her green tight fitting pants which go down to just under her knees. She is now very used to competing topless and the fact that her boobs and stiff nipples are on display for everyone to gawk at, does not bother her anymore. She also realised long ago that most girls' nipples are stiff during fights. She looks up to where Jana is sitting. She feels a bit jealous as she sees Jana's eyes wondering from half naked girl to half naked girl. She can't blame Jana though. She can just imagine how sexy this must look to the spectators. She plans to watch a few matches afterwards and she hopes that Lea will join her and Jana then. She wants to introduce her to Jana. It will be so cool if they can be friends as well.

The referee drops the ball on the centre spot and as is customary, the two forward lines engage each other in fifteen one-on-one battles. This opening move to the game is designed to reduce the number of players on the field by fifteen. The first time the ball will be played is when all fifteen fights are done and fifteen girls have been removed from the field by the referees. Eva is only allowed to watch as her forwards are all engage in fist fights just a few

metres away from her. Her instincts are to jump in and help them, but only forwards are allowed to engage in this initial fight. Fighters start to drop one by one as the fighting goes into the third minute. Each time a fighter goes down, a referee steps forward, waiting to see whether the fighter can protect herself. The moment they feel that as fighter is taking too much punishment on the ground, they step in and stop the fight. The loser is removed from the field and the winner is ordered to step back five yards. The initial fights do not go as planned for the Combat Sport Academy. They lose nine forwards to the six lost by Central City Academy. The referee blows her whistle and the remaining fifteen forwards all rush the centre spot. They wrestle for the ball and three one-on-one fights break out. The three remaining Combat Sport Academy forwards, not involved in fights, have no chance and one of the Central City Academy forwards breaks away with the ball. Eva sets herself and as the girl is about three yards away from her she lowers herself and moves forward. She hits the girl in her solar plexus with her right shoulder. A loud 'oof!' escapes the girl's mouth and she drops down, losing control of the ball. Eva jumps on her and starts punching her in the face. The girl is winded and puts up very little resistance. A referee quickly pulls Eva off the girl and leads the girl of the field. The ball is picked up by one of Eva's fellow midfielders and she quickly passed it to one of their forwards. Eva has taken her place on the field again and she feels proud of herself for stopping the attack and for reducing the opponent's numbers. She feels a pat on her shoulder and looks behind her. It is Reka, who is one of the defenders. She smiles at Eva. 'Nice play'. Eva smiles back. 'Thanks'. The three one-on-one fights are still in progress and the rest of the forwards are once again wrestling for the ball. The five Central City Academy forwards are once again too strong for their three opponents and once again a player breaks away with the ball. Eva does not have time to think and tries the same tactic again. To her amazement, it works again. She has removed another girl from the field and the Combat Sport Academy is once again in control of the ball and once again she gets a pat and smile from Reka and this time a thumbs-up as well. The three individual fights have all been stopped by referees and all three fights were won by Combat Sport Academy. The tables have turned. From being six against nine, the forwards are now six against four. One of the Combat Sport Academy's forwards breaks away with the ball and as she is being tackled, she passes the ball to another who runs around a defender and hurls the ball at the opponent's net, which spans the width of the field. Her aim is good and the ball goes between two goalkeepers and into the net. The referee blows the whistle and the fight between the girl who broke away with the ball and her tackler is broken up. The teams are ordered to switch sides as sides are swapped after each goal. Eva sees Lea walking towards her as they swap sides and as they get close to each other, Lea smiles at her and Eva smiles back. Eva's smile quickly turns into an expression of pain. As Lea passes Eva, she punches her unprotected right boob. A referee warns her and Lea throws her arms in the air, claiming innocence. Eva shouts at her. 'You sneaky bitch!'
Lea turns her head and gives Eva a big satisfied grin. Eva wants to fight her right here, right now and she looks over at Helga for permission. Helga shakes her head and mouths 'Get back to your position'. Eva's blood boils, but she slowly walks backward towards her position, staring at Lea all the time.

The referee blows her whistle again and the forwards attack each other immediately. Four pairs fight each other and one of the two remaining Combat Sport Academy forwards grab the ball and starts running. Eva and the other forward follow her and as she gets tackled, she passes the ball to Eva who heads directly towards Lea. Their bodies collide and both lose their footing. As the hit the ground they both scramble to their knees and grab each other and start landing a few punches before the fight is broken up. The other forward picked up the ball when it spilled from Eva's hands and she scored the goal. Eva is frustrated by this. 'I will get you back.'

Lea grins at her. 'Come get you some, I can't wait.' The teams swap sides again and the Central City Academy's coach decides to boost her forward line. She moves two of her midfielders to the forward line and one of her defenders into the midfield. As soon as the whistle goes, the forwards all go for each other in six one-on-one fights. Eva considers grabbing the ball so that she can run towards Lea again, but that would be against the spirit of the game. An unwritten rule dictates that when all forwards of both sides are involved in fights, the ball is dead and the rest of the players should hold their positions. The referees start breaking up the fights as girls are unable to protect themselves. Combat Sport Academy dominates the fights and they win four of the six fights. They are down to sixteen players and Central City Academy is down to twelve. The referee blows her whistle again and the remaining forwards rush the centre spot wrestling for the ball. Two of Central City Academy's midfielders join their forwards to even out the numbers. One defender moves into the midfield and Lea moves into the defence line. The wrestling match on the centre spot soon turns into four fist fights and both teams lose two more players. This forces the coach of Central City Academy to move two more midfielders to the forward line. She also moves her two remaining defenders into the midfield and one goalkeeper forward as the sole defender. Helga moves Eva and another girl into the forwards and moves one of her defenders into the midfield. Eva revels in her new role. She can't wait to get involved in the fighting and when the whistle goes, she rushes into the wrestling match for the ball. She hears a call of 'all in' and the next moment the Central City Academy's forwards stop wrestling and they each pull an opponent away from the centre spot to engage in one-on-one matches. The other six members of their team rush forward and pair off with six opponents for fights. Their head coach is now going for broke. If they win the majority of the fights, they are back in the game, but if they break even or lose the majority of the fights, the game will be all but over. Eva and her opponent tussle for position and the girl manage to get Eva in a headlock and starts raining punches to Eva's face. Eva's only defence is to take the girl to the ground, so she gets a leg behind the girl and pushes forward hard. The girl trips, but does not let go of the headlock and Eva's face is slammed into the sand. She gets to her knees with her head still trapped and pushes her left hand on her opponent's elbow and pulls back with her head. Her ears feel like they are going to tear from her head, but she carries on and eventually escapes the hold. She quickly mounts her opponent and starts landing fists and elbows to her face. A referee pulls her from the girl and she steps back. When the rest of the fights are done, Lea is the only player of Central City Academy left on the field. The coach of Central City Academy gets up and walks onto the field to forfeit the match, but Lea yells at her. 'No coach, I can take them.' The coach shakes her head in amazement,

but she knows that Lea wants a go at Eva, so she decides to forfeit after their match, should Lea manage to beat Eva. Eva steps forward and the friends tear into each other. They both land hard punches and kicks before a right hook drops Eva. She scrambles to her knees, but Lea dives on top of her, however, she cannot stop her momentum and she rolls clear of Eva. They both get back to their feet and immediately attack each other again. Neither tries to grab the other. They both rain punches on each other and both their faces are soon bruised and cut. It is Eva who goes down again as another right hook catches her flush on the chin. This time Lea waits for her to get up. She is enjoying the fist fight and does not want to end this just yet. They again start to punch each other, but as both girls start to get tired, the number of punches decreases. After a while, they end up circling each other without a punch being thrown. Both girls are gasping for air and both struggle to lift their arms. The head referee steps in and calls it a draw. She has seen enough and is convinced that neither girl is able to defend herself anymore. Combat Sport Academy is declared the winners. Eva steps in and hugs Lea and they both tumble to the ground, both too exhausted to stay upright. Lea playfully punches Eva's right boob again. 'I won this fight, you went down twice.'
Eva is almost too tired to argue, but she can't let Lea claim victory. 'Yes, but I got up again twice. I was just about to knock you out when the ref came to your rescue.' They both laugh at this and slowly get up and leave the field. Just before Eva enters their change room, she turns to Lea. 'Will I see you later. I want to introduce you to my best friend.' Lea nods her head and enters the Central City Academy change room.

In the change room, Reka comes over and sits down next to Eva. 'You were very impressive out their. I really enjoyed you fight at the end.'
Eva smiles at her. 'Thanks. Listen, I started this issue between us by slapping you in the face. I was upset by the way that you refereed my fight with Amelia and I wanted to get you back for it. I am sorry, it was silly and I will ask Helga to cancel the wall-on-wall fight.
Reka shakes her head. 'No don't. We are both in the wrong. I would love to get to know you better, but we have to sort out our issues with each other first. Anyway, the whole academy is looking forward to the match and you don't want to be the one who takes it away from them.'
Eva leans in and gives her a hug. 'I really look forward to getting to know you better and I think we may become good friends, but don't expect any friendship during the wall-on-wall match. The girl I fought at the end is one of my best friends. Friendship means nothing during a fight.'
Reka nods her head. 'And I will do my best to tear you apart during the match.' They give each other a warm smile and Eva hits the showers.

Eva hugs Jana who is still sitting in the same seat and gives her a deep kiss on the mouth. 'Did you enjoy that?'
Jana puts her hand on Eva's thigh. 'It was ok, but I have seen better.'
Eva punches her in the shoulder. 'You stuck up old cow. Do you want to watch more matches? I invited Lea to join us and I hope you do not care. I really want the two of you to meet and I think you will like each other.'

Eva could not be more wrong. When Lea joins them there is a tense atmosphere. Eva tries to get the conversation going, but her friends just can't seem to like each other. After an awkward twenty minutes, Lea get's up and excuses herself. Eva hugs her goodbye and gives Jana a dirty look once Lea has left 'You could have tried harder. I was really hoping that the two of you would become friends. You both mean a lot to me.'

Jana kisses her on her forehead. 'Sorry Babes, I will try harder, but there is just something about her I do not like.'

Chapter 18 – A Fight for Love

Eva has not given up on the idea that Jana and Lea will become friends. She does not understand why they do not like each other. She is crazy about both of them and she hates having to spend time with them individually. It would be so nice if the three of them could hang out and enjoy each other's company. She wrecked her head trying to understand why they do not like each other. May they be jealous of each other's relationship with her? She doesn't think so as her relationship with Jana is very different from her relationship with Lea. She has a sexual relationship with Jana and she is in love with her. Although they agreed to be friends with benefits only, they have a relationship as a couple in all but name. Her relationship with Lea is purely friendship and the enjoyment of fighting each other. The rivalry between them stirs something in her. They both desire to beat the other in fights and they both truly enjoy the thrill of fighting each other. There are no hard feelings after their fights, even if either or both of them used dirty tactics during the fight. It is different with Jana though. Eva believes that a fight between them will damage their relationship. She hated it when Jana beat her in a nipple tug-of-war. She was upset because of the immense pain it caused to her nipples, but she was much more upset with the fact that Jana beat her and that she did not even seem to experience any pain.

Eva discussed this problem with Margaret and hoped to get some sound advice. She does not know why she thought Margaret would be able to help her solve this issue though. She should have known that Margaret's advice would involve violence. She told Eva that she should take them to the biker bar and get them to fight each other in the octagon. This, according to Margaret, would sort out the issues they have with each other and all three of them would live happily ever after. Well she did not use those exact words, but in Margaret's mind everything turns out rosy if you throw violence at it. Eva knows that fighting is the way Margaret and Janet settle their differences and that this works for them, but she does not believe that she can get Jana and Lea to like each other by asking them to fight it out. She thanked Margaret for her advice in a sarcastic way, but her sarcasm was lost on Margaret and she smiled at Eva, impressed with herself that she was able to solve this issue for Eva. Eva made a mental note not to ask Margaret for advice again.

The issue haunts Eva and she decides to go talk with Helga. Helga can see that something is really bothering Eva and she takes her to the quiet spot at the back of the indoor training centre where she normally have private conversations with students. Helga's voice is soft and caring. 'I have noticed that you have been distracted the last few days. What is bothering you?'
'I know this may sound silly to you, but I really want my two best friends to be friends with each other as well, but they do not even get along.'
'Are you talking about Jana and Lea?'
'Yes. I don't understand why they don't like each other and its eating me up inside.'

'First of all, it is not silly to want your friends to be friends with each other as well. We all want that, but it does not always work out and forcing it does more harm than good. When did they meet each other?'

'After last week's calcio storico match. I asked Lea to come sit with us while we watched some of the other matches, but she only stayed for a short while before she left. It was obvious that neither of them wanted the other to be there'

'Do you think that Jana may have been upset with Lea for the way the two of you fought during the match? It may be that her instincts were to protect you. The fight was very intense and to anybody else, but the two of you, you look like enemies and not like friends when you fight.'

'Maybe, I did not think about it that way.'

'Also, are they both very clear on your relationship with them? Is there a chance that they are both in love with you and jealous of each other?

'Yes, I am just friends with Lea and Jana and I are friends with benefits only and not a couple.'

'It is clear to me that you are in love with Jana and she is definitely also in love with you. I think you are more than friends with benefits, you both have feelings for each other. I believe you when you say that you are not in love with Lea, but are you sure that she is not in love with you?'

'You are right about my feelings for Jana. I do not think Lea is in love with me. We enjoy each other's company and we like to fight each other, but I don't think there are any romantic feelings.'

'I suggest that you discuss this with Lea and that you reassure Jana that you do not have romantic feelings for Lea. I further suggest that you arrange a situation where the three of you can have fun together. If they see the fun side of each other, they may start to like each other. However, if they don't, do not force the friendship. You will end up harming your relationship with both of them. You can still be friends with both of them even though they are not friends with each other, as long as all three of you are clear of what each friendship entails.'

Eva hugs Helga and thanks her a few times before she walks back to her townhouse. She hugs Jana and kisses her deeply. 'I love you and I will not have a romantic relationship with anybody else.'

Jana frowns. 'Where does this come from? Have I said anything to make you believe that I think you are cheating on me?'

Eva is slightly taken aback. She did not expect a cold response like this. 'No, that is not what I meant. I just don't want you to wonder about my friendship with Lea.'

'I love you too Babes and I trust you. I am not sure whether I trust her though and I don't really understand your friendship. You try to seriously injure each other every opportunity you get. It just doesn't make sense that you are friends.'

'Margaret and Janet fight each other frequently and they are friends.'

'Difference is that they are friends and lovers who only fight each other when they get on each other's nerves. You and Lea seems to be friends because you fight each other.'

'We are friends because we like each other's company and we have fun together. The rivalry

is just something that happened. We compete hard and during a fight we are probably enemies, but we leave that in the ring. The moment the fight is over, we like each other again. I think respect for each other's fighting abilities also helps with our friendship.'
'Why do you hate losing to me then?'
Eva did not expect this question. 'I don't know. Maybe it is because I love you and I want us to be equals, but you seem to be better than me with each contest we have. I do not like competing against you and I don't ever want to fight you. I can't hurt you and I don't want you to hurt me.'
Tears are rolling down Eva's face and Jana hugs her and kisses the tears on her cheeks. 'I am sorry. I promised you that I will make an effort with Lea and I will.' Jana cuddles Eva until she falls asleep, exhausted from all the emotions.

Eva chats with Lea and she also agrees to give friendship with Jana another go. She takes Helga's advice to heart and decides on a fun night out at the biker bar. She promised Jana that she would take her to the biker bar one night and told her so many stories about it that Jana feels she already knows everybody there. Eva also knows that Lea and she had a blast the last time they were there, so she is sure that Lea will be relaxed and that she will enjoy it. Jana and Eva catch a taxi and picks up Lea on the way. Eva is relieved when Jana and Lea starts chatting to each other on the ride to the biker bar. Their conversation does not flow easily, but they are both making an effort. They walk into the bar to a heroes welcome. Roadkill is the first to ask the obvious question. 'Are you girls here to fight again?'
Eva smiles at her. 'No sorry, the three of us are here to have a good time only.'
Roadkill is not that easily convinced though. 'You fought the last time you were here and as far as I can remember you had a very good time with us.'
Spitfire has come out from behind the bar. 'Leave my little warriors alone Roadkill. I am sure they will give us a show another day, but tonight they are here to entertain us with their quick wits only.' She looks at Jana. 'You must be Jana, the lover who lasts for hours.'
Eva blushes and avoids eye contact with Jana. She cannot remember sharing this with Spitfire, but she was very drunk and they were all sharing stories with each other. Jana accepts Spitfire's hand. 'Eva has always been bad at telling time. I can last days.'
The whole bar bursts out in laughter and Spitfire turns the handshake into a hug. 'You will do well here young lassie. I have to second Roadkill though. I would love to see you fight in my octagon one day.'

As the drinks start to flow the conversation between Jana and Lea becomes easier and they actually start to enjoy each other's company. All three girls enjoy the stories told by the bikers and they laugh at these stories, even the ones they have heard before. The bikers enjoy the girls as well. They are young and full of life and they hang onto every word the older bikers share with them. This energises the bikers and allows them to be young again, bringing back memories from when they were still bulletproof. At about one o'clock in the morning Eva goes to the bathroom. As soon as she leave them alone, Jana turns to Lea. 'Do you want to sleep with her?'
Lea is immediately upset. 'That has nothing to do with you. You guys are not a couple, so

she can sleep with whoever she wants to and you will not stop me should I decide to sleep with her.'

Eva hears a big cheer in the bar and she wonders which joke or story she has missed. She smiles to herself, surely somebody will tell it again later. However, the cheers get louder and don't stop. Something is happening in the bar and she does not want to miss out. She finishes up quickly and leaves the bathroom to see that all the bikers are around the octagon. Her heart drops, fighting each other in the octagon are Jana and Lea, dressed only in their panties, they are already both bleeding from their noses. Eva runs to the octagon intent on stopping the fight. Spitfire catches her by the arm and stops her from entering the octagon. 'Let them be love, let them sort out their differences. If you interfere you will only make it worse. They are fighting for your love and friendship, both being scared that the other may take you away from her. Let them get it out of their systems. I will make sure that they do not seriously injure each other. You can have rational chats with both of them tomorrow. Their blood is too hot now and they will not hear a word you say.'

Eva watches the fight with tears in her eyes, not only because of the fact that her friends are fighting, but because she is scared that she may lose one or even both of them.

Jana and Lea are both throwing plenty of punches to each other's faces, messing up each other's noses, lips and eyes. Without any gloves their knuckles cut skin easily and blood drips from both girls' faces. This seems to just spur them on more and they both continue throwing plenty of vicious punches. Jana also manages to land a few hard kicks to Lea's ribs, turning them bright red. After another kick to the ribs, Lea grabs hold of Jana to give herself some time to recover. However, Jana has been in many fights during her time at the underground fighting clubs and she uses the proximity to each other to land a well timed uppercut, followed by a knee to Lea's crotch. Lea has never received a strike to her crotch and she stumbles back in pain and shock, allowing Jana an opportunity to attack. She does not waste this opportunity and lands two punches and an elbow to Lea's face sending her backwards and she crashes into the side of the octagon. Lea's head bounces forward from the mesh at the same time as Jana throws a straight right to her jaw, dropping Lea like a stone. Before anybody can react, Jana jumps on top of her and starts landing punches to her face. It is clear that Lea is out cold, but the biker who acts as referee is slow to realise this. Both Eva and Spitfire screams at her to stop the match, but by the time she reacts, Jana has landed another five punches to Lea's face. Eva rushes in and the sight shocks her. Lea's eyes are swollen completely shut, her lips have multiple cuts, her nose is broken and both her cheeks are cut over the cheekbones. Eva pushes Jana away as she tries to say something to her and with the help of Spitfire she carries Lea out of the octagon and to Spitfires car. They rush her to the nearest hospital, where doctors immediately take her into an operating room. Eva and Spitfire spend anxious hours waiting to hear whether Lea will be ok. Eventually a doctor comes out and shares with them that she is in a stable, but serious condition. She has a broken nose, bruised ribs, various lacerations and a serious concussion.

Eva is in a state of shock and she lashes out at Spitfire. 'You promised to keep them safe. You promised.'

Spitfire just pulls her closer and allows her to sob with her head pressed against Spitfire's chest. She suddenly misses her mother and sobs even harder. The last time she cried with her head pressed against someone's chest was as a little girl. She felt so save and cared for when her mother would hold her close until she felt better. She hates Jana at the moment and she wants to go give her a piece of her mind, but she does not want to leave the hospital before she is sure that Lea would be fine.

A while later Jana arrives at the hospital. Her face is also cut and her eyes are also both swollen shut from a broken nose, but she ignores the medical staff and heads towards Eva and Spitfire. 'I am so sorry, is she ok?'
Eva gets up and walks away from her. Moments before, she wanted to find Jana and sort her out, but her emotions overcome her and she just needs to get away from Jana right now. Spitfire stops Jana from following Eva. 'Don't, she hates you right now. Lea's condition is serious and we will have to wait to see whether she recovers. If you want to keep Eva as a friend, you will have to sort this out, but not tonight. Go get your own injuries looked at.'
Jana stands around for a while, not knowing what to do. She eventually turns around and leaves without seeking medical care. Helga, who was informed what happened by Spitfire, finds her sitting on the steps in front of the academy. She is staring into the distance and tears are streaming down her face. Helga helps her up and takes her to the clinic and waits with her until the doctor arrives.

Early the next morning, Eva is allowed to go see Lea. She is awake, but her face still looks terrible. After making sure that Lea is ok, Eva promises her that she will go sort Jana out. She is surprised by Lea's response. 'Don't, it is not her fault. She loves you and she is scared that I may take you away from her. She asked me whether I wanted to sleep with you and rather than just explaining to her that there are no romantic feelings between us, I decided to tell her to mind her own business. I knew what her reaction would be, but I was buzzed and was being a bitch. She got the better of me and I ended up here. If I got the better of her, she would have been the one in hospital. Where is she by the way? I am sure I broke her nose and did some other damage as well.'
Eva remains silent for a while. 'I don't know, she was here to ask how you were, but I did not want to talk to her. I don't know where she went.'
Lea puts her hand on Eva's forearm to make sure she has her full attention. 'Go find her, I am ok now. She loves you and you love her, don't let my stupidity come between you guys. You are a good friend and I would not be able to forgive myself if I am the cause of you guys breaking up. When we both recover enough, I will take Jana for a coffee to ensure that we sort out any remaining issues between us.'
Eva understands the points made by Lea, but she is still furious with Jana and she does not visit her while Jana is in the clinic. It may not be Jana's fault that they fought each other, but she should have stopped when Lea was knocked out.

Nancy is excited with the news that Jana was in a fight with another friend of Eva. She needs something to drive a wedge between Jana and Eva when the time comes. This is a bit early for their friendship to end though, so she asks Helga to talk to both of them to ensure that the issue between them is sorted out. She also asks Helga for Lea's details and she goes to visit her in hospital later the same day. Lea fell asleep after Eva visited her and she just woke up when a woman who she doesn't know enters her room. The woman gives her a forced smile. 'Hi Lea, I am Nancy, the owner of Combat Sport Academy. How are you feeling?'

Lea is surprised that the owner of Combat Sport Academy would visit her. 'Hi Nancy, I have been better.'

'I understand that you were in a fight with one of my girls last night and am sorry that you ended up in hospital. This was a private fight between the two of you though and I am not liable for your injuries, but I still wanted to make sure that you are ok.'

Lea wonders whether Nancy is here because she is concerned about her or about being sued. 'Is Jana ok?'

'She is in the academy's clinic. I have not yet had time to visit her, but I understand she will be ok. Sounds like the two of you were in a real brawl.'

'Yeah, things got out of hand a little bit. We were both a bit silly.'

'Do you enjoy fighting?'

'I love it. It gives me a rush like no other.'

'What are your plans after your training at the academy? Do you plan a fighting career?'

'Yes, I think so. It will be a shame to waste the skills I am learning.'

'I have plans to launch a television show to help girls like you show off your skills while you are still in an academy. This will give you a chance to promote yourself, making it easier to launch your career after you finish your academy training.'

Lea is intrigued. 'What kind of fights?'

'MMA style, but with a few changes to make it more exiting for the fans. It will be safer than your fight last night though. I will have professional referees making sure that the fighters are protected.'

'It sounds like a good idea, but I am not sure that my academy will allow me to participate.'

'Don't worry about that now. I will negotiate with your academy and if they stand in your way, you will always have a choice to join mine.'

Nancy takes Lea's contact details and gives hers to Lea before she leaves. She never goes to visit Jana in the clinic.

When Jana is released from the clinic, she finds that Eva is not home. She must still be at practice. The only visitors she had in clinic were Helga, Janet and Margaret. She knows that Eva is still upset with her and she wants to talk with her as soon as possible. Helga told her to give Eva space to work things out for herself, but she needs to look Eva in the eyes and explain to her what happened. Jana also needs to talk with Lea and she decides to go visit her in hospital now, so that she can be home by the time practice is done. When she walks into Lea's room, Lea gives Jana a big smile. 'I am glad to see you at least look like you were in a fight as well. If you are here for round two, you will have to give me a few minutes to warm up.'

Jana has to laugh at this. 'I am so sorry.'

'Don't be, we are both to blame for the fight. You kicked my ass this time and you shouldn't apologise for that.'

'I went too far though. I really hated you and I wanted to destroy you. I feel horrible for not stopping when you were knocked out.'

Lea lets this sink in for a while. 'I can't say for sure, but if I was the one who knocked you out, I may have done the same. I really hated your guts as well.'

'How do we make sure we do not kill each other? I don't think the fight resolved all our issues, but I don't want any issues between us to influence our relationships with Eva'

'I love Eva, but as a friend only. There are genuinely no sexual feelings between us. I should have told you this when you asked, but to be honest, I am jealous of you. She can't help but talk about you. Even when the two of us are enjoying each other's company, it always feels like you are there as well.'

'I am jealous of you as well. When I first saw you, I could not believe that she would not be in love with you.'

Lea blushes under her bruises. 'Thanks, you are not too shabby either. Don't you fall in love with me now. I don't want Eva to also kick my butt.'

They both smile.

'She loves fighting you and she can talk about your fights for hours. Yet, she seems to hate competing with me. It feels like she trusts your friendship more than she trusts ours.'

Lea thinks for a while. 'I don't think so. She just has more to lose with you.'

Jana hugs Lea before she leaves. 'I would really love to fight you again one day, but this time as friends. You hurt me a lot during our fight and if you did not leave your pussy open to attack, the outcome may have been different.'

'I would love to fight you as well and that move is ingrained in my brain now. I can't wait to return the favour one day.'

They hug again and Jana returns home with a lighter heart. She still needs to fix her relationship with Eva though.

Margaret pulls Eva aside after practice. 'I need to talk to you about Jana. I have been quiet up to now, but you are both friends of mine and I want you to sort out this issue between you.'

'You are wasting your time if your advice is for us to go punch some sense into each other, I don't want to fight her. Well perhaps I do, I just don't know anymore.'

'No, but if you two do not at least talk about this, I will punch some sense into both of you. Seriously, this has gone on too long now. I know she pissed you off, but not even visiting her in the clinic is not cool. Grow up and go talk to her.'

Margaret says this with tears in her eyes. She turns around and walks away. Eva is shocked by this. She did not expect such harsh words from Margaret. She walks around for a while, alone with her own thoughts. Eventually she makes her way to Janet and Margaret's townhouse. She walks in without knocking, go straight to Margaret where she is busy in the kitchen and gives her a hug. 'Thanks Margaret, you are a true friend.'

'No problem Eva.'

Janet watches in silence as Eva leaves their townhouse again. 'Pray tell.'

'I verbally kicked her butt. It is time she makes up with Jana.'
Janet just shakes her head. She can't believe Margaret interfered with their friends' relationship even after she told her not to. 'It's time again. After the wall-on-wall.'
'I agree. I will arrange with Helga.'

Eva and Jana have a long heart-to-heart. After a lot of tears, hugs and serious discussions, they fall asleep in each other's arms. Both happy that their relationship is back on track, both knowing that time is needed to fully restore it to a point where they will be lovers again.

Chapter 19 – Wall-on-Wall

The last two calcio storico games of the season are both tough affairs. Both Eva and Reka still bear the scars of the last match when the night of the wall-on-wall match arrives. Their respect for each other has grown during this time, but they both know that a fight is required to totally clear the air between them. Jana is still booked off by the doctor, but she managed to convince Helga to let her fight. Helga agrees against her better judgement, but she knows that this fight is important for Eva and Jana's relationship and she decides to take the chance. Although she likes to keep contests as historically accurate as possible, she insisted that the girls fight with MMA gloves and mouth guards. Although the original fights were bare knuckle affairs, girls used to fight with MMA gloves at the beginning of the twenty-first century when there was a resurgence of this sport.

Helga lines up the two teams on either side of the sandpit. Eva's team are all wearing short shorts only, while Reka's team are all wearing long jeans only. Reka's team has covered their upper bodies with baby oil, making it more difficult to grab hold of them. Helga decides to allow this. She did not see any rules against this during her research. The many spectators lined up on the one length of the sandpit also seem to appreciate the effect the baby oil has on their upper bodies. Topless girls, exited by the rush of preparing for battle, are sexy enough, but the oil accentuating their curves makes them even sexier.

Nancy is watching from her office and she also appreciates the look of the oil on the girl's bodies. This will be one of the features she will introduce when her show, Grudge Fights, starts. She suggested to Amelia that they cover their bodies in oil as she wanted to see whether this makes the girls look sexier during a real fight and whether the fight will still be competitive, even with slippery bodies. She regrets not telling Eva's team to do the same as well. She considers telling Helga to oil them up before the fight starts, but decides against it. She does not want everyone to know that she is watching this fight.

As was customary, the two teams line up in columns of two lines of two girls each. The idea being for the columns to collide with each other before the girls split off into pairs for individual fights. Eva makes sure that she lines up against Amelia. Not only is Amelia the biggest girl in the other team, but she is also Eva's bully and Eva wants to break any psychological hold Amelia has over her. Helga gives the sign to start and the two columns charge each other. Just before they collide, Eva jumps as high as she can, bringing both her knees up and hitting Amelia flush on her large boobs. Amelia goes down screaming out in pain and Eva dives on top of her to secure full mount. She lands two punches to Amelia's face, but is suddenly pulled off her. Reka managed to avoid Janet's attempt to tackle her and she wrestles Eva to the ground. This two-on-one move is allowed as long as the second girl joining uses only wrestling moves and do not strike the opponent before they are paired off and the third girl is no longer involved in the tussle. Eva is frustrated as she was in a good position to finish off Amelia, but she is also excited to face Reka in a one-on-one fight. Reka allows Eva to get to her feet as she wants a fair fight between the two of them. They square off, fists raised and eyes focussed on each other. Eva lands two stiff jabs and is rocked by a straight right by Reka. She recovers and retaliates with a kick to Reka's ribs. She follows this up with another to Reka's thigh and a right hook to her chin. Reka stumbles back and Eva moves in to grab hold of her, but her slippery body makes it difficult to hold onto Reka. Eva losses her balance and Reka punishes her with a knee to the face. Eva manages to block the second knee, but blood is dripping from her nose from the first knee. She manages to get away from Reka and they square of again. This time Reka is the aggressor and she land a combination of three punches, two to Eva's body and the third to her left eye, the same eye which is already black from the last calcio storico match. This punch stings a lot and Eva covers her face, which allows Reka to step in and land a knee to Eva's lower belly and another to her ribs. Eva pushes Reka away and Reka falls over Margaret and her opponent. Margaret is in full mount and is landing elbow after elbow to her opponent's face eventually breaking her nose. Eva's first instinct is to jump on top of Reka, but she decides that this will not be fair as Reka is only down because of another pair fighting behind her. Eva waits for Reka to get back on her feet and her focus is still completely on Reka. She never sees the punch coming from behind her and Amelia lands a full force punch to the side of Eva's face from behind. Eva is out cold before she hits the sand. When she gets to, Amelia and Reka are punching each other a few yards away from her. She is not totally aware of what is happening around her, but she can see that Reka is taking a lot of punishment. Then Jana rushes over and starts punching Amelia, while Margaret grabs Reka, wrestling her to the ground where she controls her without throwing any punches. Eva looks back to where Jana and Amelia are fighting. Amelia lands punches, but they do not seem to have any effect on Jana. At the same time Jana's punches rock Amelia's head back every time she connects. It is not long before Amelia goes down and Jana mounts her. Jana is relentless, landing punches and elbows to Amelia's face without any pause and Helga has to fight to get Jana away from Amelia. Margaret has calmed Reka down and she gets up, helping Reka to her feet as well. Helga awards the fight to Eva's team as Jana and Margaret are still in the fight against only Reka from her team. It is clear to Helga that Jana and Margaret has no intention to fight against Reka and she is happy to call the match as things got a bit out of control already.

As the fighters clear the sandpit, Reka joins Eva's team. 'Do you mind if I hang out with you guys tonight. They will kill me if I go back with them.
'Yes sure, what happened, why was Amelia punching you?'
Jana laughs at her friend. 'That bitch knocked you out from behind. She beat Janet and was waiting for an opportunity. It came when you pushed Reka away and you were technically no longer involved in a fight. Like the coward she is, she punched you from behind. Reka jumped in and attacked Amelia and after I finished my match, I decided to help her with that fat cow.'
Eva looks at Reka. 'Thank you.'
'No problem, but you know the two of us still need to finish our little chat.

Eva just smiles at her as the five of them start to make their way back to Eva and Jana's townhouse. After a few drinks, Janet and Margaret excuse themselves and Eva and Reka are left alone while Jana takes a shower. Eva gives Reka a playful punch in the shoulder. 'So why did you really attack Amelia?'

'To protect you.'

'I know that may be part of it. Thanks again. But she did not technically break the rules when she punched me from behind, so why not just use the situation to win the match for your team? Why attack your own teammate and give the match to us?'

Reka gives a deep sigh. 'Well it's a long story. As I told you before, I was often bullied at school and I was too small in size to do anything about it, so I joined the academy straight after school in order to learn some skills to protect myself. Helga decided that I should share a townhouse with Amelia. At first, I was scared that she would bully me, but instead she protected me. She is actually very kind to her friends and she once told me that she will not allow anyone to ever harm her friends or her roommate. I felt save with her and really enjoyed having her as a roommate. I started realising that she bullies others, but to be honest, I actually started enjoying the fact that I was part of the group bullying and not the group being bullied. With your initiation fight, I was instructed by Helga to stretch the rules and to make sure that you took a lot of punishment. Once again, I truly enjoyed the fact that I was in control of your punishment. I enjoyed the fact that Amelia was bullying you and that I was the one controlling it. When you slapped me while I was pinned down, it brought back all those feelings I felt when I was bullied at school. I told Amelia afterwards and she told me that the only way I would get over those feelings was to get you back. I took it as challenging you to a fight, but she told me that me fighting you would not be enough and that the only way you would stop bullying me was if you were taught a good lesson. Her plan to hold you to ensure that I could properly punish you, did not sit well with me, but I still went along with it and I actually felt great afterwards. I was sure that you would never try to bully me again. When we had the chat on the bus and you told me why you slapped my, I realised that you never bullied me, but that you were fighting back against your bullies. I still wanted to fight you as I felt that we both needed to face a bully one-on-one. And I know that you were not really bullying me, but your slap made me feel that way and I needed to face you the right way. At that stage the wall-on-wall match was already organised and I decided to make sure we would face each other. This worked out and I enjoyed the fight with you. It made me feel very powerful. Then Amelia once again interfered and once again bullied you by going against the spirit of the fight and punching you from behind while you were giving me a chance to get up. You were fair to me and for that you were punched out with a cheap, cowardly shot from behind. I snapped and attacked her. So there you have it, my full sad story.'

Eva hugs her and kisses her cheek. 'I am glad you told me. Let's go face her.'

'What do you mean? Fight her? She is probably strong enough to beat us both, but she will get the rest of her friends involved and we will be beaten to a pulp.'

'No, I do not want to fight her, but if it boils down to that, I will. I want to go chat with her and clear the air.

Reka shakes her head, but she follows Eva. Amelia is truly surprised when she opens the door. Her first instinct is to punch Eva in the face, but she is curious why the two petite girls are here without any backup. She also wants to know why Reka attacked her during the fight. She is furious at her and she really wants to punish her, but she also really likes her roommate and she did not expect her reaction during the fight and she wants to understand why she did what she did. She invites them in and Eva can hear her heart bounce in her chest when she sees Amelia's other two friends sitting inside. Eva wonders if she should turn and run, but decides to push through. She takes a deep breath. 'I am here to clear the air with you. You broke the rules during my initiation fight and you put me in the hospital and out of action for a long time. You then grabbed me from behind and allowed Reka to punch me without me being able to protect myself or to fight back. To make it worse, you hit me from behind when Reka was done with me. Tonight, I was in a one-on-one fight with Reka and when I waited for her to get up, as I felt that it was unfair to attack her on the ground after I pushed her over another pair of fighters, you knocked my out from behind. I am sure that in a fair one-on-one fight you will kick my butt and if that is what you want or need to do, I will face you in a fair one-on-one fight. I just want you to stop attacking me in unfair ways.'

Amelia thoughtfully nods her head without saying anything and looks at Reka. Reka looks at Eva first trying to find some strength. 'You have only been good to me, but the two of us have bullied Eva and a few other girls and I cannot do that anymore. I am moving out for a few days to allow us all to come to terms with what has happened tonight. After that I want to take you for a beer so that we can discuss whether I should move out permanently, or whether we will both be happy to remain roommates.'

Eva is surprised to see tears in Amelia's eyes. Her voice trembles as she starts to talk. 'I don't want to lose you as a friend. Let me know when you want to go for a beer.' She looks at Eva. 'I want to have a beer with you as well, if you would have one with me.'

Eva can't help herself. She moves in and hugs Amelia. After collecting a few things, Eva and Reka walk back to Eva's place in silence. Jana just shakes her head in amazement when they tell her where they were. 'I really don't understand you.' She says to Eva.

Reka goes back to her own townhouse a few days later after she had a chat with Amelia. Amelia also had a beer with Eva and they managed to straighten things out. Amelia followed Helga's instructions with their first fight and after that her motivation every time she hurt Eva was to protect Reka. Eva accepts this and Amelia's apology, although she still believes that Amelia has a nasty streak in her. She doesn't believe that Amelia's life as a bully is really over, but only time will tell.

Chapter 20 – Betrayal

Nancy is ecstatic, the oil enhanced the sexiness of the fight and she identified a few more rivalries which she will be able to exploit in her new show. She makes a few entries on her computer before she calls Helga in. 'I know that Janet and Margaret arranged with you for another fight. I want this to be in a MMA octagon on my new live television show, so delay their fight for a month.'
'What television show? And we don't have an octagon.'
'I needed to get a few agreements signed before I could tell you. The show is called 'Grudge Fights' and the octagon is in the television studio of my partner in this venture. The fights will be mostly MMA style and it will give our girls some much needed exposure.'
'Janet and Margaret fight in a very specific style. They stand in front of each other and punch till both of them had enough. They don't kick or grapple, so it will not be a true MMA fight,'
'That is the beauty of it. I will give the audience a few variations on the MMA theme. There style of fighting is perfect for my opening match on episode one. I also want fights between Eva and Reka and between Jana and that girl she fought in the club a few weeks ago. I already cleared it with her academy and she is keen to fight Jana again.'
'This is not a good idea. Their last fight almost destroyed the relationship between Eva and Jana. This is too soon to let them fight again.'
'They are all nice and grown up. Life is complicated and they should learn how to deal with the bumps in the road. By the way, Olga will be the head coach for the new show. I want you to work with her to get the girls ready for these kinds of fights.'
'Why did you get her involved? I will not work with her.'
'I had no choice, my business partner insisted on her. Anyway, the two of you should really make up as well. You are sisters and grown women.'

Helga is devastated and goes directly to the biker bar for some drinks. She needs time to think about this and to discuss it with her best friend, Spitfire. Spitfire is happy to see her friend, but she can see that something is eating her up from inside. She gets one of the bikers to run the bar, grab a few beers and the two of them goes to her office to talk in private. Her office is quite small and she sits on her desk and offers the chair to Helga.
'What's up with you, it looks like you saw a ghost?'
'Nancy decided to start a television show and she is bringing Olga in as the coach for this show. She wants me to help Olga to get the girls ready for the show.'
'Have you still not sorted out your issues with Olga?'
'I tried, but she did not want to accept my challenge to a death match on Duel.'
Spitfire smiles at her friend. 'I know, but that happened long ago. I meant, have you not forgiven her yet?'
Helga shakes her head slowly. 'You know me better than that. You know I can never forgive her for what she has done. How am I supposed to work with her again? I don't trust her and

I still want to kill her. I don't understand why Nancy wants to bring her in. She knows that I am more than capable of training the girls myself.'

Helga is nursing a headache the next morning. She still arrives at the academy early, although she was having beers with Spitfire until about four in the morning. She goes through her training plan for the day and she sets up the equipment required. When the first girls arrive, one of them tells her that Nancy wants to see her. Helga instructs one of the senior girls to warm up the rest as soon as all are there. She opens the door to Nancy's office and finds Nancy and Olga chatting inside. She is furious. 'What is she doing here?'
'I told you Olga will be the head coach for the Grudge Fights show. We only have a month left before the first show and she will need to get the girls ready for the new format.'
'I still don't understand why we need her. I am more than capable to get the girls ready by myself.'
'You still have to train the rest of the girls for their sport matches and I told you that my partner insisted on Olga being the main coach for the show.'
'I want nothing to do with her or the show then.'
Olga has been silent till now. 'I am here because you are not willing to do what is required sister.'
'What is she talking about?'
'You may as well tell her Nancy, she will find out sooner or later.'
Helga glares at Nancy. 'Tell me what?'
Nancy sighs. She did not want to share this with Helga just yet. 'We will eventually launch another show called Pit of Death.'
'That's why you insisted on allowing Eva to join.'
'Yes, she is part of my plans to launch the show.'
'Does she know what you have planned for her?'
'You know that she is here to train for revenge. I am not forcing her to do anything that she does not want to do. I really want you to stay, but I knew that you will not train women for death matches and I had to get the best coach who trains women for these kind of matches to help me.'
'I will not be involved with an academy which trains young girls for death matches and I will not work with her. If you want a death match on your show, why not have the two of us launch your show for you. I have challenged her before, but she was too scared to face me.'
Nancy did not know about the previous challenge and her head immediately starts to work on how she could use this information to her advantage. 'I may arrange that one day if Olga wants that too, but not for the launch. Is there anything I can do to convince you to stay?'
'Get rid of her and cancel the plans for the death matches.'
Nancy does not answer and Helga walks out and leaves the academy. She immediately feels bad for not explaining her decision to the girls and she feels guilty for leaving them at the mercy of Nancy and Olga. But she has to get away from here. She cannot stand to be at the academy any longer.

Eva is busy warming up with the rest of the girls when Helga and Nancy walk into the indoor training centre. Eva wonders why Nancy is with Helga. She never comes to training. She looks at Helga again and she does not know what it is, but there is something different, something not quite right about Helga. She realises that her hairstyle is different and she is wearing clothes Eva has never seen her wear before and she starts to think that this is not Helga. Her suspicion is confirmed when Nancy tells them that Helga has decided to leave the academy, but that she was lucky enough to secure the services of her twin sister Olga. Eva is shocked. She did not know Helga has a twin sister and why would Helga decide to go. Before she can ask this question, Nancy turns around and leaves the training centre. Eva decides to ask Helga herself and she thinks she knows where to find her. Olga's way of working with the girls is very different from Helga's. She does not show the same level of care for the girls and is a lot more impatient. Her technical skills are very good though and she picks up on small mistakes and quickly makes the girls aware of it.

That night Eva visits the biker bar and finds Helga chatting with some of the bikers. Helga motions her over and buys her a beer. Eva gets straight to the point. 'Why did you decide to leave the academy?'
'I will not be involved in training girls for death matches and I will not work with my sister.'
'But you knew that I will have death matches one day. You said you will still train me.'
'I know, but I was still hoping that I could talk you out of it. Now Nancy will start her own death match show and she will convince many of the academy's girls to fight in these when they reach the legal age.'
'And your sister, why do you not want to work with her?'
'That, my dear Eva, is a very long story which I may share with you one day. Please don't go on with your plan for the death match. You have everything to live for. You are young, beautiful, have many good friends and a girl who really loves you. Live for her, live for your friends. Don't throw it all away for revenge. It is not worth it.'
Eva looks at her for a long time. 'I have to. It's a promise I made to my mother when we buried her.'
'I didn't know your mother, but I can guarantee you that she would not want you to revenge her. She would want you to live and have a better life than hers.'
'I have to.'
Helga does not want to push too hard. She wants Eva to be comfortable to come and talk to her. 'Promise me one thing though. Promise me that you will talk to me whenever you need advice or whenever you feel uncomfortable about anything at the academy.'
Eva gives her a hug. 'Thank you, I promise to visit you often.'
'And please promise me one more thing. Promise me you will never trust Nancy and that you will think hard before you agree to anything she wants you to do.'
Eva smiles. 'I promise.' She does not want to tell Helga that she already signed an agreement for three death matches on the day she joined the academy.

Chapter 21 – Grudge Fights

Olga starts training the girls who are scheduled to fight on the opening show of 'Grudge Fights' in MMA techniques. She makes time to train Lea in the evenings and Eva helps out when they need a sparring partner. She did not want to get involved at first as she does not really want Jana and Lea to fight again, but both assured her that this would be a match without hatred for each other and that they would both abide by the rules. Jana knew that Eva would want to spend time with Lea while she was training at their academy and she suggested to Eva to help her out as a sparring partner.

When the night of the fights arrives, the girls are all well prepared to do battle. They are all taken to the recording studios of Kelly Yates where their hair and makeup are done by professional makeup artists. They will all be interviewed and Nancy wants each of them to be as sexy as possible. She instructed Jana and Eva not to remove their nipple rings as she believes that these will add something to their fights. Both girls are afraid that their nipples may get damage if their nipple rings get caught in the opponent's hair, so they both use a staff with little balls on each side, hoping that these will not easily get caught. Each pair of opponents has outfits and equipment picked by Nancy with their style of their fight in mind.

Janet and Margaret will fight first in a punching only match. They will wear MMA gloves, mouth guards and short boxing shorts with a metal ring woven into the front of it. A thick metre long cord with a carabiner on each end will keep them close to each other during the fight. They will fight for five rounds of three minutes each. Nancy played with the idea of unlimited rounds, but she has a ninety minute slot only and this includes interviews before and after each match.

The second match will be between Eva and Reka and it will be three rounds of five minutes each. All MMA rules are allowed, but each round starts with a trade of slaps to the face. One slap each for the first round, two slaps each for the second and three slaps each for the last round. They will wear MMA gloves, a mouth guard and MMA shorts.

The last match scheduled for the live television show will be between Jana and Lea, fighting each other in a no rules fist fight with no rounds and a time limit of fifteen minutes. They are each offered five thousand credits for every clean knee strike to the opponent's crotch. They will wear a mouth guard and a thong.

Nancy has also lined up four more girls on standby in case any of the matches do not go the full distance. They will fight each other whether or not their fights will be broadcasted on live television. The studio audience has been promised at least five fights. Each of them has also been made aware that they are welcome to participate in amateur fights after the five main fights are done. She did her homework and had discussions with all six girls beforehand to understand what happened between them. She told them to play along with the background story which would be shared with the audience before each fight. They were coached general interview techniques and were instructed on what to say during the interview before the fights. Although there is enough history between the girls, Nancy wanted the first programme to really be memorable, so she decided to add a few threads to the background stories.

The studio has been set up with the octagon close to the back wall, an interview area, complete with a host desk and two couches either side of it and two custom made pavilions with a leather seat for each of the sixty audience members. Each seat offers a clear view of the action in the octagon as well as the interview area. Nancy advertised audience member tickets for five thousand credits each and had no problems selling them out in just a few hours.

The ten girls, including the four backup fighters, are warming up in a room fitted out with wrestling mats, punching bags and a few couches for the girls to relax on. They are all dressed in their fighting gear and their bodies have a thin sheen of perspiration from their warm up routines. The six girls participating in the main fights will all enter the studio before the first fight and each pair will only have about two minutes to loosen up before their fight starts. The rest of the time, the four girls who are not fighting will watch the fight between the other two girls from the couches in the interview area. Eva is glad that she will at last see Margaret and Janet fight each other. She is not so keen on seeing Jana and Lea fight each other again as she is scared that they will put each other in hospital again. She is further scared that the incentive to knee each other in the groin area may result in serious damage to their pussies. She was kind of hoping for a passionate night of lovemaking with Jana later, but considering the rules of their fight, Jana may not be in a condition to enjoy sex at all.

A studio assistant comes in and tells the girls that the six girls fighting in the main fights will be introduced to the audience in five minutes. Eva walks over to Jana and gives her a hug. 'Good luck. Please don't injure each other.' She whispers in Jana's ear. 'Don't get kneed too much, I have big plans for later tonight.'.
Jana just smiles at her. 'It's a fight, we are going to hurt each other, but within the rules.'
This does not comfort Eva much. The rules of Jana's fight against Lea open both of them up to serious punishment. Eva gives each of the other girls a hug as well, leaving Reka for last. She gives her a long hug. 'Good luck and fight hard. I hope we hit the shit out of each other.'
'Oh I plan on that and I hope you give it back to me. I need to have a fight to the finish with you.'
They hug again and Eva goes back to Jana, giving her another long hug and a passionate kiss.

The studio assistant opens the door again and motions to the six fighters to follow her. She waits for the host to start with the introduction.

'Good evening and welcome to the inaugural episode of 'Grudge Fights'. We have a very special line-up tonight with at least three live matches for our television viewers on both Apollo and Artemis and five fights for our studio audience. Our audience members will also be allowed to try their hand in the ring after the main matches. If you want to view girls sorting out their grudges only metres away from you, or if you want to challenge a friend or rival for a fight in front of an audience, make sure that you book well in advance for our next episode.'

After details of the next episode and how to book for it are shown on the television screens, the announcer carries on where she left off. 'Our combatants for the first fight are friends, lovers and rivals. They've had many fights against each other in the past, each sparked by insane jealousy. A glance in the direction of another girl; an innocent compliment from another girl; the mere mention of another girl's name and these two attack each other like wildcats. They are close friends and to ensure that they stay close during their fight, they will be bound together. This will be a fist fight at close range. Ladies and gentlemen, Janet and Margaret.'

The studio assistant opens the door and Janet and Margaret walk towards the interview area. When they come into view the studio audience erupts as they see the two beautiful, half naked girls walking towards them. Most expected larger and older women to fight in these types of fights. The producer slows the speed of the live video feed down, giving the television viewers an artistic view of their boobs bouncing and jiggling as they walk towards the interview area. The girls each take a seat on opposite couches. The host waits until the applause dies down. 'Welcome ladies. Janet, are you ready for the fight and do you have anything to say to Margaret before the fight?'

'I can't wait to get in the octagon Beatrice. I have been waiting a long time to punch some sense into her.' She looks at Margaret. 'You will regret your flirting ways tonight.'

'Thank you Janet. Margaret, are you ready and do you have anything to say to Janet before the fight?'

'Beatrice, I love fighting and the audience are in for a hell of a fight tonight.' This draws a new round of applause from the studio audience. 'Janet, your jealousy will bring you buckets of hurt tonight.'

'Well there you have it ladies and gentlemen, Janet and Margaret.' The studio audience applauds again and the producer switches to a commercial break.

After the commercial break the camera slowly moves in from a wide angle shot of the interview area to a close-up of Beatrice. 'Welcome back. Our combatants for the second fight have been rivals for months. One of them ended up in hospital after a fight. She blamed the other, who acted as referee for that fight, for giving her opponent an unfair advantage and the rivalry was born. The rivalry was renewed when the unhappy loser humiliated the unfair referee in front of many girls during training. The unfair referee cried foul play this time and challenged her rival to a fight. Unfortunately, the loser of this fight claimed that she only lost due to interference from other girls and another fight was organised. This time the loser of the fight was knocked out by a bystander. We will give these girls an opportunity to fight each other without any interference tonight. Ladies and gentlemen, Eva and Reka.'

The studio assistant opens the door and Eva and Reka make their way to the interview area. Once again the audience are surprised by the lovely petite girls walking towards them. The producer is consistent and the movement of Eva and Reka's boobs are showed in slow motion. Eva sits down next to Margaret and Reka next to Janet. When the applause dies down, Beatrice turns to Reka. 'Your opponent has accused you of cheating during your previous matches. What do you have to say about that?'

'Well Beatrice, thousands of viewers and the studio audience will be my witnesses tonight. She can cry as much as she wants to after this match. Everyone will know that I beat her fair and square.'

'Eva, Reka accuses you of being a cry-baby. How do you respond to that?'

'She is a little nasty cheating bitch Beatrice. When that door closes tonight, nobody will be able to come safe her butt again. She will learn what a fight is about if you do not have anybody to back you up.'

'Ladies and gentlemen, Eva and Reka.'

During the applause, the producer cuts to another commercial break.

This time the producer switches from a close-up of Margaret and Eva to a close-up of Janet and Reka and then to a close-up of Beatrice. 'Welcome back to 'Grudge Fights'. The next two combatants are in love with the same girl, who cannot choose between the two of them. They fought each other once before as she watched the fight. The fight was brutal and the girls tried to destroy each other's vaginas. Both ended up in hospital and their love interest could still not choose between them. Tonight they will fight for her love again and any hard, clean knee to an opponent's vagina will earn the owner of that knee five thousand credits. The winner will get the girl. The loser will not be capable of making love for a very long time. Ladies and gentlemen, Jana and Lea.'

Jana and Lea are applauded into the interview area and the producer sticks to his slow motion boob focus. Jana sits next to Reka and Lea sits next to Eva. This was carefully planned by Nancy as she wants to use any small opportunity to manipulate the relationship between Jana and Eva. Using Lea in these little games she plays with them may also pay off in future. Beatrice turns to Jana. 'You were in a happy relationship until Lea made a play for you lover. How will you ensure that you do not lose your lover permanently?'

'I love her and will do anything to win her back.' Jana glances at Eva as she says this. 'I will not only put Lea in hospital tonight, I will also make sure that she will never be able to make love to somebody else's girlfriend again.'

'Lea, you are accused of being a home wrecker. Why not rather get your own girlfriend?'

'Beatrice, I take what I want and no love struck bitch will stand in my way. If Jana wants a pussy war, she will get one. Question is, can she handle it?'

'Ladies and gentlemen, Jana and Lea.'

Once again the producer cuts away to a commercial break during the applause.

After the commercial break the producer starts with a wide angle view of the octagon and then slowly moves in on a table with two bottles of baby oil on top of it. He then cuts away to a close-up of Beatrice. 'Welcome back to 'Grudge Fights'. For your enjoyment, all fighters will be covered in baby oil and they have agreed that lucky members of the audience will have the opportunity to oil them down. If you want to make use of this opportunity, enter the amount you are willing to pay on the pad in your left armrest. To give everyone a fair chance, an audience member will only be allowed to oil down one of our lovely combatants, so choose wisely. The first silent auction will be for Margaret. Ladies enter your bids now.' The winner is announced and she hurries down to the octagon where Janet and Margaret is busy warming up in their corners. The woman starts to apply oil all over Margaret's body. The same process is followed for Janet and soon both girls' bodies are glistening under the studio lights. Eva has never been so exited to watch a fight. She has been waiting for this since the first day she joined the academy when she saw a few seconds of their fight in the sandpit. That image enters her head often when she touches herself and although she will never share this with anyone, a few times while she was making love to Jana. She forgets about her own fight which is only about twenty minutes from now. Her full attention is on the two half naked, oily bodies now only feet apart as Olga attaches the rope to the rings on their shorts. Their eyes have been locked since the moment Olga called them to the centre of the octagon. Anybody who doesn't know them will swear that they hate each other and when the bell rings, the ferocity with which they attack each other seems to confirm this perceived hatred for each other. Eva knows better though. She has seen this absolute all-in war between them before, albeit only for a short time when she was walking past them. It seems that this never affects their relationship. The first round flies by and when Olga removes the rope at the end of the round, both girls are gasping for air. Margaret sports a cut above her left eye and blood drips into her eye, forcing her to keep it closed. She has managed to cut both Janet's top and bottom lips on the left side. Blood trickles down her chin. The doctors appointed for these matches have their hands full stopping the bleeding between rounds. The second round starts off as energetic as the first round. Both girls still land to the face often, but they also start to attack each other's bodies. Eva knows that none of their fights have lasted much longer than three to five minutes. She also knows that there has never been a clear winner in any of their fights. That has never been important to them and they both were satisfied after a while of punching the living daylights out of each other. The fights would generally stop at this stage and both girls would go their own way to clear their heads, before they carried on as if nothing happened. Eva wonders whether their relationship will be affected should either of them manage to win the fight before the end of five rounds. There is a loud cheer as Janet's knees buckle after a right hook to her chin. She manages to stay upright and has to cover up with both her arms as Margaret continues to pound her fists into her face. Margaret changes her point of attack and lands a few brutal punches to Janet's unprotected breasts. As soon as Janet's guard drops, Margaret's fists find their way back to her face. Janet is in serious trouble and she tries to put some distance between them, but the rope holds her back. Margaret is relentless and she continues with a barrage of punches to Janet's upper body and head. Janet is out on her feet, but she refuses to go down and somehow manages to stay upright. Olga watches her closely and is about to stop the fight when the bell rings. When the rope is released, Janet stumbles back and drops to the floor. Her doctor rushes in and examines her. She waves her arms, giving Olga the sign that her fighter is unable to continue. Only the rope kept her from going down during the last portion of the round. Margaret does not celebrate her victory, but instead she sits quietly in her corner, watching to see whether Janet is ok. When she comes to, Janet is very unsteady, but she lifts her fists, ready to fight on. Only when Margaret hugs her and whispers something in her ear, does she relax. A tear starts to flow down her cheek. She is devastated by the loss and Margaret starts to cry as well. Hurting her friend with her fists is one thing, hurting her emotionally is too much for her to take. The producer focuses on Janet's bruised breasts then on her cut and bruised face and then back to her breasts before she cuts to a commercial break.

After the commercial break Janet and Margaret has taken their spots on the couches while Eva and Reka entered the octagon to start warming up. Beatrice puts a consolatory hand on Janet's shoulder. 'Janet, you have been well and truly beaten by Margaret. How will this affect your relationship?'
'I am gutted and very disappointed with my performance in this match. This does not change the fact that I love Margaret. We will fight again, but fights will never change my love for her.'
'Margaret, you tore her apart in the second round. Am I right to say that there were at least a little bit of hatred between the two of you?'
Margaret is furious and forgets all her interview training. 'No! You are totally wrong. There is nothing but love between us. We will fight each other again, but never again by forced rules like this. We will settle our differences our own way.'
'Well there you have it ladies and gentlemen. It is clear that all issues have not been sorted out tonight and that new issues have probably surfaced during this brutal beatdown. It is time to enter your bids for the silent auction and the opportunity to oil down our next two combatants.'

The woman who oils down Eva is very handsy and spends most of her time oiling her boobs and toying with her nipples. Eva is upset at first, but blocks this out as she focuses on the fight at hand. During their one-on-one in the wall-on-wall match, Reka was getting the better of her. She is faster than Eva and she punches very hard for her size. Eva will have to fight smarter this time. She outweighs Reka by about five pounds and intents using the weight advantage in her ground game. The woman is now spending a lot of time on Eva's thighs and when she brushes a hand over Eva's pussy, Eva pushes her away. Olga realises what happened and she quickly steps in and tells both women that its time to leave the octagon as the fight is about to start. She calls the two girls to the centre of the octagon. She orders Eva to keep her hands behind her back and to keep her head still. Reka makes full use of her free slap and Eva's left ear rings after the slap. It takes her a second or two before she is able to focus again. When it is Eva's turn she slaps Reka with all she has and she is chuffed when Reka has to take a step to her right side to stop her from falling. The bell rings and Eva uses the moment Reka needs to recover to land a straight right to Reka's face before she grabs her around her middle, lifts her up and smashes her to the ground. She lands on top of Reka and tries to get full mount, but Reka twists her body slightly and traps Eva's right leg between her thighs. She also grabs Eva around the neck and pulls Eva's body into her own. Eva forces her left forearm between their bodies and across Reka's boobs. She pushes herself up with her right arm, while her left arm is pushing down on Reka's boobs. The force and Eva's slippery body soon results in Reka losing her grip around Eva's neck. Eva immediately tries to land some punches to Reka's face, but she covers her face well with her arms. Eva remains patient and she starts picking her shots, landing two fists and an elbow to Reka's face. The elbow cuts Reka just under her left eye and blood starts dripping from the wound, rolling down her cheek past her mouth. It is difficult for Eva to keep control of Reka's body as the oil makes holds all but impossible. As Eva lines up another elbow, Reka is able to worm her body between Eva's thighs and for a split second her mouth and nose brushes against Eva's pussy. This momentary distraction is enough for Reka to roll clear of Eva. They both get to their feet and start circling each other. Eva lands a few hard kicks to Reka's thighs and Reka scores by dancing in, landing a one-two and dancing out before Eva can tag her with punches of her own. Eva times an attack by Reka correctly and lands an elbow to Reka's forehead as Reka lets go with a straight right which also catches Eva in the face. Reka stumbles forward and grabs onto Eva's body in order not to go down. She regains her composure quickly though and pushes Eva back until her back hits the fence. She moves her legs back slightly and lands a knee to Eva's thigh. Eva tries to wrestle her way out of the hold and Reka lands another knee to her thigh. When Reka strikes with her knee again, Eva turns her body slightly and she immediately regrets this. The knee catches the inside of Eva's thigh and carries through to her pussy. Pain shoots through her body. She pulls Reka closer to herself to avoid any further knees. When the pain is under control she bends her knees slightly and forces her head under Reka's right arm. She straightens her knees with force and manages to lift Reka's feet off the ground and they tumble to the ground. Eva lands on top of Reka, but her head is trapped under Reka's right arm. Reka tries to put force on Eva's neck, but she is not in a position of strength and Eva is able to pull her head away. As Eva comes up, she starts swinging and lands a number of punches to Reka's face. Olga gets closer to make sure Reka is able to protect herself. She is satisfied when Reka manages to protect herself with raised arms. She even manages to land a few punches from a defensive position. The bell goes and the girls both let go of each other and go back to their corners.

Eva watches Reka as the doctors start to clean their faces and offer them water to drink. Neither of the two girls has serious cuts and the doctors leave the ring with about half of the break time left. Reka looks Eva straight in the eyes, then diverts her eyes down to Eva's crotch and she gives her a naughty smile. The little bitch knows exactly what she has done. This spurs Eva on to punish her during the second round. She can't help but wonder how much pain her two friends will be in during their match. They will target each other's pussies after all. Olga calls them to the centre of the octagon and each are allowed two free slaps. Reka lands a hard slap to each side of Eva's face and Eva slaps her twice on the same side. Both girl's cheeks are stinging after the slaps and they are both ready to beat each

other up again. The bell rings and the two girls cautiously circle each other. Eva goes back to kicking Reka's thighs and Reka uses her speed to land a few stiff jabs and a few combinations. As Reka comes in again, Eva hits her with a front kick, catching Reka on the sternum. Reka's legs are still going forward as her body is forced backward. She lands hard on her back and the back of her head slams against the ground. Everything goes dark for a second and by the time she regains her focus, Eva is on top of her in full mount. Eva lands two punches to Reka's face before Reka is able to lift her arms in defence. Her defence is weak though and Eva is able to pick her punches. Olga allows three punches to Reka's face before she pulls Eva off of Reka. The doctors rush in and examine Reka before they help her to her corner. After a few minutes she is helped back to the couch. Beatrice turns to Eva first. 'Eva, you proved that, without help, Reka is not a match for you.'
'It was a hard fought match and I only got the better of her by landing that straight kick to her breastbone. She had me in trouble as well and in fights like these, one sometimes needs a bit of luck to win.'
'Reka, your butt was handed to you tonight. Do you agree that you can only compete against a girl like Eva if your friends are holding her down?'
Eva jumps in to defend her opponent. 'Reka was brave enough to enter that octagon for a one-on-one fight. Not many girls have the guts to do that. If you want to run your mouth, you should probably try it at least once. Otherwise, you should show some respect for the fighters.'
'Ladies and gentlemen, now you know why the next pair will be fighting for Eva's love. Let's get the bids going for our first lady, Jana.'
Jana and Lea are both tense as they warm up in the octagon. Both were hurt in their previous match and they know that their pussies will be targeted tonight. Eva can see the tension on their faces and she can almost not bear to watch this match. She knows that they will hurt each other, but she can only hope that neither will be seriously hurt.

After they are oiled down Olga calls the fighters to the centre of the octagon. 'There is a slight change to the rules. The fight will continue for the full fifteen minutes. There will be a one minute break between every knock out or submission. Knock outs will earn three points and submissions one. The winner will be the fighter with most points after fifteen minutes. Oh, I almost forgot. Every knee to the groin will earn two points and every punch one point. Do you understand?'
They both nod their heads and the bell is rung. While the focus is on the match, Nancy comes over to where Eva sits. 'I know you had a hard fight, but the host is instructed to ask controversial questions. This helps with the ratings. Do not attack her again. When the current fight is done, I need you to play the roll of the lover who was won by the winner and to kiss the winner passionately. During the interview also play along and confirm that the winner won your love.'
Eva does not like this, but she understands that television shows are all about ratings, so she nods her head. In the ring, Jana has pressed Lea against the fence and is landing knees to her thighs, trying to target her pussy. Lea keeps her body angled though and Jana has to settle for her thighs. She presses her forearm into Lea's neck, trying to choke her, but Lea's

chin is low enough and Jana is unable to make the move count. She pulls her arm back and lands a short elbow to Lea's face. It does not do a lot of damage, but in fights like these every bit helps. Lea manages to get her left leg between Jana's legs and she pushes Jana back just far enough that both tumble down. Jana turns her body and is able to roll Lea off as soon as they hit the ground. They both get to their knees and Jana grabs Lea's hair with her left hand and start punching her with her right. Lea eats a few punches before she manages to tie up Jana's right arm with her left. Her right arm is free and she punches Jana as hard as she can between the legs. Jana screams in pain, releases her hold on Lea's hair and grabs Lea's right arm to stop her from punching her again. With both their arms locked, Jana is happy to take some time to recover from the punch to her pussy. She looks up just in time to see Lea's head coming forward towards her face. The headbutt catches Jana on her right eye which starts to tear up and swell close immediately. She is blind to a second headbutt which catches her on the same eye. It opens up a cut under her eye and blood starts to stream down her face. Jana's right arm is still trapped by Lea and her only choice is to release Lea's right arm. She uses her left hand to push Lea in the face in order to control her head. A second punch to her pussy drops her to the ground. Lea rolls on top of her and start punching the back and sides of Jana's head. Olga grabs Lea and pulls her of Jana after a couple of punches. The first submission goes to Lea and she also scored two points with punches to Jana's crotch. After four minutes Lea is leading three to nil and Jana is in real trouble. Her right eye is completely swollen closed and she has a deep cut under the same eye. The doctor manages to stop the bleeding, but the cut is an easy target for Lea as any punches to it will come from Jana's blind side.

Eva cannot understand why the fight is not over as Olga stopped it. She looks at Nancy, but she just motions to her to stay put and relax. Eva is getting scared quickly. Her lover is badly hurt and it looks like they are going to fight on. The clock is not stopped during the break and it rolls on to five minutes when the bell is rung again. Jana keeps Lea away from her with stiff jabs and Lea circles to Jana's right to try and attack her from her blind side. To counter this, Jana turns her head slightly to her right to enable her to see further to her right with her left eye. Lea gets impatient and she steps in to attack Jana with a few punches to her face. Jana has been waiting for this and she is prepared to take a punch to be able to get close to Lea. The punch opens the cut under her right eye again and blood starts to flow down her face again. However, Jana has successfully managed to grab Lea around her upper body from where she lifts her and slams her to the ground. This knocks the air from Lea and Jana has no problems claiming full mount. After a flurry of punches, Lea manages to tie up Jana by grabbing onto her arms. Jana pulls back, pulling both their bodies to about a forty-five degree angle with the ground. She falls forward, slamming Lea back to the ground. However, Lea manages to maintain her hold on Jana's arms. Jana does this another three times, but decides that this is taking more energy out of her than it is hurting Lea. She dummies another lift, but just as Lea's shoulders start to life, Jana relaxes and slams her head into Lea's face, breaking her nose. Blood streams from Lea's nose and she releases her grip on Jana's arms, allowing Jana to swing to her head at will. Olga jumps in and pulls Jana off. The score is three to one with five minutes to go. After the break, Jana will have only four minutes to gain at least two more points. She needs a knockout to win or a knee to Lea's crotch to draw even. She decides to go for broke when the fight resumes. Eva is very concerned. Both her friends are injured and she knows that both will go at each other with all they have during the last few minutes.

The bell rings and both girls rush each other. They collide with a thud, neither being able to gain an advantage. They push each other away and start swinging without caring about defence. Lea's nose and Jana's cut are soon bleeding freely again. Both soon have cut lips and Jana also has a cut above her left eye. The blood dripping into her eye makes it very difficult to see any punches coming her way. Both girls' arms feel like lead at this stage, but both keep swinging. With about thirty seconds to go, Jana lands a right uppercut to Lea's jaw rocking Lea's head back. Lea drops but is not knocked out. As she tries to regain her feet, Jana jumps on top of her and lands elbow after elbow to her face. Olga jumps in and pulls Jana off. She has won another point, but has lost the match due to the two punches she took to her pussy early in the match. The two girls are a bloody mess and they both struggle to stay upright as they hug each other in the centre of the octagon. Both have been in a war and both respect the other for a hard fought fight. The doctors work on the bleeding and clean the blood from their faces. Eva walks into the octagon, goes past Jana and hugs Lea before she gives her a deep kiss. Lea is surprised but plays along as she is sure this is just part of the show. When Eva turns around she sees tears in Jana's eyes. She is not sure whether Jana is a very good actress, or whether she is really hurt. Before she can go over to Jana to find out, the host, who has come into the octagon, starts the interview with her and Lea. 'Lea you won a brutal fight against Jana and won the love of Eva. How does that feel?' Lea plays along. 'I love Eva and am very happy to have her back in my life. The fight was very tough and I am glad that it was only fifteen minutes. If there were more time left after the last fall, I would have been in serious trouble.'
'Eva, these girls fought hard for you love, how does this make you feel?'
'Beatrice, I love them both and it is difficult to see them hurt each other, but it's always flattering when girls are prepared to fight over you.'
Beatrice walks over to Jana and the doctor insists that Lea comes with her so that she can start working on her broken nose. Olga takes Eva by the arm and tells her that Nancy wants to talk with her. Eva protests and tells Olga that she wants to make sure Jana is fine first. Olga tells her that, for the sake of the show, they should only show affection in the dressing room. Nancy is in a small office at the back of the studio, with a clear view of the octagon and the interview area. She has a huge smile on her face. 'Great matches Eva. I am in the debt of you girls, the opening show could not go better. We have time for one more match on live television and I have decided to take a bit of a chance. One of the audience members paid a considerable amount to fight you in an oil wrestling match. No striking will be allowed, but anything else goes. I decided to do this match on live television instead of a match between our backup fighters.' She hands Eva a small g-string. 'Quickly put this on, your match starts in a few minutes.'
Eva is not too happy with this, but she understands why this will be good for the show and she pulls down her MMA shorts and slips on the small g-string. When she enters the

interview area, the other five girls are no longer around and a woman in her late twenties is sitting on the one couch. She is wearing small lacy panties only and has a very sexy body with C cup boobs and long dark nipples. Eva sits down opposite her and the woman takes her time checking out Eva's body. Beatrice welcomes the viewers back after another commercial break. 'We have a special match to close out tonight's live episode. A member of our studio audience has challenged one of tonight's combatants to an oil wrestling match. Although no striking will be allowed during this match, anything else will be within the rules. Jenny, why did you specifically challenge Eva?'

'Just look at her Beatrice. She is gorgeous. Who wouldn't want to roll around with her in the ring? Wrestling another girl in a competitive match has been on my bucket list for a long time. This is the perfect opportunity to do that and being on live television will not be bad for my modelling career either.'

'Eva, this will be your second match of the night. Do you have enough energy left to deal with this new challenge?'

'I am definitely up for it Beatrice. She looks fit and strong, but I fight fit, strong and young woman on a regular basis.'

Eva and Jenny follows Olga to the octagon and each takes a bottle of oil and starts to oil the other one down. Olga orders them to start the match on their knees and they face off in the centre of the octagon, sitting on their knees only inches apart. When the bell rings, they grab each other around the neck and they struggle to force each other down. Jenny grabs hold of Eva's hair with her left hand and starts to yank on it. Instant pain goes through Eva's scalp and she yelps in pain and surprise. The combination of the hair pulling and the grip around Eva's neck is enough to force Eva over to her right side. Jenny slips on top of her and does not release her grip on Eva's hair. With her right hand she grabs Eva's left boob and sinks her fingers deep into it. Her long nails digs into Eva's skin and Eva grabs her arm and pulls it away from her breast, leaving deep scratch marks all over her left boob. This stings like hell and Eva realises that she is in for a hard match. Jenny pulls her arm free from Eva's hold on it and immediately attacks Eva's left boob again. This time she deliberately uses her nails to scratch Eva's chest area, leaving long deep scratch marks from above Eva's boobs, across her left boob and onto her tummy. Eva is furious and grabs both Jenny's boobs and squeezes with all she has. Her nails are too short to effectively scratch Jenny in retaliation, but she still presses them into Jenny's tit flesh and Jenny pulls back to get away from the pain. Eva twists her body and dislodges Jenny, but Jenny maintains her grip on Eva's hair as they both struggle to their knees. Eva grabs a handful of Jenny's hair and start pulling as hard as she can. With her free hand she grabs hold of Jenny's right boob. Jenny does the same and the girls are locked in a painful standoff. Each twist and maul her opponent's boobs while yanking on her hair. Neither girl wants to show weakness and they both maintain their hold on each other rather than protecting their own boobs. Eva feels Jenny's nails breaking skin on her boob and also on her scalp and she can only hope that she is inflicting similar pain to Jenny. The painful standoff is only broken when the bell rings for the end of round one. Eva nurses the scratches and bruises on her boobs and is satisfied when she sees the deep bruises on Jenny's boobs. There are only small scratch marks though and she knows that Jenny will win the battle of leaving scratch marks on the opponent. She suddenly realises that she does not know how to win the match. All she was told was that they will wrestle for three rounds of two minutes each. She does not know whether pins count or whether she should try and submit Jenny. She motions Olga over and asks her this question. Olga informs her that there will be no winner or loser. Jenny wanted three rounds of inflicting pain and pins or submissions do not count.

Eva's plan to finish this match quickly will not work. She will just have to inflict as much pain as possible in the next two rounds. The fighters take their position on their knees again and when the bell rings they each grab a handful of hair again. Jenny sinks her nails into Eva and leaves long, deep scratch marks on her upper body, this time targeting Eva's right boob. Eva grabs Jenny's left nipple and twists and pulls at the same time. The oil makes it difficult to hold onto it, but she still gets a scream from Jenny. Jenny retaliates immediately and she uses Eva's nipple ring to gain a good grip on Eva's right nipple. The pain is excruciating and Eva fears that Jenny may tear the nipple ring out of her nipple. She does not want permanent damage to her nipples and she grabs Jenny's hand and pries it away from her breast. Once Jenny's hand are away from Eva's nipple, she controls Jenny's hand, making sure her fingers stay away from her boobs. They keep on yanking on each other's hair and neither is prepared to let go. Then Jenny leans forward and sinks her teeth into Eva's shoulder. Eva lets go of her grip on Jenny's arm and forces Jenny's head away from her shoulder and punches Jenny in the face, drawing blood from her bottom lip. Olga jumps in and separates the girls. She warns Eva for foul play. Eva protests that Jenny bit her, but Olga points out that biting is not against the rules. Jenny is grinning at Eva. She enjoys the fact that she made Eva lose her cool. The girls tear into each other's hair again and Jenny grabs hold of the front of Eva's g-string and pulls up hard. It wedges into Eva's slit and she screams out is pain. She tries to remove Jenny's hand, but she has a death grip on the small garment. Eva's only defence is to loosen the strings on either side of her hips and the g-string is yanked off of her body by Jenny who tosses it to one side. Eva did not plan to fight naked, but that is the least of her problems now. Her clean shaven pussy is not only on display for thousands to see, it is also Jenny's new target. Jenny grabs Jana's clit and starts to pull and twist it. Eva screams out in pain again. She grabs hold of Jenny's arm and pulls it away. She tries to take the initiative by letting go of Jenny's hair and sinking her free hand into Jenny's left boob. This far in the match, she has been playing second fiddle. Jenny initiated each new area of attack and Eva has just reacted to it each time. She slips her fingers around Jenny's ample nipple again and digs in her nails for better grip. She twists it hard and forces Jenny to let go of her hair to protect her nipple. This time Eva uses her teeth as weapons and she sinks them into Jenny's left boob, biting down hard. Jenny screams and forces her thumbs into Eva's eyes. Eva is once again surprised by this move and releases her bite and pulls back. The girls are a few feet apart and glaring at each other when the bell rings.

Eva wants to put her g-string back on, but Olga has tossed it out of the octagon and a woman in the front row has claimed it as a momento. She will have to fight the last round naked. She crosses her legs when she sits down. She gently strokes the bite marks on her shoulder and the deep scratch marks on her upper body. She looks over at Jenny and is surprised to see that she has also removed her panties. She does not bother to cross her legs though and her clean shaven pussy is on full display. Eva looks at her stiff clit. She must get her own back this round and Jenny's clit must be one of her main targets. She smiles at the bite marks on Jenny's left boob. Jenny has left her mark on Eva's body, but at least she is marked as well.

Olga allows the fighters to start on their feet for the last round. The bell rings and they grab hold of each other. Eva uses a hip toss to get Jenny down and for the first time in the match she feels in control. She has a grip around Jenny's neck and is able to pin her down. With her free hand she grabs hold of Jenny's pussy lips and twists them from side to side. She then grabs hold of her clit and starts to maul it. Jenny screams with pain and scratches Eva's back with her left hand. Her right arm is trapped under Eva's body and she can do nothing with it except for digging her nails into Eva's inner thigh. The scratching hurts Eva, but she knows that she is inflicting more pain to Jenny and she maintains her grip on Jenny's clit. Jenny tries to bite Eva's nipple which is only a few inches away from her mouth, but it is just out of reach. She screams out in pain again and taps twice on Eva's back. Eva is confused when Olga breaks them up. She was in full control and was inflicting a lot of pain by tearing into Jenny's pussy, but Olga is satisfied that this was a genuine submission and she allows both girls to get back to their feet before she instructs them to fight again. Eva goes for a hip toss again, but Jenny anticipates this and counters pushing Eva back and tripping her up. She falls on top of Eva and pins Eva's arms down with her own. She slowly moves her body upwards until her knees are pinning Eva's arms. This leaves her arms free and she reaches back and renews her attack on Eva's nipples. Eva is screaming in pain and Jenny maintains the attack on Eva's nipples for a while. She does not want to give Eva the opportunity to submit though, so she lets go and starts scratching Eva's body and boobs again. Eva kicks up with her legs, trying to dislodge Jenny, but she does not succeed. Jenny mixes her attacks between twisting Eva's nipples, scratching her and mauling her boobs. Eva is helpless and can do nothing but to absorb the pain. With about fifteen seconds left in the last round, Jenny moves her body forward slightly and plants her pussy on Eva's mouth and nose. She grabs Eva's hair and forces her face into her pussy. Eva is struggling to breath and starts to panic when she hears the bell rings. However, Jenny takes a good five seconds before she gets off of Eva's face. She helps Eva to her feet and gives her a hug before she stands back a bit to admire her handiwork. Eva's whole upper body is covered in deep scratch marks and she will have lots of pain over the next few days. Her boobs have dark bruises all over them from the mauling they took. She knows that her own body is showing signs of the battle as well, but she knows that her young opponent will remember her for a long time.

After a short interview with both girls, Beatrice thanks the television viewers for watching and promises them more excellent fights for the next episode. She then tells the studio audience that they will be entertained by two more matches before she opens the octagon for amateur matches. Jenny walks with Eva to the changing rooms. 'Good fight there youngster.'

'Thanks. You too. This was not really your first wrestling match, was it?'

'No, that was just for the show. I do this for a living at some clubs in town. I live off the price money I win and by wrestling rich women who are looking for a thrill. Nancy hired me for this fight and it was always going to be part of the show.'

When they enter the changing room, all the girls, except Jana, are still there. Margaret is the first to react. 'Fuck Eva, what happened to you? I though you were having an oil wrestling match. Where are your bottoms?'

Eva almost forgot they were both stark naked. She covers her pussy with her hands. 'Hi guys, this is Jenny. She is a professional oil wrestler and she taught me a lesson in how to inflict pain during an 'innocent' oil wrestling match. Where is Jana?'

The girls exchange greetings with Jenny before Margaret answers her last question. 'She went home. I tried to convince her that everything you did after their fight was just part of the show, but she felt humiliated and wanted to be on her own.'

While they shower and dress, Jenny tells Eva more about the tournaments she fights in and Eva promises her that she will come and support her in future. Jenny also gives her the name of a cream she should use to ensure that the scratch marks do not get infected and to help with the pain. The other girls decide to watch the last two matches and the amateur fights and Eva excuses herself as she needs to go find Jana. As she leaves the studio, Margaret catches up with her. 'I'm coming with you.'

'Thanks, but I need to be alone with Jana.'

'I know, but you need some advice on our way to the academy.'

'Do I? Let me guess, when I find her we should punch some sense into each other?'

Once again Margaret seems to be immune to sarcasm. 'That may work, but I think there is a better approach tonight. You have done nothing wrong, but your actions really humiliated and hurt Jana. You need to tell her that it was just for the show, but more importantly, you have to show her that you love her, and only her.'

Eva is surprised that Margaret is actually capable of giving good advice. She hugs her friend in the back of the taxi and rests her head on Margaret's shoulder all the way to the academy. Margaret gently strokes her hair and Eva feels too bad to tell her that even that hurts her scalp, which is still burning like a hot coal.

Jana is not in their room and nobody has seen her around. She also does not answer her phone and Eva is very concerned. She also phones the biker bar, but Jana has not been there either. Margaret supports her and a crying Eva falls asleep late that night with her head pressed against Margaret's chest.

Chapter 22 – Family

Jana knows that Eva is acting the part as she walks past her to hug and kiss Lea. She is disappointed in herself for losing the match. She made Olga stop the match twice to safe Lea and was only saved once herself, but the rules of the match and the fact that Lea punched her in the pussy twice cost her the win. It was a good fight though and she respects Lea's fighting ability. The moment when Eva kisses Lea, it suddenly becomes too much for Jana and tears start to flow down her cheeks. She needs to hug Eva and be close to her, but Eva leaves the octagon with Olga and Beatrice grabs her for the post match interview. 'Jana you have lost this close fought match and with that the love of your live. I can see that you are very upset. Where do you go from here?'
'I am devastated and will do whatever it takes to get her back.'
The doctor comes over again and wants Jana to stay a while so that she can have a look at her eye and the cuts to her face, but Jana declines the offer and promises her that she will go to the clinic to have it looked at. She leaves the octagon and is disappointed not to find Eva in the change room. Margaret comes over and gives her a hug. 'Nancy called for her. You know that her actions after your fight was all just a show right?'
'I know, but I still felt humiliated. I would never do the same to her, no matter who told me to do it and no matter whether it was part of the show or not.'
'I know you wouldn't, but we are not all the same. She was not trying to hurt you. In her mind this is all just part of the show.'
'I know, but I just need to be on my own for now. I need to clear my head.'
Jana showers quickly and gets dressed. Lea comes over and puts a hand on her shoulder. 'I am sorry. The idea of Eva picking me after the match was stupid. Please have your injuries looked at.'
Jana hugs her before she leaves. 'Thanks, I will. We really know how to destroy each other's faces, don't we?'
They smile at each other and Jana leaves the studio and catches a taxi. She first asks the taxi driver to take her to the academy, but halfway there she changes her mind. She does not want to argue with Eva tonight. Deep down she knows that she overreacted and that she will probably be over it in the morning. She also realises that she is probably just feeling sorry for herself at the moment and that she will take it out on Eva, should they talk about it tonight. She considers going to a pub for a few drinks, but the state of her face will draw unwanted attention and she is not in the mood to explain what happened to her to complete strangers. She has been toying with the idea of seeing her mother again for a while now. She has a lot of anger built up toward her mother and she wants to confront her for what she has done to her as a child. She may as well take out her current frustrations on her mother. She gives the taxi driver her mother's address.

Emily Theron is just about to go to bed when there is a knock on her door. She considers ignoring it as it is just about half-past-ten in the evening and she is not expecting any

visitors. She hesitates for a moment, but when there is another knock she decides to answer the door. She is elated to see Jana, but shocked by the state of her daughter's face. Her right eye is swollen totally closed and dark purple in colour. She has a cut under her right eye and another above her left eye. Both her lips are cut and she can see bruises on Jana's arms and her chest. She grabs Jana by the arm and pulls her inside before she locks the door behind them. 'Who attacked you, are you ok?'
Jana can't help but to smile. 'I am fine. I had a fight earlier.'
'Why are you getting involved in fights, you can get seriously injured.'
'I am in an academy, remember? Fighting is a contact sport and we do get injured, but generally not seriously.'
'I don't understand why you want to do a dangerous sport like this?'
'Should you of all people ask that? I had to find a way to make money when I was homeless and fighting was one of my few choices.'
'I am sorry. I did not mean to judge you. I am just very concerned about your welfare and I don't want you to be hurt like this.'
'You were not concerned about my welfare when I got beaten up much worse than this as a sixteen year old, why are you now suddenly concerned?'
'You are right, I was a terrible mother and I wish I could reverse time, but I cannot. All I can hope for is to try and make up for the past.'
Emily motions to a couch. 'Please sit. Do you want anything to drink?'
Jana sits down. 'A beer please.'
'Sorry Jana, we do not have any alcohol in the house. A coffee or tea perhaps?'
Jana feels a bit embarrassed. Her mother has told her that she is no longer drinking and that she is in a support group for alcoholics. 'I am sorry, tea is fine thanks.'
Emily disappears and Jana can hear the water starting to boil in the kitchen. She is surprised when Emily comes back with another woman following closely behind her. Jana remembers her mother telling her that she has a roommate, but she did not expect her to introduce the woman to her this time of night. The woman is covered by a nightgown and has a medical kit in her hands. 'Jana, this is my roommate Andrea.' Andrea puts down the medical kit and offers her hand to Jana. 'Hi Jana. I have heard so many good things about you, it feels like I've known you for years.'
Jana accepts her hand. 'Hi Andrea. She looks at her mother. 'I was kind of hoping that we could have a private conversation.'
'We will, I just want Andrea to have a look at your wounds first. She used to be a matron in a large hospital.'
Andrea cleans Jana's cuts before she smears an ointment into them, while Emily goes back to the kitchen to make the tea. Jana twitches her face as the work on her cuts hurts a lot. However, she does not complain. She has been cut many times before and she knows that it is important to disinfect open wounds. When Andrea is done she sticks plasters over the two cuts around Jana's eyes. She instructs Jana to go to the clinic the next morning to get these wounds stitched up and for a doctor to properly examine her right eye. She excuses herself and makes her way to her room.

When Emily returns with the tea, they chat about Jana's fight earlier the night. Emily is still concerned about her daughter's choice of sport and although she tries not to push too hard, there is something that she needs to know. 'Please tell me that you will not compete in death matches when you turn twenty-one.'

Jana sees the concern in her mother's face and decides not to get testy with her. 'No, that has never been my plan, but I am a good fighter and I will probably use fighting to make a living until my late twenties or early thirties.'

Emily does not want to upset Jana, so she changes the topic. 'Tell me about your friends. Is there anybody special?'

'Yes, but I am mad at her at the moment. I know that I'm overreacting though and I will probably make up with her soon.'

'Don't let small issues get between the two of you. Don't waste you life fighting with those you love. Rather just enjoy the time with her. You are young, but time flies by quickly and you do not want to realise that you wasted your life on stupid things by the time you reach my age.'

'Why did you do it?' Jana just blurts this out without thinking.

'What?' This question out of left field really confuses Emily.

'Why did you challenge that woman? Why did you pay a professional fighter to kill her? Why did you ruin my childhood?' Jana can't hold back the tears.

Emily knew for a long time that this moment would come at some stage and she has thought about how she should handle it many times, but now that the question was asked, her mind blanks out. All her rehearsed explanations are suddenly gone, so she just starts talking. 'I was very ambitious and very self-centred. Megan joined the corporation six months after I did and we got along at first, but as we both started moving up the ladder we became very competitive with each other. When the branch manager post became available, I was sure that I would get it. I was better qualified for it than anybody else, including Megan. When she was promoted, I snapped. I knew she was involved with the vice-president, but I stupidly believed that the fact that they were sharing a bed would not influence the decision. I wanted to humiliate her. I wanted to show everyone at the office that she is a coward, so I challenged her to a death match in front of everyone at the office. I never thought that she would accept the challenge. I never seriously wanted to fight her. I just wanted to make a point. When she accepted the challenge in front of everybody, I could not back down. I never called the show though. I was hoping that everybody would eventually forget about the challenge. When the show phoned me a few days later to confirm the challenge, I assumed she phoned them and I had to go along with it. I was only told later that the call was made by one of our co-workers. With Megan killed and me drinking everyday, she was soon promoted to branch manager. Anyway when the day of our fight arrived, I could not go through with it. I phoned them and the owner of the show personally tried to convince me to fight. When she realised that I was not going to fight, she suggested that she would get a replacement for me so that I could get out of the fight without losing face. The owner promised me that they had a woman without any fighting skills who has been begging them for a fight. I was convinced that Megan would win the match and that everything would blow over soon. At the time, this seemed to be the perfect

plan. Now, I cannot believe that I was naive enough to go along with the plan. Perhaps fear blinded me, perhaps I knew all along that they would kill her, but ignored it to safe my own life and my own honour and self-respect. I just don't know anymore. Well, I took something to upset my stomach and went to the doctor to get a note. I mailed this together with an explanation that I am too ill to fight, but that a friend of mine agreed to take my place. I wanted to come clean after I realised that they pitted a professional fighter against her, but I was cornered. They had my mail and all evidence pointed in my direction, so instead of coming clean I started to drink heavily. My life was destroyed and I was in a very dark place. Instead of being a mother to you and helping you through that difficult time, I spent my time drinking and feeling sorry for myself. When you left, I did not even realise it for a few days. I was a terrible mother and I can only hope that you will forgive me one day.'
Jana does not know how to respond to all this information. She needs time to process it. 'I am very tired, may I sleep here tonight.'
'Yes, of course dear, will you be ok on the couch?'
Jana lies awake for hours, thinking about her relationships with Eva and with her mother.

Eva wakes up at five in the morning with pain all over her upper body. She needs that cream Jenny told her about to disinfect the scratch marks that criss-crosses her chest, boobs and tummy. Hoping that Jana returned during the night, she walks to Jana's room, but Jana is still not home. She phones her again and to Eva's surprise, Jana answers. Eva wants to have a go at her, but she just does not have the energy for a fight. 'Are you ok?'
'Yes, I just needed to be on my own for a while, but I missed you a lot last night.'
'Why did you not come home then?'
'I had a lot to think about and I needed to be away from you. Sorry, that came out wrong.'
'Its ok, I understand. I love you, but I sometimes have to be away from you as well.'
'Thanks, I was not sure that you would understand. How are your body feeling this morning?'
'Very painful, I got scratched up in my second fight. Will you bring me a cream when you come home? I will message you the name.'
'I Will do. I did not know you had another fight?'
'Yeah an oil wrestling match against a so-called fan.'
Jana hears her mother in the kitchen and decides to hang up. 'Have to go now, will see you later.'
She is not sure that she wants to involve Eva in this at the moment. She is not even sure where her relationship with her mother is going, but she knows that she wants to visit her again. Her mother brings her tea and they chat for a while. Jana asks whether she may take some of the ointment home and her mother gives her a full tub. When she leaves about thirty minutes later, she gives her mother a hug and suddenly she finds it difficult to leave.

Eva is sitting topless on the couch when Jana arrives just after six in the morning. She is shocked by the extent of the scratch marks on Eva's body and realises that Eva was not in an oil wrestling match against a fan, but probably in a cat scratch match against a professional. She has seen these matches during her days fighting in underground clubs.

Girls would file their nails to a point where they were as sharp as knives, in order to do as much damage as possible to their opponents. Tournaments were brutal as women whose bodies were scratched raw in earlier matches had to face each other for more scratching to their bodies. The winner of a tournament really deserved the price money. She gives Eva a kiss, but decides not to hug her, fearing that she may hurt her. She takes out the ointment and gently applies it to all the scratch marks. Eva feels instant relief as the ointment dulls the burning pain. She leans forward and kisses Jana on her swollen right eye and Jana flinches as even the gentle kiss hurts a lot. Eva gives her a sad smile. 'We both need to get to the clinic, don't we?'

'It only opens at eight on a Saturday. You are stuck with me for a bit longer.'

'You want to fight?'

'What! You must be joking?'

'Sex fight, I want to sexfight you. I planned it for last night, but as you were not available then, now will have to do.'

Jana is intrigued. 'What do you have in mind?'

'I bought some toys yesterday before we went to the fights. They are in my room.' Eva takes Jana by the hand and leads her to her room. While she gets their new toys out of the cupboard, Jana takes off her clothes and is completely naked by the time Eva reveals them to her. Eva takes out a vibrating double dildo and holds it up for Jana to see. 'This will be our main weapon. The woman at the shop told me that she and her partner get each other off within five minutes with this. We will fight until one of us submits. Not only will we thrust this into each other, we will also control each other's vibration settings, and Ö' She takes two magic wands out of the bag. 'We will use these on each other's clits at the same time. Do you accept the challenge?'

Jana is so turned on by how sexually aggressive Eva is that she almost jumps Eva's bones there and then, but she keeps her composure and with a husky voice answers in a very formal matter. 'I accept your challenge.' What does the winner get?'

'I thought about that. The loser has to go down on the winner whenever she tells her to for the rest of the weekend and she gets to control the remote for these.' She takes a pair of vibrating panties out of the bag. 'There are four more pairs in there and the loser has to wear vibrating panties for the rest of the weekend and she is at the winner's mercy, anytime, any place.'

Eva takes her g-string off. 'Shall we warm each other up for two minutes before we start? Hands only.'

Jana is so wet that she definitely does not need any 'warm up' and when she touches Eva's pussy she feels that Eva is in the same condition. They ignore this and start rubbing each other anyway. Eva has to fight her urges to ensure that she does not cum before the main event starts. She feels Jana's pussy contract around her fingers as well and she works her even harder. The two minute limit is soon forgotten and they carry on till both shudders with orgasms. After a few moments to regain composure, they insert the double dildo and start to thrust there hips rhythmically. Both start to play with the other's vibration setting on the remote controls, trying to find the setting and speed which cause the most pleasure to one another . Jana is the first one to pick up a magic wand. She pushes it against Eva's clit and the vibrations have an immediate effect. Eva starts to buck her hips and cries out as a huge orgasm takes over her whole body. Jana does not let up and Eva's body jerks in orgasm after orgasm. She begs Jana to stop, but she is relentless and after a few more orgasms Eva's clit is so sensitive that she has to submit. She hates losing, but this felt like a win. Eva lies back and is rocked by a few aftershock orgasms. Jana watches her with a satisfied smile for a few moments before she takes the other magic wand and uses it to attack her own clit. She soon squirms in absolute ecstasy, but she carries on and Eva is sure that she does this just to prove her superiority in sexual contests. When she is eventually done molesting herself, she lies down next to Eva and lets out a satisfied sigh. Eva sometimes hates the competitive nature of her lover, but she has to respect her sexual prowess.

Jana makes Eva go down on her twice while they shower together. Eva starts to regret the forfeit they agreed on already and she is sure Jana will make use of her benefit often this weekend. Eva puts on a pair of vibrating panties and Jana immediately revs her up. Jana has an evil grin on her face and Eva knows that she is in for a long and very interesting weekend. She makes Jana promise that she will not switch the vibration on while they are checked out at the clinic, but her friend has a short memory. The doctor is checking out Jana's eye and cuts first and Eva is sitting behind the doctor's back. She takes in quick breath as the vibrations start to tickle her clit. Luckily the doctor does not suspect anything and she continues to examine Jana. Unlike earlier when Jana was just revving her up, the vibrations continue until Eva has to grab hold of her chair to keep her composure. When the doctor is finished with Jana, she switches the vibrations off. The doctor calls Eva over, but she is unable to stand up for a few seconds as her legs feel like jelly. The doctor calls Eva over again and she slowly gets up and shuffles over to the examination bed. After a proper examination the doctor books both of them off for a week to recover from their injuries. She instructs them to keep on using the ointment Jana brought from her mother's. As they walk out Eva starts to wonder where Jana got the ointment. 'Where did you get that stuff, it was not what I asked you to buy.'
'The shops were still closed, so I could not get the stuff you wanted. I got the ointment from a friend who used to work in a hospital.'
'Is she beautiful?' Eva surprises herself with this question and immediately hopes that she can take it back. She is relieved when Jana gives her a sweet smile before she revs her up again. As neither of them has the energy to prepare something to eat, they decide to go to a nearby street cafÈ for breakfast. It's a beautiful day and they walk the short distance to the cafÈ talking about their matches and Eva is relieved that Jana does not harbour any bad feelings against Lea. She wants to face her again to set the record straight though. This does not concern Eva nearly as much as when she learned that they would fight each other on 'Grudge Fights'. She knows that their rivalry is built on respect for each other's fighting skills and not on any bad feelings towards each other. She wants to fight Lea again as well, but it seems that she will have to compete with Jana for the opportunity to do so. Jana activates the vibration a few times during breakfast and Eva is so horny after a while, that she rips Jana's clothes off as soon as they get back to their townhouse. The rest of the weekend is full of fun and games. Janet and Margaret are soon invited by Jana to come and

watch the show. They almost fight each other for an opportunity to try out the remote. They yell out with pleasure each time Eva reacts to her clit being vibrated. When they learn about the unused vibrating panties in Eva's room, all four girls are soon wearing a pair and controlling a remote control of one of the other girls. These are passed around until all four girls are soon panting with pleasure.

Chapter 23 – Special Training

Over the next few months, Olga starts to spend more time with Eva than with any of the other girls. Some of the girls notice this and she becomes the object of some catty remarks, but she ignores these. The fact that the academy will become involved in death matches is not known to any girl but Eva and she was sworn to secrecy. The 'Pit of Death' will pit women against each other in unarmed fights to the death. It is therefore important that Eva learns different techniques she can use to kill her opponents. More importantly, she needs to learn how to avoid situations where her opponent is able to use some of these techniques, such as choking and neck breaks, on her. They practice both offensive and defensive techniques over and over again until they become second nature to Eva.

Olga starts teaching these techniques to Jana as well. Jana is a quick study and most of the moves come naturally to her, but she soon grows suspicious and confronts Olga about the training. 'Why are you teaching me how to kill? I have no wish to compete in death matches, why would I need to learn these techniques.'
'These are life skills I teach to many women. You never know when you may need to defend yourself, when you are in a situation where it is your life or the life of your attacker.'
Jana gives her a quizzical look, but does not argue any further. She attends special classes often, but not nearly as often of Eva. Eva is very concerned when Jana tells her about the special training Olga is giving her. She knows that the training is meant for her as she will compete in three death matches one day. Jana told her that she will never compete in death matches, but why is she receiving training in death match techniques then. She asks Olga about this and Olga assures her that there is no plan for Jana to compete in death matches. She explains that she decided to train a few other girls to ensure that there would be no suspicions should anybody find out about the training Eva receives. This makes sense to Eva and she stops worrying about it.

After about a year of training, Olga introduces Eva to a psychologist. Olga explains to Eva that killing another person is not natural and most humans are unable to do this, even when their own lives depend on it. The psychologist starts working with Eva on a weekly basis, starting with her motivation for wanting to compete in death matches and slowly building to the actual feelings involved when her life is in danger and when she has to kill another person. After a few months of therapy, Olga takes Eva to the 'Duel' show. She bought them ringside seats as she wants Eva to look in the eyes of the fighters, to see the fear when they realise that they may die and the utter devastation when they realise that they lost the fight and death is only a few moments away. She wanted Eva to deal with these feelings now, and not when she is in a life or death struggle with another woman. The psychologist suggested this to Olga as she was not sure that Eva really grasped the fact that she will have to end somebody's life, or the fact that she may die during these matches.

There are two matches scheduled for the show, but Olga tells Eva that they will have at least two more women lined up in case the main matches do not last long enough. She tells Eva that there are women who are prepared to fight to the death for price money. Eva finds it difficult to believe that woman will be willing to kill each other for money. At least her motives are pure, she will carry out the sentence that Emily Theron was supposed to get for murdering her mother. She will ensure that justice is served.

The host welcomes the studio audience and the television viewers and informs all that the first fight is between two neighbours. The one is thirty-five and a successful businesswoman and the other one is twenty-two and a dancer in a club. The older woman has been complaining for months about loud parties, trash being thrown into her garden and somebody keying her vehicle after she called the police to come break up a fight during one of the wild parties. When she went over to confront her neighbour, she was jumped by three women and badly beaten up. After she was released from hospital a few days later, she found her cat gutted and hanging from her porch. She challenged the younger woman in front of her friends and she accepted, telling the older woman that she would gut her like she gutted her cat.

The challenger is introduced first and a slightly overweight thirty-five year old woman, wearing panties only, enters the cage. Olga looks at Eva. 'Look at her face. What do you think?'
'She looks very focussed to me.'
'Yes.'
The younger woman is introduced and she enters the cage completely naked. She is used to stripping naked for her job and she loves to show off every inch of her beautiful toned body.
'And her?'
'She looks a bit nervous.'
'You are right, she probably only realised a short while ago that she may die. At the moment she is probably preoccupied with her own safety and not focussed on killing her opponent. In most fights, she will end up dying, but fights are unpredictable. If she has successes early in the fight, her focus may change. Similarly, the older woman may lose focus if she is hurt early on. She may start to fear for her own life and forget to attack. When you see fear in your opponent's eyes, make sure that you take advantage. Keep the pressure on her and force her to face the fact that she will die soon. Do not play around with her, kill her with the first opportunity you get. You do not want her to realise that she has a chance to survive if she attacks you with all she has.'

The younger woman is about ten pounds lighter than her older opponent, but her muscles are well defined and she looks the stronger of the two. She also looks fitter and this may count in her favour if the fight carries on for a while. As with all fights on 'Duel', the first ten minutes are fought without any weapons. After that weapons selected by each fighter will be dropped in the cage. Each fighter will receive her own weapon as well as the weapon chosen by her opponent. The host announces that both women chose knives as their preferred weapons. When the fight starts the older woman rushes in and tackles her opponent to the cage floor. She pins the younger woman down and starts punching her in the face. The weight advantage makes it difficult for the younger woman to escape her opponent's hold. She covers up as best she can, but many punches find their way through her defences and blood soon starts to flow from her nose. The sight of her own blood seems to spur her on and she grabs hold of the older woman's hair and starts to shake her head from side to side while letting out a gut wrenching scream. This seems to intimidate the older fighter and she stops punching, being frozen for a few moments. This is enough for the younger woman to dislodge her and they both scramble back to their feet. They both felt the power of the other and they both realise that they are in a serious fight and that only one will survive this. A few minutes go by with very little action. Both woman circle each other, both throwing the occasional jab. They are both afraid to make a mistake and the fight quickly turns into a boring dance of survival. The studio audience quickly start to jeer. They are here to see woman kill each other and they are getting impatient with two women not willing to attack each other. The jeering has the desired effect and the older woman grabs her opponent by the hair, pulls her head down and lands a knee to her face, busting the younger woman's nose. She looks confused and bewildered and she tries to get away from her attacker, but the older woman's grip on her hair is solid and she throws another less effective knee. Most of the force is absorbed by the younger woman's arms covering her face. The older woman is frustrated by this and she throws her younger opponent to the cage floor. The younger woman scrambles to her feet and tries to run away from her opponent, but the cage stops her from fleeing. Her eyes are full of fear and she is screaming for help, but nobody is allowed to help her. The rules are clear, once the cage door is locked, it will only be opened, when one woman is dead, or when a woman is unconscious and her opponent decides to spare her life. The woman in control has to indicate clearly that she does not wish to kill her opponent before a doctor is allowed inside. The only other situation where a doctor is allowed inside the cage is when a woman indicates that she believes her opponent is dead. However, should the doctor find that she is not dead, she will leave the cage to give the winning fighter the opportunity to finish the job. The younger woman's screams seem to delight the studio audience. They shout their encouragement to the older woman to catch her and to kill her. The older woman eventually manages to catch the opponent, but she is out of breath from running after her. She wrestles the younger woman down and controls her, but she is too tired to throw any punches or to manoeuvre her opponent into a position where she is able to choke her, so she lies on top of her opponent, pinning her arms to the floor. The younger woman is whimpering, pleading with her to let her go, but this falls on death ears. When the knives are dropped into the cage, the older woman lets her opponent go and rushes back to the nearest corner to pick up the two knives dropped there. The younger woman is panic-stricken and she does not even try to get hold of the two remaining knives in the opposite corner. Instead, she runs to the cage door and pleads with those outside to open it. Eva is shocked by this and cannot stand it when the woman looks straight at her while pleading for her life. The younger woman's eyes grow wide as her opponent sinks a knife into her back. She drops to her knees and grabs hold of the side of the cage, her fingers protruding through the mesh. The older woman withdraws the knife and plunges it into her opponents back a few more times before she leaves it there. With the other knife she slits the younger woman's throat. Blood streams down her chest and she tumbles over, her body convulsing a few times before she lies silent on the cage floor. The victorious fighter drops the knife and leaves the cage as soon it is unlocked, her face emotionless.

Eva is in a state of shock. She tries to make it to the bathrooms, but starts throwing up halfway there. An older woman gives her a sympathetic smile. 'Your first time dear? It gets easier to stomach after a while and once you do, only the excitement of two women fighting for their lives remains.'
Eva gives her a dirty look, but says nothing. Instead, she hurls again. Olga catches up with her and helps her to the bathrooms. After Eva has regained a level of composure, Olga pulls her in close and holds Eva against her chest. 'I know that was traumatic to witness, but if you wish to compete in these matches, you have to be willing to kill your opponent, even if she is hysterical with fear, even if she pleads with you not to kill her. This is enough for tonight. I have called your psychologist. She will meet us at her office.

After many sessions, Eva asks Olga whether they can attend another episode of 'Duel'. She is determined to kill Emily Theron in a death match and she has to face her fears. She remembers the words of the old woman and hopes that she will get used to witnessing woman die during these fights. She never does and it always affects her deeply, but she manages to watch both fights in the next episode, without throwing up and without having to get away from the slaughter happening a few feet away from her. Olga is very pleased with her progress in this regard and her development as a fighter. She is not too concerned with Jana's feelings about death matches. It is well known that Jana has a large collection of these fights and that she enjoys watching them. Jana's training is also going well and Olga reports back to Nancy that their fight will have the potential to be an epic encounter, as long as Nancy is able to convince both to fight each other to the death. Nancy is sure that her plan will work, but she has also made a few backup plans, just in case. She is also very satisfied with how close Jana and her mother has become. Andrea keeps her informed and the mother-daughter bond is growing stronger and stronger.

Chapter 24 – Choked Out

Eva has competed in many 'Grudge Fights' episodes, but has never been pitted against Lea in any of her fights. She is delighted when Olga informs her that she will fight Lea during the next episode in a choke out challenge. It will be a bare fisted affair with limited rules and the only way to win the fight will be to choke the opponent until she loses consciousness. Olga explains that this will give Eva practical experience in how to win a death match. It concerns Eva a little that she will fight Lea in a simulated death match, but she needs the experience as there is only six months left before she is old enough to compete in death matches. She is also excited to renew her rivalry with Lea. They are still very close friends and both have been looking for an opportunity to fight each other.

The academy has become a lonely place for Eva. First, Janet and Margaret moved out after they decided to go into business together. They have moved to the other side of town and Eva seldom sees them, but they do call each other regularly. A week ago, Jana broke the news that she was moving out as well. She was moving in with her mother and will make a living fighting in different television shows and fighting clubs. Eva was devastated. Somehow she believed that they would always be together, but although Jana clearly loves her as well, she has made it clear from the start that she does not want to be tied down. They remained friends with benefits only. Eva finds it difficult to cope without her and she throws all her energy into training. She hangs out with Reka and Amelia occasionally, but although Reka is always exited to see her, Amelia merely tolerates her presence. Eva calls Jana every night and every night she cries herself to sleep. She misses Jana and she feels sorry for herself because Jana does not seem to need her nearly as much as she thought. She is too proud to tell Jana how the separation really affects her though.

The decision to leave was one of the most difficult decisions Jana had to make in her life. She hopes that Eva and she will move in together in future, but her mother needs her more at the moment. She has been going through tough times at her job and is really finding it hard to stay on the wagon. Andrea called Jana one night and told her that her mother has tried to overdose on sleeping pills, but that she managed to stop her from doing it. She told Jana not to bring this up as her mother made Andrea promise not to tell her. She also told Jana that she has dealt with many cases like this and that her mother may further harm herself if she convinces herself that she lost Jana's respect for her. Jana believed this and was unaware that this all was part of Nancy's scheme to drive a wedge between herself and Eva. Jana considered to tell Eva everything regarding her childhood and her mother, but decided to do this one day when her mother has control over her own life again and when she will be able to share a place with Eva.

Nancy has a lot of control over Emily Theron's life. Unbeknownst to Emily, Nancy controls her job and her closest friend and confidante. The problems Emily experienced at work were all carefully orchestrated by Nancy. These were slowly resolved after Jana moved in with her mother and she even received a small raise soon after Jana moved in with her. Andrea has also included small amounts of alcohol in Emily's meals and drinks, just enough to give her a craving for alcohol. This also stopped when Jana moved in and Andrea redoubled her commitment to make sure Emily attends meetings and stay away from situations where alcohol is available. Jana can see the difference in her mother and she is glad that her presence helps her mother and Emily is soon convinced that she could not cope without her daughter being close to her.

The week that Eva spent alone in the townhouse seems like a year to her and she asks Jana to join her at the biker bar, but Jana has plans with her mother and is unable to make it. Eva is very disappointed and considers cancelling her plans, but she really needs a night out. Lea is also not available as her academy has exhibition matches as a fund raiser for an orphanage. She would love to spend some time with Reka, but Amelia will want to tag along and she is not in the mood for her. She remembers Jenny, the girl she oil wrestled on the first episode of 'Grudge Fights'. She promised her that she would go see some of her matches, but with the death match training taking up a lot of her time, she never got around to that. She phones Jenny and is surprised that the older woman still remembers her. Jenny says that she has a fight at eight, but that they could go for a drink afterwards, if she is still able to go out after the fight. Eva is glad when Jenny asks her whether she wants to watch her fight at one of the underground fighting clubs and she accepts the invitation immediately.

Eva arrives at the address she was given by Jenny, which is only a few blocks away from the biker bar. The building is dilapidated and only a small sign with the words 'Spartan Pub & Grill' identifies the establishment inside. She opens the door and enters the dimly lit pub. The pub is empty except for a woman who is busy behind the bar. Eva walks over to her to find out whether she is at the right place. It is half-past-six and Jenny said she is fighting at eight. Eva came through earlier to grab something to eat before Jenny's fight starts. She also wanted to make sure that she finds a nice table close to the fights and that she doesn't miss any earlier fights. She expected the pub to be busy by now. The woman looks up at her as she gets close to the bar area.
'You're a bit early honey, we are not open yet. Are you wrestling tonight?'
'No, I am here to support a friend who is wrestling later though. What time do you open?'
'At seven only, who is your friend?'
'Jenny.'
The woman gives her a big smile. 'Welcome, Jenny should be here soon. You are welcome to sit down at one of the tables so long. Can I get you something to drink?'
'Thanks, a beer please. Do you have a menu? I would love to order something to eat as well.'
The woman shakes her head. 'The grill portion has been closed for a very long time. People come here to watch fights and to drink. Nobody eats here anymore. If you are hungry, I can share my sandwich with you.'

Eva declines the offer, but the woman insists and she slowly eats her sandwich and sips on her beer at a table right next to the fighting area, which is no more than a tatty old wrestling mat.

Just before seven the first three wrestlers arrive. They are chatting with each other and all three waves at the bar lady on their way to the change rooms. The pub falls silent again for a few minutes. Then, just after seven customers start to stream in and all tables are soon occupied. Two women in their early twenties ask Eva whether they may share her table as there is very little space still available. Eva is happy to have some company and begs them to join her. They introduce themselves as Marian and Dana and tell Eva that they are both students and that one of their lecturers mentioned this place to them when she overheard them discussing who of them would beat the other in a wrestling match. They have been here a few times and tonight is the night when they will find out who the better wrestler is. The pub allows audience members to wrestler after the arranged matches are finished and many women make use of the opportunity to experience a wrestling match in front of a live audience. They ask Eva whether she has wrestled before and they are in awe when she tells them about some of the fights she participated in. She is busy telling them about her fight against Jenny when somebody hugs her from behind and kisses her neck. She turns around to see a broad smile on Jenny's face. She is thirty now, but as gorgeous as she was when they fought almost two years ago. 'Don't believe a word she is telling you, I totally kicked her butt. I am sure she still has scars all over her body.'

Eva laughs and lifts up her shirt to proof that her body is scar free. 'Yes, she kicked my butt, but only because I didn't know that we could scratch, bite and maul any part of each other's bodies. She even stuck her thumbs in my eyes.'

Marian's mouth is literally hanging open. 'Wow, I would love to see you guys wrestle each other again. Any chance of a rematch tonight?'

'Sorry, I have to kick another bitch's butt tonight, but I would love to fight Eva again.'

Marian and Dana both look at Eva with expectation in their eyes. 'I would love to fight her as well, but I have a big fight on 'Grudge Fights' next Friday, so I cannot fight before then, but maybe after that. Who knows, if you guys give us a good show tonight, Jenny and I may return the favour in a few weeks time.'

'I know. Dana and I are in charge of a fund raiser for our three hockey sides. We can arrange wrestling matches between our teammates and the two of you can be the main attraction. Please say you will.'

Jenny laughs. 'How can anybody say no to that face? I am in if Eva agrees.'

'Yeah, why not.' Eva does not care so much about the fundraiser, but she really wants to wrestle Jenny again and the fundraiser seems to be the perfect opportunity for a rematch.

The two students are beaming with excitement. This will be the best fundraiser ever. Jenny excuses herself as her match will be the first of the evening and Eva is left to entertain the two women with more stories of her fights and they hang on to her lips, soaking up every little detail she shares with them. They insist on buying her drinks and, as students they are students, most of these are shooters.

Eva already has a nice buzz going by the time Jenny and her opponent are introduced. Her opponent is in her late twenties and carries a bit more weight than Jenny. They are both nude to allow full access to each other's bodies for this cat scratch match. Marian and Dana finds the fact that Jenny and her opponent will face each other without any clothes very exciting and starts discussing what they will wear during their fight. Both came here wearing thong bikinis under their clothes, but now they are contemplating whether they should fight topless or even nude. Eva can tell that both want to fight nude, but that neither of them wants to be the one who makes that decision first, so she pushes them a bit by telling them that fighting nude is the purest form of female combat. She read in an old history book that Spartan women competed in wrestling, boxing and pankration in the nude and they saw themselves as superior to other women. So she adapts history a little bit to fit in with her objectives. It works and a blushing Marian tells Dana that she wants to fight nude. Dana quickly agrees. Jenny and her opponent locks up and immediately starts to scratch and maul each other. Their fight are scheduled to continue without rounds until one submits and both women try to do as much damage as they can as fast as they can. They are soon both full of bruises, scratch marks and bite marks. Eva is convinced that Jenny took it easy on her in their match. She seems to be a lot fiercer now and her opponent is soon trying to get distance between them, but Jenny is relentless. It sometimes seems that she has more than two hands. Her opponent would cover her breasts and Jenny would maul her clit and scratch her face. As soon as her opponent tries to defend these areas, she would leave deep scratch or bite marks on her breasts. After just six minutes her opponents taps out in tears. Jenny is also covered in scratch marks and bruises and it is clear that she received a lot of punishment as well. She comes over to where Eva sits and asks her to help her put cream on the scratch marks. Eva makes Marian and Dana promise that they will not fight each other before she is back as she really wants to watch their match.

Jenny's opponent is sitting in the corner of the change room, with her legs curled up to her chest. She is sobbing as the pain is too much for her to take. Jenny walks over to her. 'Sorry about hurting you this badly, but it is you or me out there. Come, we have to shower to clean the wounds. I have a cream that will take the pain away quickly, but we have to shower first.' She takes the woman by her arm and pulls her up and leads her to the showers. She turns on the taps for two showers and starts washing the other woman with soap, causing the woman to cry out in pain. 'I know it hurts, but we have to clean the wounds properly, be strong.' After washing herself she helps the woman to dry off before she gently applies cream to all her wounds. The instant relief calms the woman down and she leaves the change rooms after dressing herself. Eva and Jenny are the only women left in the change rooms and Jenny gives her a naughty look. 'Come, your turn to apply some cream on me. My nipples and clit took a lot of abuse, so make sure you rub them good.' She winks at Eva with a huge smile.
Eva gives her an embarrassed smile. 'Stop it, I have a girlfriend.'
'Why are you here on your own then, why did you ask me for drinks tonight if you have a girlfriend?'
'Well we are more friends with benefits than girlfriends and she needs to look after her

mother tonight. I don't want to cheat on her though, I love her.'
'I'm not talking about a relationship between us. We are both sexy women and we are both attracted to each other. I want to pleasure you and I want you to pleasure me, no strings attached. We have been playing with each other's pussies and tits before. This time we will just be a bit gentler.' She winks at Eva again. 'Think about it, the night is still young.'
Eva applies the cream to Jenny's wounds and she can't help but notice how sexy this woman is. Her body wants her to accept the offer, but she tries to fight her urges. She has not had sex for two weeks now and she misses the feeling of another woman's body against hers. She finishes applying the cream and looks Jenny straight in the eyes and has to force herself not to tell Jenny that she wants to make love to her too.
'We should go watch Marian and Dana fight each other.'
Eva can see the frustration in Jenny's face and she feels guilty for leading her on, that was never her intention. She just wanted to spend time with somebody tonight. Jenny dresses herself and they join Marian and Dana again to find shots are lined up on the table. 'The two of you are behind, Dana and I have finished a few shots already, you have to catch up.' The two students each wait with a shot in their hands until Eva and Jenny has downed the other four shots waiting for each of them. The four women down the last shot together. Alcohol flows as they watch the remaining organised wrestling matches and by the time the mat is opened for audience participation, Marian and Dana jump up, strip off all their clothes and rush to the mat. They eagerly oil each other's bodies down and jump on each other as soon as the referee tells them to fight. They are clumsy from the liquor intake and it is also clear that they have no fighting experience, but they throw all at each other and try to apply the techniques they saw during the previous matches. Their nails are too short to do real damage, but this does not stop them from scratching each other. They soon have marks all over their upper bodies. They squeal every time a breast or clit gets mauled, but they both stay at it. After two minutes the referee stops them for the end of the first round. They are both exhausted and their chests are heaving up and down. Eva finds this sight very sexy and she places her hand on Jenny's thigh. She knows that she shouldn't, but her mind is no longer able to control her body. She is extremely horny and she wants to make love to Jenny as soon as possible. They both start stroking each other's inner thighs as they watch the last two rounds. The occasional brush of a hand against a clit makes them both breath in deeply. Marian and Dana are pretty worked-up themselves when they return to the table. As they all want to get out of the club in order to go enjoy each other's bodies, they agree to meet each other the next morning at ten for breakfast in order to discuss arrangements for the fundraising fight.

Eva and Jenny continues their foreplay in the back of the taxi and by the time they reach Jenny's flat, they are both ready to explode. They rip off their clothes and start kissing and fondling in her lounge area. Fingers soon explore each other's pussies and Eva sighs deeply as two of Jenny's fingers enter her. She tries to return the favour, but her brain is too occupied with the pleasure she feels to control her fingers. Eva explodes with a huge orgasm and she sinks to her knees. She wraps her arms around Jenny's waist and start kissing her pussy gently. When she recovers enough, she starts working Jenny's slit and clit with her tongue. Jenny grabs hold of Eva's hair and pulls her face deeper into her pussy. She pants as her orgasm approaches and her whole body shudders as the orgasm causes ripple after ripple of ecstasy. They move to Jenny's room and make love until they are both exhausted. After cuddling for a while, Jenny leaves Eva in her bed and goes to sleep on the couch. Eva wakes up early in the morning and lies awake, wrestling with her guilt until she hears Jenny move around in the lounge area. She gets up and joins her. 'This was a once off. I feel very guilty for cheating on my girlfriend. I cannot do it again.'

'Morning. I don't know why you feel guilty. You said you are friends with benefits only. We had sex and that is all. I don't want to take you away from her. Anyway, how do you know that she is not also having sex with other girls?'

Eva has not even considered this, but Jana is the one who wanted to stay friends with benefits only. She is the one who moved away. Perhaps the relationship is over. Perhaps there never was a real relationship. 'I don't know, but I do not want to cheat on her again.'

'And I will not force you to, but I really enjoyed sleeping with you, so you are welcome to my bed anytime. Either way, I would love to spend time with you. I enjoy your company and I hope we can be friends.'

'I would like that as well.'

They meet Marian and Dana at a cafÈ near the university at ten the next morning. The two students look rough. Hangovers from the heavy drinking and the damage they inflicted on each other's bodies during their fight have caught up with them. The women order breakfast and the two students order beers to drink. This seems to revive them and they are soon their chatty selves again. They discuss various options for the fights between the hockey teammates and Jenny suggests that they have a tournament with normal oil wrestling rules. Scratching, biting and mauling may be too much for most of the girls. Dana feels certain that they will be able to get sixteen girls of similar weight to participate in an elimination tournament. To finish the night off, Eva and Jenny will fight each other in a five minute exhibition cat scratch match. Everybody is happy with these plans and Jenny offers to give the fighters some basic wrestling training. Eva immediately offers to help her with the training. She also pledges some price money for the winner of the tournament. This should ensure that the matches are competitive. Dana raises the question on how to deal with matches where neither girl scored a pin after the three rounds. Eva suggests a fourth round to control only. The moment a girl manages to get the other down and in any control hold, she will win the match. After the meeting Eva goes back to the academy excited about this new venture, but still feeling guilty for cheating on Jana. She does not know whether or not to come clean.

On the day of Eva's 'Grudge Fights' match against Lea, she arranges to go to the studio early. She is excited to find Lea already there when she arrives. They go to the small coffee shop at the studio to catch up. They laugh and joke and it is difficult to believe that they will be trying to destroy each other in a couple of hours. When the time comes for them to prepare for their fight, Eva takes Lea's hand. Lea's first reaction is to pull her hand away, as they have never been tender with each other before. She sees the confusion in Eva's face.

'Sorry, I am not a touchy-feely person. I did not mean to pull away.' She gives her hand back to Eva and they awkwardly hold hands for a moment. Eva lets go of Lea's hand. 'I did not want to get soft with you. I just wanted to make sure I have your attention. I need your advice, but only after our fight. Please don't go before we had a chance to talk.'

Lea tries to break the tension with a joke. 'I can give you advice before the fight as well. Don't get in the ring with this killing machine.' They both smile. 'I will wait for you to become conscious again after I choked you out, before I go. Is everything ok?'

'Yes, I am fine. I just need some advice. Good luck for the fight.'

'Good luck to you too.'

They hug each other and go to their separate change rooms.

Eva is used to the interviews before the fight by now and she answers the questions in a way that reinforces the made up grudge between her and Lea. Lea does the same and they are both soon in the octagon. They will not be oiled down for this fight as Olga wants this to be as close as possible to a death match. Many women in the audience are disappointed as they would have loved to oil these young, athletic thong clad bodies down. Lea has never seen such focus in Eva's eyes before and she knows that she is in for a tough fight. The bell goes and they both move forward in a controlled manner. They both use jabs to keep the other at bay while they are looking for an opening. Eva also lands some kicks to Lea's legs. Olga instructed Eva to finish this fight as quickly as possible and she takes a chance by following a jab up with a couple of hooks. Lea sees the opening and lands a straight right to Eva's face. This rocks Eva and she takes a step back. Lea jumps forward letting her fists go and Eva eats four more punches before she goes down. Lea still punches as hard as ever and Eva needs a few seconds to clear her head, but Lea is on top of her before she has a chance to get away. She gets greedy though and immediately goes for the double handed choke. Eva grabs her arms and pulls her towards herself and as Lea's momentum moves forward, Eva twists her body and dislodges Lea. They wrestle on their knees for control until Eva lands an elbow to Lea's face, opening a cut under her left eye. She grabs Lea around the neck and forces her onto her back and starts to punch her in the face from a side control position. Lea's right arm is trapped under Eva's body and she tries to stop the punches with her left arm. Eva lands at least ten punches to Lea's face before Lea manages to grab her arm. By then Lea's face is a mess. The cut under her eye is wide open and bleeding freely. Her nose and top lip are also bleeding. She holds on to Eva's right arm and they are in stalemate for a few seconds before Eva slowly moves her body forward until she pins Lea's left hand to the ground. Lea knows what is coming and turns her face away to ensure that Eva does not break her nose. The headbutt opens a cut on Lea's cheekbone under her other eye. Lea is open for another headbutt, but Eva uses the few moments of confusion to roll her onto her side. She rolls her own body behind Lea's and wraps her left arm around Lea's throat. She locks her left arm in position with her right arm and pulls back. Lea grabs her arms, but soon realises that she has no way out. She taps and Eva almost releases her hold, but she remembers the rules just in time and maintains the choke until Lea's body goes limp. The doctor rushes in to attend to Lea and Eva stays close to her until the doctor revives her. Lea is still groggy and the doctor has to help her to sit on a stool. After the

doctor managed to stop the bleeding, Eva helps Lea back to the couches where they are interviewed. After the interview, Lea is able to make her own way to her change rooms, but Eva joins her to make sure she is fine. Her own clothes are in a different change room, but she decides to shower with Lea so that they can talk. Lea shakes her head. 'Fuck, you were clinical in there. I have never seen you this focussed.'
'Thanks, I have been training hard for this.'
'To fuck me up?'
'No. Will you promise me that what I am about to tell you, will stay between us? You cannot tell anybody, not even if you think you can save me by telling another person.'
'What's going on? You know you can trust me. If you tell me something in confidence, I will never tell another person.'
'In about six months I will fight in my first death match of three.'
Lea is silent for a long time. She does not know how to process this news. 'Why?'
'I made a promise to my mother that I will revenge her murder.' I will be given the opportunity to do that, but only if I compete in two other death matches for Nancy.'
'Don't do it. It is not worth it. I do not want to lose you.'
'I have to and I do not plan to die. I have to win my first two matches to get my chance at revenge and I will definitely kill her when I get that chance. I made that promise to my mother.'
'Please don't.' Lea cannot hold it in any longer and starts to sob. 'Why would you tell me something like this?'
'I am sorry. I have been living a lie for the past two and a half years and I needed to share this with somebody I trust and I was hoping that you would understand why I have to do this.'
'You said you wanted my advice, but you do not want to listen to anything I say.'
'I was not talking about this before our fight. I was not planning to share this with you, but our fight was so close to the real thing and for a moment I thought that I killed you. I just had to share this with you.'
'Does it get worse, what else do you have to tell me that can even compare to this?'
'I cheated on Jana and I do not know whether I should confess to her or not.'
'What? How is that even important in the bigger scheme of things?'
'It is to me. I love her and I don't want to hurt her, but I also do not want to keep secrets from her.'
'Have you told her about the death matches?'
'No, she will not understand it at all. I also cannot deal with her trying to convince me not to do it.'
'But you can deal with me?'
'You are unfair now. You know it's not the same.'
'Sorry, I am just very mad at you now. I wish I could take you back to the octagon to knock some sense into you.'
Eva has to smile at this.
'Why are you smiling? I am dead serious.'
'That is just something that Margaret would say. Her advice for everything is to go knock

some sense into each other.'

Lea does not see the humour in this. 'Don't tell her. Not before your death matches are done anyway. If she decides to leave you, you will be a mess and you will surely get killed. We will discuss this again after your death matches.'

'Thanks, I appreciate your advice. Your friendship is very important to me.'

'Do not cheat on her again. I want to help you prepare for these fights.'

'You did tonight. I will love to have you in my corner, but I cannot afford for Nancy to find out that I told you. When the first fight is announced, I will tell Olga that I need your help.'

They hug each other for a long time before they make their way to their separate academies, both with a lot to think about.

Chapter 25 – Lovers from the Past

Both Eva and Jana are very busy the next couple of weeks and they only manage to see each other about a month after Jana left the academy. Jana comes over to the academy before they go out for the night and the two make passionate love for about an hour. As they lie in each other's arms afterwards, Eva feels as if her life is complete and she does not want Jana to leave again. She plays with Jana's hair and gives her a soft kiss on the forehead. 'I miss you so much. Do you have to leave again?'
'I miss you too, but I have to be with my mother at the moment. She is doing a lot better, but she is still fragile and I am still very concerned about her.'
'When will I meet her?'
Jana is silent for a long time. 'Not yet, I want my relationship with her to be solid first and I want her to be herself again before I introduce you to her.'
'Is she better now?'
'She is still struggling with her craving for alcohol. We are working hard to keep her on the wagon. When I am not practising or fighting, I am pretty much making sure her mind is occupied to ensure that she does not think about drinking. Luckily Andrea helps a lot with this. Without her my mother would still be a mess.'
'Do you still love me?'
Jana looks at her for a long time and Eva feels that she is looking into her soul. She is suddenly afraid that Jana is seeing her deceit. 'You know I love you Babes. We will be together again in a few months time. You will graduate soon and we will get a place of our own then.'
Eva wants to tell Jana that she has a further commitment to the academy, but she just cannot get herself to do it. Instead she changes the topic. 'You will love the pub we're going to tonight. The fights are fierce and there are normally quite a few amateur fights afterwards. I love these. The women generally do not have a lot of skills, but they make up for this by really tearing into each other.'
Jana smiles, she likes to watch a fight as much as the next woman, but Eva is totally into it. Watching fights totally turns her on and Jana knows that she is in for a wild lovemaking session later tonight.

Jana is not surprised that she knows this pub. As a youngster she fought in many underground fight clubs and this is one of them. She does not share this with Eva as she does not want to spoil the night for her. Eva is clearly excited to share this experience with her and she does not want to take that away from her. Eva leads Jana to her regular table, which she asked the owner, Elsa, to reserve for her. Since her first visit here, she has been back every Friday to watch the matches and Elsa has become fond of Eva. She is always here early and she always sits at the same table. She is close friends with Jenny, who tells Elsa that Eva is a very good fighter herself, yet she has never accepted a challenge here, although she has been challenged at least twice that Elsa is aware of. Before they sit down,

Eva decides to introduce Jana to Elsa. Elsa smiles at Jana and gives her a wink. She knows exactly who Jana is, but she does not give the game away. It is obvious that Jana has not shared this part of her past with Eva and who is she to interfere. How can anyone forget a little hellcat like Jana? She had many tough matches here way back when she still had a few girls who were willing to fist fight each other for cash. She heard that Jana has graduated from the Combat Sport Academy and that she is in the fighting circuit again. Perhaps she should start fist fights in here again. Jana will draw in many spectators, so she just needs to convince Jana to come fight for her again. Jana is glad that Elsa did not tell Eva that she knows her. She has never really shared her past with Eva. She has told her that she used to fight in underground clubs, but never shared her experiences in detail with Eva. To be fair, she has not shared these with anybody, not even her mother. Well especially not her mother. She will probably never share this detail with her mother as she is already carrying enough guilt on her shoulders.

Eva and Jana sit down after Elsa hands them each a beer and Eva starts reminiscing about some of the previous fights she witnessed here. She recalls small details of some of these fights, the look in a woman's face when her clit got mauled or the scream of pain of another as her breasts were viciously scratched. Her excitement is contagious and Jana can't help but to get excited about the fights to come. She remembers why she loves Eva so much and decides that she has to share her past with her. She will stay over tonight and they can have a nice breakfast tomorrow morning. That will be the perfect time to tell her about how her mother ruined her life when she was a kid and her subsequent life as a sixteen year old fighter in underground fighting clubs, including this one.

While Eva is telling Jana about one of the amateur fights, a beautiful woman comes over to the table and kisses Eva on the lips. Eva blushes and avoids eye contact with Jana. She introduces the woman as her friend Jenny. Jenny looks Jana up and down before she smiles and sticks out her hand. 'Please to meet you. I understand you are the girlfriend slash friend with benefits.'
Jana accepts her hand. 'And you?'
Eva jumps in as the situation is getting a bit tense. 'Jenny is the woman who fought me in the oil wrestling match on the opening episode of 'Grudge Fights'. She fights here often and we have become good friends.'
Jenny gives her a sarcastic smile. 'There you have it, good friend. Will I see you later Eva, I need to go warm up for my fight.'
'Yes, come join us after your fight.' Eva knows that this is a bad idea, but she does not know how to otherwise deal with this situation. The conversation between Eva and Jana flows a lot less after Jenny leaves them. Jana stops herself from asking the obvious question as she does not want to ruin their night together, but she can't help but wonder whether Eva is sleeping with this woman.

Half an hour later a totally nude Jenny makes her way to the fighting mat. Everybody, except Eva and Jana applauds and shouts their support for this sexy woman. Eva does not want to upset Jana further and Jana is even more jealous than before as she stares at Jenny's perfect body. She is now certain that Eva is sleeping with her. She is about to confront Eva, when her heart skips a beat. Jenny's opponent is her ex-lover Lexi Moore. They broke up about two weeks before Eva joined the academy and even after she started sleeping with Eva, Jana was still hoping that she and Lexi would get back together again. With time she realised that this will never happen and she slowly got over Lexi. She does not want to deal with this complication now and she hopes that Lexi will not see her, however, the naked Lexi takes her place on the mat right next to their table. As an audience member starts oiling up Lexi's body, she looks over and recognises Jana. She grins at her and comes over, giving Jana a deep kiss on the lips. 'Hello lover, who is this little slut with you? I will fight her for you as soon as I am done fucking up the old cow over there.'

Eva does not know how to react to this. She wants to be furious, but she is so surprised that she is unable to manage to say anything. Jana has a guilty grin on her face. 'Eva this is my ex-girlfriend Lexi. Lexi this is myÖ'

Eva cuts her off. 'Friend with benefits. I am a friend with benefits only. Eva's voice reveals the hurt she feels inside and Jana gives her a concerned look. She has not realised that labelling their relationship as such was hurting Eva. Lexi is enjoying the situation. 'Good for you honey. Just remember, no woman will ever be able to pleasure Jana the way I did. You are just a disappointing substitute until I decide to fuck her again.'

With that Lexi turns around and takes her place on the mat again. Eva jumps up to go rip her head off, but Jana catches her from behind and constraints her. Lexi has a huge grin on her face. Their relationship ended on a bad foot and fucking up Jana's night really gives her a lot of pleasure. Elsa comes over and tells Jana that she and Eva should go talk in her office. She does not want the situation to get out of hand, but her head is full of plans for potential match ups. Eva struggles against Jana, but as she starts to calm down she allows Jana to march her to Elsa's office. Jana tries to calm her down further. 'We had a bad break up. I caught her cheating on me a few times and decided to cheat on her with the same girl. While we were still in bed, I sent her a message from the girl's phone to come over. She was furious when she saw the two of us in bed and we had a big fight. We probably would have killed each other if the girl did not call her neighbours to come break us up. She is probably still bitter and trying to damage our relationship.'

'She is a demented bitch and the two of you were girlfriends, yet I am only good enough to be a friend with benefits. Were you hoping to get back together with her?'

Jana does not want to answer this as she does not want to lie to Eva. Eva starts crying harder as she sees the truth in Jana's eyes. 'You really wanted to get back together with her. You were just using me until you could get her back.'

'No, well yes when we first started sleeping together I was still in love with her, but that ended when I fell in love with you.'

'I don't believe you.'

This upsets Jana. She has been trying to explain to Eva that nothing is going on and she does not feel that she is in the wrong, but Eva is not only blaming her, she is also calling her a liar. 'While we are talking about lovers, are you sleeping with Jenny?

Eva is not prepared for this. 'No. Yes. Only once. I slept with her only once and that was a mistake.'

Before she can think, Jana punches Eva in the face, knocking her down. 'I thought you were better than that. I trusted you.' She turns around and leaves the club. Eva wipes the blood from her lip and the tears from her eyes. As Eva leaves the club in search of Jana, she sees their ex-lovers tearing into each other on the fighting mat.

Eva could not find Jana outside. She was not sure whether she wanted to fight her or talk to her, but she needed to sort the issues between them out. Jana has not answered any of her calls for a week now and Eva decides not to call again for a while. It is obvious that Jana needs a break from her and she can only hope that she would give her a chance to explain what happened and to prove her love to her. She does not want to lose Jana, but she also has to focus on her training for her upcoming death matches. Her life depends on this.

Nancy cannot believe her luck. She was looking for an opportunity to drive a wedge between Eva and Jana. She was thinking of using Lea for this, but was not yet sure how she would manage to do this. Now Andrea reported back that Jana is devastated with the fact that Eva cheated on her. She finds this ironic. She always thought that Jana would be the one to cheat on Eva, now a cheating Eva has done her work for her. She instructs Andrea to use every opportunity to drive the wedge in further.

At first Eva decides to withdraw from the fund raiser of the hockey sides. She blamed Jenny for breaking up her relationship with Jana. It took her some time to realise that the only person to blame is herself, so she phones Jenny back and tells her that she changed her mind and that she wants to help her train the fighters and that she wants to fight Jenny in the main match. They have drinks together and Eva apologises to Jenny for being a bitch. Jenny is quick to forgive her and on a Saturday morning, just over two months from her first scheduled death match and a week before the fund raiser, the two of them have a training session with the students. Eva truly enjoys the training session. They show the students the basics of wrestling. There is no time to turn them into proper wrestlers, but that is not the idea anyway. The fighters just need some moves to enable them to have competitive matches against each other. She also enjoys demonstrating some of the moves with the help of Jenny. They have both taken their tops off in the hot indoor arena and Eva finds their naked upper bodies pressed together a big turn-on. After the training session Jenny invites her for drinks at her place. Eva knows what this means and she feels a bit guilty for accepting, but she has given up on reconciling with Jana. The one time Jana answered her call she told her in no uncertain terms to fuck off and to stop bothering her. Eva and Jenny make love all afternoon, before Eva goes back to the academy. Jenny made it clear to her again that she only wants to make love to her and that she does not want a relationship. She also told Eva that she will make love to other girls as well. Eva is fine with this, she also does not want a relationship and she is not sure whether she ever wants to be in a serious relationship again.

The fund raiser is a huge success. The tournament between the sixteen students has drawn a huge crowed and they do not disappoint. Sixteen sexy bodies, some topless and some not ready to discard with their tops yet, struggle against each other in fifteen competitive, hard fought matches until a winner is crowned. She has a big smile on her face, proud of her achievement and happy with the ten-thousand credits she earned. It was decided that Eva and Jenny will fight each other in a five minute exhibition match. No scratching is allowed, but they are allowed to maul each other, to pull hair and to slap anywhere. The fight starts fast and Eva lands a hard slap to Jenny's face. This brings a nasty grin to Jenny's face before they lock up and tumble to the mat where they wrestle for position. Jenny buries her left hand in Eva's hair and pulls with all she has. Eva has to move with the pull, or lose a handful of hair. This allows Jenny to get on top of her and she starts raining slaps to Eva's pussy. Eva screams out and crosses her legs, forcing Jenny to move her attack to Eva's upper body, but not before she gives Eva's clit a nasty twist, causing her to scream out in pain. Before Eva has time to refocus, Jenny sinks her fingers into Eva's left breast and squeezes with all she has. Eva yelps out in pain and grabs Jenny's hand with both of hers. She manages to dislodge the hold on her breast, isolating Jenny's right hand. Jenny increases the pressure on Eva's hair again and Eva releases her grip on Jenny's right hand to try and dislodge the grip on her hair. She lives with the slaps to her breasts and face for a while until she realises that she is not able to get Jenny's hand out of her hair. Her training kicks in and she goes on the attack, slapping Jenny's breasts with her right hand while latching on to her clit with her left hand. Jenny tries to stop the slaps first, but then grabs Eva's left hand and pulls it away from her clit. Eva stops slapping and grabs Jenny's left nipple, twisting it while she is pulling on it. Jenny lets go of Eva's left hand to pull her right hand away from her nipples and Eva's left hand goes straight back to Jenny's clit. Jenny releases her hold on Eva's hair and grabs hold of her right hand. She realises that they are in a stalemate and that the crowd did not pay to see that, so she rolls off of Eva and they both get back on their feet. This time they both get a grip on each other's hair and start raining slaps on each other's breasts, legs and sides. By the time the referee stops the match both are glowing with red marks all over their bodies. Eva gently takes her left breast in her hand and tries to sooth it. Jenny sees an opportunity and kisses Eva's breasts and gives her a quick wink. They spend the night making love to each other again. Eva knows that this may be the last chance in a while to spend a night with Jenny. Her training camp for her first death match starts soon and she will be isolated for most of it.

Chapter 26 – Pit of Death

Jana is missing Eva a lot, but she is still very disappointed in her. After her disastrous relationship with Lexi, she was not keen to be in a relationship again. She really loved Lexi, but the girl broke her heart so many times. Eva just happened. She was a sexy little thing to enjoy in bed at the start, but as their friendship grew stronger, so did Jana's love for her. What they had was very special and Jana thought that they would be together forever. She thought that they were on the same page and that it was not necessary to re-label their relationship as being girlfriends. She had no idea that Eva had insecurities about this and if she knew, she would have asked Eva to be her girlfriend a long time ago. She could have handled her move to her mother's place better as well, but it was very difficult for her to move out and she could not allow Eva to convince her to change her mind as her mother really needed her. An emotional drawn-out discussion about this would have been too much for her to deal with. The first month with her mother was hectic. When she was not practising or fighting, Jana was going to the support group with her mother, having long discussion with her mother or with Andrea to ensure that her mother stays positive, or helping her mother with hobbies to distract her from her craving for alcohol. She probably could have made a plan to visit Eva earlier, and she now thinks she should have, but she was scared that if she went back to Eva too soon, she would not be able to go back to her mother again. Lexi's actions at the pub upset her a lot and she understands Eva's reaction to Lexi, but she was not ready to learn that Eva was no better than Lexi. The first chance Eva got, she cheated on her. She betrayed her and Jana does not think that she will ever be able to forgive Eva for this. Maybe they can be friends again someday, but it will never be the way it used to be. Margaret has been trying to convince Jana to forgive Eva for the mistake she's made and Lea even came to see her. She told Jana that she advised Eva not to tell Jana about her infidelity and she apologised to Jana for this. Jana appreciated this, but it was still Eva's decision to cheat on her and it was still Eva's decision not to come clean before she was confronted by Jana. Andrea pointed this out to her when she overheard Jana sharing her discussion with Lea with her mother. Andrea made a good point. Eva still made the final decision, even though she received advice from Lea.

Nancy inspects the purpose built studio for her new show 'Pit of Death'. The building work was supposed to be done two weeks ago and with only two weeks left before the airing of the first episode, everything better be perfect. She is very pleased with what she sees and she gives a sigh of relief. She had many sleepless nights about this development as she did not want to move the launch date of 'Pit of Death'. The fighting area is an oval pit sank two metres into the floor of the studio. Its floor area is seven metres in length at its longest point and four metres in width at its widest point. Its glass walls angle outwards at sixty degrees and a pavilion with a gradient of sixty degrees start on the edges of the two long curves and one of the short curves of the pit. It is eleven tiers high and each tier, except the bottom one, which is a foot rest only, has thirty seats on it. Cameras are installed inside the glass walls and more cameras are suspended from the ceiling and can be raised and lowered as required. The other short curve has a desk behind which the host sits and a couch for the medical staff to sit on and another for guests. The doctor has to confirm whether the loser of a fight is dead and will also treat the winner if required. The only entrances for the pavilion are on either side of this short curve. The dressing rooms for the fighters are on the first floor and the fighters will be lowered into and removed from the pit with lifts suspended from the ceiling. These lifts automatically open in the corridor outside the change rooms and in the pit. There are two sets of change rooms either side of a wall to make sure that opponents do not accidentally meet up before their matches. A further feature is a glass divider across the width of the pit, dividing the pit in two. This divider will be up until the fight starts, when it will be lowered into the floor.

The recruitment of fighters started three months ago and this process is ongoing. As women apply to compete, they are classified per weight class and skill level. Each applicant has to fight against one of the academy's girls for a few minutes to gage their skill levels. Tournaments per weight class will be held. Each tournament will be in the format of an eight women elimination competition. The eight most skilled women per weight class will qualify for a tournament, while the other will be afforded an opportunity to receive some training in order to qualify for future tournaments. Each tournament will be held over four weeks. Two quarter finals will be fought in week one and the other two in week two. The semi-finals will be in week three and the finals in week four. The winner will win a large amount of credits and the other seven will all be dead, unless a clear winner chooses to spare the loser's life. Nancy had to include this rule in order to comply with the conditions of the court decision which allowed women to compete in death matches. However, to ensure that this will not happen often, she also included a rule that only winners who killed their opponents will advance in the tournament. Further, if the winner of the final does not kill her opponent, she will not win any price money. To make provision for women who may be excluded from the tournament for not killing their opponents, or for winners who are too badly injured to continue in the tournament, four substitutes will be on standby for each tournament. Each episode, except for the finals episode will therefore have two death matches. During the finals week, a non-tournament death match will be included in the programme. Eva will fight her first death match during the fourth episode of the first tournament. Her second will be during the fourth episode of the second tournament and Nancy believes that her plans to ensure that her second opponent will be Jana, are well on track. Should Eva survive the fight against Jana, her last match will be against Emily Theron during the fourth episode of the third tournament. After this, Nancy hopes to include celebrity matches during the finals week of each tournament. She knows of enough celebrities with grudges and she already has people working to plant the seed with a few of them. However, if this does not pay off, she will replace it with a grudge match. 'Grudge Fights' will be cancelled as soon as 'Pit of Death' starts and each 'Pit of Death' episode will also feature a number of non-lethal matches in the same style as the fights currently on 'Grudge Fights'. These fights will be fought before the death matches, but will not be broadcasted live. The live television show will start with the two death matches and the producer will pick the best non-lethal matches to make up the rest of the two hour time slot every Friday night. Nancy is sure that she will be able to use these non-lethal matches to build up rivalries and to turn her fighters into minor celebrities. She is also sure that she will be able to convince some of these rivals to fight in the celebrity death matches.

Nancy is not only here to inspect the structures, she has also arranged for a test of the cameras and production studio today. She thought of getting some of the academy girls to wrestle or catfight each other for this purpose, but rather decided to do the test with the real thing, a death match. She asked Olga to pick two lightweight women who did not qualify for the first tournament. She told Olga to make sure that their skill levels are good enough to survive a while in a fight against Eva, but not good enough that they may be able to beat Eva or to injure her seriously. She called both these women in and explained to them that they did not qualify for the tournament, but that the winner in a death match between the two of them will fight in the celebrity fight during episode four of the first tournament and that the price money for this fight will be half of the amount the winner of the first tournament will win. She knew off course that she will probably not have to pay this amount as Eva should win this match and she will not be fighting for any price money. She will be fighting only to get her chance to kill Emily Theron. Both women jumped at this opportunity and they are currently in the change rooms warming up for their fight. Nancy allowed twenty women, mostly friends of the production staff to watch this match. They are spread around the pavilion and have to report back on any issues with not being able to see all the action. Nancy goes to the production room in order to review their performance and to check the video quality. The two naked women enter their lifts and the cameras zoom in on their tense faces. The lifts slowly make their way to the pit and the cameras follow them down, still focusing on the woman's faces. The producer switches over to the cameras mounted in the glass walls of the pit. Nancy is happy to see that the pictures are clear, despite the angle of the walls. The women get out of their lifts and the lifts return to the first floor. The divider is slowly lowered and the moment it disappears into the floor, the women attack each other. They are both quite good at defending themselves, but neither of them has a lot to offer in attack. Nancy is happy with Olga's choice for Eva's first opponent. The winner of this match should be able to defend herself for a while, but Nancy is not concerned that either of them will be able to hurt Eva. The fight carries on for almost twenty minutes before exhaustion causes one of the women to slip. The other jumps on her back and locks her arm around her neck. The woman being chocked kicks and swings her arms wildly for a while, before she goes limp. The other woman maintains her hold for a while and when she releases her opponent, her lifeless body drops to the floor. The doctor enters the pit with a rope ladder dropped over the side of the pit. She examines the woman and declares her dead. The lifts are brought down and the rest of the medical staff members also enter the pit to load the body into her lift. The winner enters her lift and both lifts return to the first floor. Nancy orders the producer to cut a two minute highlight package from the fight so that she can use it to promote her new show. She leaves the studio a very happy woman. Everything is in place for the first tournament and she can relax for the first time in months.

Jana is excited by the fact that a new death match programme is at last airing on television tonight. She enjoys watching 'Duel', but the new programme has a different format altogether and she likes the fact that no weapons are allowed. She has been looking forward to tonight and as her mother does not want to watch death matches and does not like it when Jana does, she arranged with Janet and Margaret to watch the first episode with them. Neither of them is really into death matches, but they are both happy to see their friend. They decide that this is close enough to a special occasion and promised Jana a proper show after the episode. When the taxi drops Jana off at their home, the three of them hug for a long time. They do not get time to see each other often and they have missed each other a lot. Janet has told Margaret beforehand not to bring up Eva, but she should have known that Margaret will follow her own stubborn mind. 'So have you made up with Eva yet?'

Janet kicks Margaret in the shin. 'What?'

Jana knows Margaret too well to get upset by this. 'No, please accept that we will never be a couple again. She cheated on me and I will never trust her again.'

Margaret shakes her head to make it clear to Jana that she does not approve, but she does not push it further than that. They drink wine and chat about their current lives, the good old days at the academy and the fact that none of them knew about Nancy's plans to produce death matches. Janet switches on the television when its time for the episode to start. The camera focuses on the host as she welcomes the viewers and explains the format of the tournament. When she gets to the part of a celebrity death match during episode four, the camera zooms out to reveal Eva and her first opponent sitting next to each other on a couch. She introduces them and announces that they are the opponents in the first celebrity death match. The three friends are all shocked into silence and Margaret has tears in her eyes. She is the first to speak. 'Why would she do that? Why didn't she tell us about this? It is our fault? We pushed her away afterÖ' She stops herself from completing the sentence.

'I don't know, do you think it is because I broke up with her?'

'Stop it both of you. Eva will not do something like this because you broke up with her. We will go see her tomorrow and talk her out of this.'

Janet switches off the television and Jana excuses herself. She just needs to be on her own to think about what just happened. She is still concerned that the way she broke up with Eva and the way she treated her when Eva phoned her, influenced Eva's decision. She tells the taxi driver to head to the Combat Sport Academy. She does not have her key anymore and she has to wait in front of the academy until some girls arrive back from a night out to be let in. The townhouse is also locked and she considers phoning Eva, but she does not want to do this over the phone, so she decides to wait outside the townhouse until Eva gets back from the show.

Eva has to stay at the studio until the interviews with her and her opponent is done. She leaves as soon as she is allowed to as she needs a good night's rest before she leaves with Olga for a training camp tomorrow. The training camp will continue until the day of her fight. She will call Janet, Margaret, Jenny and Reka tonight to tell them about the death match, or to explain to them if they watched the episode. She would have preferred to go see each of them, but with the timing of the announcement and her training camp, it is just not possible. She has already told her aunt and Helga and she spent time with both of them during the week. Lea will join her on the training camp as Olga has agreed to this. She was upset with Eva for telling Lea, but promised her that she wouldn't tell Nancy. Eva checks her phone for messages, but there are none. She is not sure whether she should also call Jana as they have not talked since Jana told her over the phone that she wanted nothing to do with her. Even after Jana made it clear to her that she wants nothing to do with her, Eva still considers Jana as her friend and she still loves her.

The taxi drops Eva off at the academy and she walks to her townhouse deep in thought and almost bumps into Jana. She did not expect to see her here. 'What are you doing here?'
'I saw the episode and wanted to talk to you in person. Are you doing this because of me?'
'Don't flatter yourself, you made it very clear that you do not want to be part of my life and I have moved on. Perhaps you should too.' Eva knows that she is unfair, but she is not ready for an emotional discussion now and she cannot afford to let Jana back into her mind so close to her first death match. She needs to be focussed until her three death matches are done. Hopefully, Jana will be willing to let her explain everything then.
'Don't do it, don't fuck up your life.'
'I cannot do this with you right now. Maybe we can talk after my fights.'
'Fights? Will you have more than one fight?'
"Yes, but I cannot discuss this with you right now. I cannot afford to get distracted by you before these fights. Please leave. If you want, we can talk after the fights.' Eva cannot hold back the tears any longer and she opens the door and closes it behind her. She feels bad for leaving Jana like that, but she just cannot get distracted now. Jana considers knocking on the door, but decides against it. She slowly walks away and spends the rest of the night drinking heavily at a nearby pub. Although she broke up with Eva, it just became very clear to her that there will never be a relationship between them again and she is not ready to deal with this yet. Eva cries herself to sleep and never phones the rest of her friends. Olga takes her phone away the next morning as she needs Eva to be totally focussed on her training until she fights in her first death match. Eva feels very lonely, but at least she will see Lea at the camp.

Chapter 27 – Killer

Eva finds the first two weeks of the training camp very tough. Olga concentrates mostly on her fitness and core strength and Eva spends long hours running and exercising in the gym. She also has long wrestling sessions against Lea, who joins Eva in the gym and running sessions, even though she is not required to. Eva also has regular sessions with her psychologist to prepare her mind for the death match. They are too tired at night to really enjoy each other's company, but their friendship grows even stronger than before during this period of suffering together. During the third week, the gym and cardio sessions are reduced and Olga starts to concentrate on technical issues. Lea is the victim of many choke holds applied by Eva. However, she gets to sit out when Eva practices neck breaks on a dummy. Lea is concerned by the ferocity of the neck brakes. If Eva's opponent possesses these skills, Eva could be killed in an instant during the fight. Lea does not share her concern with Eva, but Olga calls her for a chat after practice. 'Does the neck break training make you uneasy?'
'Yes, I am scared that Eva's opponent may kill her using a similar move. Eva would not even know what happened.'
'These techniques are lethal when used by a well trained fighter. Eva is a well trained fighter and she will be able to use them during the fight, but she is also trained on how to defend against moves like these and it will be very difficult for her opponent to apply these on her, even if her opponent is well trained and her first opponent is not.'
'What about her other two opponents, are they well trained?'
'We don't know yet, but I will make sure that she is physically ready to face any opponent. You are helping a lot with this. Please also make sure that you help to keep her head in the game. Any uncertainty or distraction may cost Eva her life.'
'I will do whatever it takes to make sure that she is focused on the fight.'
'Are the two of you sleeping with each other?'
'No, we have never been sexually attracted to each other.'
'If I ask you two to wrestle naked against each other, while covered in oil, may that lead to any sexual feelings.'
'No, I don't think so. Why do you want to do that though, I have never wrestled naked?'
'All the death matches are fought in the nude and the fighters in the celebrity fights will be covered in oil. I want to prepare Eva for this and I need you to help me with that.'
'I understand and as I said before, I am willing to do whatever it takes.'
'Thanks.'
Olga decides to give Eva a break on the Friday before her fight. She tells the two girls to go enjoy themselves, but not to drink or to get into any fights. She also makes Eva promise that she will not go visit any of her friends or family as she does not want her to get distracted now. Eva is disappointed with this and decides to rather relax at the training venue. She asks Olga whether Lea can take some messages on her behalf to a few of her friends. She explains that she was not able to talk to them before the training camp begun. Olga agrees to this, but tells Lea in private to withhold any messages from Eva's friends which may

distract her. Eva asks Lea to explain to Janet, Margaret, Jenny and Reka that this is something she has to do and that her reasons will be revealed soon, but that she cannot share it with them now. She also asks Lea to tell them that she loves all of them and that she is sorry she could not discuss this with them earlier and in person.
.
Lea visits Reka first and then Jenny. Both of them have many questions, but both accept that Lea cannot give them any further information. When she gets to Janet and Margaret's home, Margaret opens the door. She is surprised to see Lea and is immediately concerned that something happened to Eva. Lea sees the concern in her face and tries to calm her down immediately. 'Eva is fine. She could not contact you guys and asked me to bring you a message.'
'Why is she not here? Is she doing this against her will? Did you put her up to this?' Margaret has grabbed Lea's shirt with both hands and is pushing her up against the wall. Lea lifts her hands up next to her head to show that she is not here to fight. Hearing to commotion, Janet rushes over to find out why Margaret is attacking Lea. 'What's going on, what have you done?'
'I am just bringing you a message from Eva.'
'Margaret, calm down and let Lea go.'
'Not before she tells me who put Eva up to this.'
Janet sighs. 'Lea did you put Eva up to this.'
'No.'
'Margaret, let her go.'
Margaret slowly releases her grip on Lea, but she does not move away, staying a few inches in front of Lea, ready to pounce on her at the slightest provocation. Janet gently pulls her away. 'Sorry Lea, we all love Eva a lot and Margaret has taken the news of the death match very hard. Come inside so that we can talk.'
Lea follows Janet inside and sits down on a couch. Janet brings them each a beer and Lea relays Eva's message to them. When Margaret asks her why Eva talked to her and not to the rest of them, Lea tells her that Olga asked her to help with Eva's training. She does not want to upset Margaret further by telling her that Eva told her about her death match before the announcement on live television. When Lea is ready to leave, Margaret gives her a hug. 'Sorry about earlier. Please look after my friend.'
'I will.' Although Lea sounds confident in saying this, she knows that there is very little she can do to keep Eva safe. When Eva enters the pit, nobody will be able to help her. She will have to protect herself.

Lea knows that Eva will be very upset with her if she finds out, but she decides to go visit Jana anyway. Eva told her about Jana's visit the night before the training camp started and she knows that Eva regrets the way it went down, but she also knows that the wounds of the breakup is still very raw and that Eva is not ready to have a serious discussion with Jana yet. Jana is glad to see her and to receive news from Eva. They talk for a long time and Lea once again appeals to Jana to give Eva another chance when this death match is over. Jana does not give her an answer on this. Eva has hurt her a lot and she is not ready to contemplate a

relationship with her again. When Lea is ready to leave, Jana gives her a very serious look. 'Please be honest, does this fight have anything to do with our breakup?'
'No, this has been planned the day Eva joined the academy. She told me that she joined the academy in order to get training to improve her skills for a death match. She did not want to give me more information on the reasons though, but your breakup is not the reason for this fight.' They hug each other for a long time before Lea returns to the training camp.

The intensity of the training programme is reduced a lot during the last week before Eva's fight. She and Lea do a lot of light wrestling, oiled up and in the nude. Eva practices how to get into specific positions, over and over again. The first time the two friends wrestled each other naked last week, both were very uncomfortable. Each time one of their pussies would come into direct contact with the other's body, both would pull away. Olga sat them down and told them to get over it and that such little distractions could cause Eva to get into trouble during her match and that she may even lose the match and her live due to it. They both still found it awkward to feel a body part of the other rubbing against their pussies, but they bit the bullet and concentrated on the wrestling moves. Now, after about two weeks of wrestling naked against each other, Eva barely notices it, but Lea still feels very uncomfortable, but she does not show it. She decides that she will have to have a serious talk with Eva when this is all over. She wants to make sure Eva understands that these were special circumstances and that her pussy is off limits to women. She likes guys only and has never had sex with another woman. She understands why it will be lots of fun, but it is just not her thing.

The night of her first death match arrives sooner than Eva anticipated. The four weeks since the announcement was made flew by. She is told that her opponent received training from one of the academy's assistant coaches and that she should not underestimate her. What Olga does not tell her is that they only concentrated on her opponent's defence to try to ensure that the match lasts a bit longer. Eva is not aware that this woman is no match for her and only pitted against her to ensure that she has her first kill in order to build up her reputation and to give her some confidence for the planned fight against Jana. Like her mother, this woman will have no chance against a well trained professional fighter. Nancy and the assistant trainer have been building up the confidence of Eva's opponent and she believes that she is a much better fighter than she really is. She has been told that she has a death match record of one win and her opponent has never been in a death match. She truly believes that she has a very good chance to win this match and with it a large sum of money.

Lea oils down Eva's naked body and finishes the job with only a few minutes to go before her fight. This will be the first death match of the evening and will be followed by the final of the first lightweight tournament. Lea hugs Eva and tells her to make sure she wins the fight. She has to replace some of the oil on Eva's body as a lot rubbed off on her clothes. Olga repeats her instruction that Eva should be patient and not go for a kill too early as any mistake may cost her the match. She tells Eva to wear her opponent down and to wait for her to make a mistake. The green light goes on and Eva waits in the corridor until the lift door opens and she walks in without any hesitation. After all the training she received, she just wants to this fight to start now as this is the first obstacle in the way of getting her revenge.

Janet and Margaret were not sure whether they wanted to watch the fight. Neither of them wanted to see their friend die in a fight, but they knew that Jana would watch the fight and did not want her to do this on her own, so they asked her to come watch it with them. They watch with almost disbelief as their naked friend exits the lift and starts swinging her arms before she practices some combinations, while staring down her opponent on the other side of the glass divider. The woman is older than Eva, probably late twenties, and carries a bit more weight around her waste. She looks softer than Eva, who is in peak condition. The divider starts to lower and all three of them take a deep breath in anticipation.

Eva waits until the divider is completely down before she starts to move towards her opponent with short measured steps. Her opponent is frozen for a moment and only starts to move to her right when Eva is just out of range. Eva kicks out with her left leg and catches her opponent on her right thigh. This stuns the woman and she takes a step backwards. Eva's first instinct is to rush forward to take advantage, but she holds back, remembering Olga's instructions. The woman starts to circle Eva again and Eva manages to land some stiff jabs with her left hand. She realises that her opponent's defence is slow and that she is able to hit her almost at will. She lands a few more jabs before she unleashes a straight right, opening a cut on her opponent's upper lip. The woman takes a step back and immediately covers her face with her hands. Eva again resists the urge to rush her opponent and she moves forward slowly, trying to corner her opponent, but she quickly moves to her right and gets away from Eva, who continuous to stalk her. Eva uses her jab again and lands a number of stiff jabs to the woman's face. Her opponent realises that she is no match for Eva in a striking match and she suddenly rushes Eva, trying to grab Eva around the neck. Eva sees her coming and punishes her with a hard right to the face before their bodies collide. Eva grabs the woman around her upper body and the woman manages to grab Eva around the head, but before she has a proper grip, Eva lifts her and smashes her to the floor. Eva tries to mount her opponent, but her left leg is trapped between her opponent's legs and the woman pulls Eva's head into her chest, making it difficult for Eva to punish her.

The three friends are on the edges of their seats. Eva is in control and seems to be hitting her opponent at will, but she allows the woman to recover every time she has her in trouble. None of them say anything, but all three are concerned with Eva's seeming reluctance to go on the attack.

The oil makes it difficult for Eva to get a good grip on her opponent and after a while of trying to manoeuvre her body into a better position, she decides to try another tactic. Her left thigh is resting against her opponent's pussy and she thinks about slamming it into her pussy, but she is unable to pull it away far enough to do any damage. She works both her arms under the arms of her opponent, tugging her elbows against her opponent's sides of her upper body. When she is in position for her next move, she starts rubbing her thigh against her opponent's clit, waiting for her to make a movement. The woman twists her lower body to her right to try and avoid this distraction and Eva immediately rolls her body in the same direction, lifting her opponent's left shoulder with her right arm. She kicks back with her left leg and tries to slide her body over her opponent's body to get behind her, but her opponent realises what she is trying to do and rolls her body away from Eva. The oil causes Eva to lose her grip and both women get back to their feet. Eva now knows that her opponent is a good wrestler, but that she is vulnerable in a stand up fight. The woman knows it too and tries her best to get close to Eva again, but Eva keeps her at bay with stiff jabs and hard kicks to her thighs. The thigh kicks are quickly paying off and the woman starts to move with a limp as her left thigh is no longer able to take the strain.

Jana gets to her feet when Eva slams her opponent to the floor. She knows that Eva is very good at inflicting damage from a mount position and this fight may be over soon. The woman defends well though and after a few minutes of struggling for position, the fighters roll clear from each other. It is not clear whether Eva tried a move or whether she decided to stand them both up again. Eva starts punishing the woman with jabs and kicks again and Margaret shouts at Eva's image on the television to keep this up.

Eva concentrates her kicks to her opponents left thigh and punches her with a hard right to the face every time she drops her left arm to try to protect her thigh. The woman realises that she is fighting a losing battle and decides to go for broke. She rushes Eva as fast as her damaged left leg allows her to. Eva plants herself and lands a devastating right elbow to her opponents face, opening a deep cut under her left eye and knocking the woman to the floor. This time Eva does not hold back, she moves in and tries to grab the woman from behind to get a chokehold on her, but although the woman is stunned she manages to turn her body enough to make sure Eva does not get behind her. They both end up on their knees facing each other. The woman grabs Eva's hair as this is one of the few places with good grip on their bodies. She wants to pull Eva's head down in an attempt to move her own body behind Eva's to try and choke her to death. Eva sees an opportunity to end this fight though and she places her left hand on her opponent's forehead and her right on her opponent's chin. With a sudden movement, she pulls her opponents head to the right with her left hand while she pushes upwards and to the right with her right hand. Her opponent's neck snaps and she drops to the floor without realising that she breathed her last breath. The rope ladder is lowered over the side of the pit and the doctor confirms that the woman is dead. Eva has won her first death match and she has become a killer for the first time. She shows no emotions as she gets back in her lift, which returns her to her change room. She wants to put on some clothes, but Olga tells her that Nancy wants her to make the announcement in the nude as this would make a much better statement. She shakes her head, but does not resist against this instruction.

Janet. Margaret and Jana are hugging each other, all three of them in tears. Margaret gives Jana a kiss on her cheek. 'Admit it, you still love her.'

Jana pulls away from the hug. 'I honestly don't know, but I know that I don't hate her anymore.'

Janet is about to switch off the television when the host announces that there will be a quick interview with Eva after the commercial break. When the commercial break is over, Eva is sitting on the couch next to the host. The friends laugh at the fact that she is still naked and that she does not even seem to realise this. They are all watching the television attentively as the host starts to speak. 'Congratulations Eva, you have won your first death match and I understand that you want to challenge your next opponent on live television.'

Janet and Margaret cannot belief that Eva will fight in another death match. Jana was aware of this, but she never mentioned it to her friends. She assumed that Lea shared this with them. They are all caught up in their own thoughts when Eva gets up on her feet and looks directly into the camera. 'Ten years ago a woman challenged my mother to a death match in order to try and take over my mother's position at the firm where they both worked. She chickened out and arranged for a professional fighter to murder my mother'

At this point Jana realises what Eva is talking about. Her whole body goes cold and her legs go weak. She sits down on the couch. 'No, this cannot be. Please, this cannot be.'

'What?' Janet is very concerned.

'She is going to challenge my mother to a death match.'

As if this was synchronised, Jana hears the words she was hoping not to. 'I challenge this woman, Emily Theron, to a death match in this pit in eight weeks time. Emily, you were too much of a coward to face my mother, even after you challenged her, so you murdered my mother and ruined my life by hiring a professional fighter to do your dirty work. Don't be a coward again. Agree to face me and to pay your debt to society.'

The host touches her ear and listens for a moment. 'Our producers have been able to get hold of Emily Theron. Good evening Emily, I understand that you have watched while Eva Hajnal challenged you to a death match in 'Pit of Death'. Do you want to respond to her challenge?'

Jana hears her mother's voice, she sounds very tired. 'I accept. I have to face the consequences of my actions and I will face her, as I have wronged Eva and her mother.'

Janet switches off the television as the host starts repeating what just happened. Jana is devastated. Her former friend and lover has just challenged her mother to a death match and her mother has just accepted the challenge. Her mother has no chance against Eva and she will definitely be killed during the fight. She phones her mother's number, but her mother does not answer. She immediately orders a taxi and takes it to her mother's home. She has to convince her mother not to go through with this. Her mother is not home when she arrives, so she phones Andrea, but she also does not answer her phone. Jana feels helpless and decides to phone Eva. She is sure that she will be able to convince Eva not to fight and kill her mother, but Eva also does not answer her phone. When Jana's mother later arrives home with Andrea, she looks a lot older than when Jana saw her earlier today. She listens to what Jana has to say, but answers every argument Jana makes with the same response. 'I have to. I owe her that after what I have done to her.'

Chapter 28 – A Perfect Plan

Three months before the challenge on live television, Andrea convinced Emily to visit a psychologist. Emily did not want to go at first due to the costs involved. However she agreed to it after Andrea told her that the psychologist agreed to see her on a pro bono basis. She immediately liked the psychologist who is friendly, warm and attentive. She made Emily feel at ease and she was soon comfortable enough to share all her deepest fears and regrets. The psychologist suggested weekly sessions and assured Emily that she would see her free of charge. The psychologist allowed Emily to do most of the talking, subtly steering her in a direction of accepting responsibility for what happened between her and Eva's mother. She further manipulated Emily into believing that the only way she would ever be able to forgive herself and to truly be free from guilt is to make amends to the victims of her actions. Andrea reinforced this with every opportunity she got and the belief that she had to pay for her role in Megan Hajnal's death became ingrained in Emily's psyche. Both the psychologist and Andrea started planting the seed that Megan's daughter may want revenge and that the only way to make amends may be to face her in a fight. When they were satisfied that Emily made peace with the fact that she may be challenged to a fight and that the honourable thing would be to accept such challenge, Andrea asked her one night what she would do if the daughter wants to challenge her to a death match. She was not sure what to do should this happen and she asked the psychologist for advice during their next appointment. The psychologist did not give her an answer, but instead asked her questions designed to lead her to a conclusion that she will have to accept such challenge. The questions started with the way she felt after she decided not to face Megan. How everyone else reacted to this. What this did to Jana and how she felt knowing that she was a disappointment to her daughter and that Jana was embarrassed to have her as a mother. What Jana will think of herself if she does not accept a challenge from the daughter of the woman she had a roll in killing, the daughter whose life was ruined because of her actions. Whether she would be able to live with herself if her daughter loses respect for her again and probably leaves her forever this time. They knew that losing Jana was Emily's biggest fear and they played this card only when really required. Most women would probably see through this ploy, but Emily fully trusted the psychologist and was totally under her spell at this stage. She knew exactly what to do should Megan's daughter challenge her. It felt like a big weight was removed from her shoulders and she almost hoped that the challenge would come. This would give her an opportunity to demonstrate to Jana that she has honour and integrity. Her daughter would always respect her if she loses the fight and if she wins, the whole world, including herself and Jana would look at her through different eyes.

Nancy did not want Jana to be with Emily when she receives the news of the challenge as she feared that Jana may be able to convince her not to accept the challenge. She was sure that Emily would not change her mind after she accepted the challenge as Emily knows that this would not only destroy herself, but also Jana. When Andrea learned of Jana's plans to watch Eva's fight at her friend's place, she informed Nancy of this. At first they decided that Andrea and Emily should spend the night at home and that Andrea should switch over to 'Pit of Death' when she receives the message on her phone to do so. However, there would be a chance that Jana would come home early, so Nancy instructed Andrea to make sure that they go out to a restaurant near the studios. To assist with this plan, Andrea 'won' a dinner for two at the chosen restaurant for the evening of the fight.

Nancy did not want to take the chance that Emily may panic when she receives the challenge during a call broadcasted on live television, so she phoned her about half an hour before Eva's fight started and told Emily that she urgently needs to see her as she received information that concerns her. Emily told her that she could not as she was having dinner with a friend, but Andrea convinced her that she should meet with Nancy so that she would not be concerned about what Nancy wanted to discuss with her for the rest of the evening. She agreed to see Nancy and five minutes later Nancy and one of her assistants joined them at the restaurant. Nancy told her that one of her fighters was about to fight in her first death match and that she informed Nancy that Emily killed her mother years ago and that she wished to fight Emily in a death match, should she survive her fight. She told Emily that she doubted that Eva would survive the fight as she was not one of her better fighters, but that she always tried to honour her fighter's last wishes. Emily already knew who her challenger was and when Nancy handed her the fight contract signed by Eva Hajnal, she did not need any further convincing. She knew that she had to accept the challenge and she signed the contract without any further questions. Nancy asked them not to inform anybody of the challenge before it was made on live television. She asked whether her assistant could hold their phones until the challenge was made and accepted. Andrea immediately gave her phone to the assistant and Emily followed suit. Nancy went back to the studios in time to watch Eva's fight. While Eva was challenging Emily on live television, the producer phoned the assistant and when it was time, Emily confirmed that she accepted the challenge. Andrea switched off both their phones and explained to Emily that the media would be calling her and that it was not a good idea to talk to them at that stage. She took Emily to the psychologist's house and they had a long session during which the psychologist made sure that Emily was convinced that she made the right decision and that she would not start to doubt herself. When Emily and Andrea left late that night, the psychologist was convinced that nothing would change Emily's mind and she informed Nancy accordingly. Nancy also made sure that Eva's phone stayed switched off and in possession of Olga. Olga was instructed to take Eva and Lea straight back to training camp and to ensure that both remained offline until she instructs otherwise. She knew that Jana would try to convince Eva not to fight her mother and she was not sure how Eva would react to this. She needed more time to ensure that there is no trust left between Eva and Jana.

Getting Emily to agree to the death match was only the start of Nancy's ambitious plan. A death match between Eva and Emily will make headline news and people will talk about it for a while. However, a fight between the daughter of a woman who was killed because her challenger was too scared to fight her and therefore organised a professional fighter to take her place, and the daughter of such challenger, would be something people will talk about for years, especially where such daughters were best friends and lovers until a few months before the fight. Emily was used as bait to convince Jana to fight Eva, but should Eva beat Jana during their fight, a fight between Eva and Emily would be a very nice bonus. Nancy is sure that Jana will try to convince her mother to change her mind first, failing that, she will try and find Eva to convince her to withdraw her challenge. Andrea and the psychologist will help to ensure that Emily will not change her mind and she knows that Jana will not be able to find Eva. Her hope is that a desperate Jana will approach her to either tell her where Eva is, or to cancel the fight. If she does not come to see Nancy within a few days, Andrea will plant that seed with Jana. She needs to confirm this fight as soon as possible as she wants Jana to go on a training camp to ensure that both women are ready for an epic fight.

Eva is disappointed that she could not see her friends before being whisked back to training camp. She knows that there will be another death match before she will finally face Emily Theron to revenge her mother's murder. She therefore understands that it is important that she does not lose her focus, but she really misses her friends and she also wants to apologise to Jana for the way she treated her the night before she first came to the training camp and for cheating on her. She accepts that their relationship will never be the same again, but she has to at least try to clear the air with Jana. The psychologist visits her a few times during the first week after her match, to ensure that killing another woman does not affect Eva negatively. She is pleased to find that Eva views that as part of the process of ensuring that she will be able to fight against Emily. She is satisfied that the woman knew what she signed up for and that she had a fair fight against her. The psychologist knows that her next session with Eva will be more challenging. She will have to break the news to Eva that Jana challenged her and convince Eva to fight her former best friend and lover. She will also have to ensure that Eva regains her focus as soon as possible after this news.

Jana continues to try and convince her mother not to fight Eva, but she has little hope that her mother will change her mind. She needs to find Eva to convince her to withdraw her challenge. Jane and Margaret have been trying to get hold of Eva as well, but without success. The evening after the challenge, Jana visits the biker bar to find out whether anybody there knows Eva's whereabouts. She knows it's a long shot, but she is desperate to find Eva, but nobody at the bar has any idea where Eva is. Helga can see the concern on Jana's face and calls her aside. 'What is going on? You look like you haven't slept for days.'
'I need to find Eva to convince her not to fight my mother.'
'Is that your mother? Does Eva know that Emily is you mother?'
'I don't think so. We never talked about my mother as I wanted to keep that part of my life private.'
'Does Nancy know about your mother?'
'Yes, I told her before I joined the academy.'
It all makes sense to Helga now. She never understood why Nancy was so keen to sign Eva. 'Your best bet to find Eva is Nancy. She will know where Eva is training. Do you want me to go to her with you?'

'No, I will go see her on my own.'

'Just promise me that you will be careful with her. Do not trust anything she tells you.'

Jana thanks Helga and goes outside to phone Nancy, who tells her that she cannot give her Eva's location, but that she is willing to meet with Jana at the academy. Jana orders a taxi and while she is waiting, she decides that she does not want to go see Nancy on her own after all. She phones Janet and she agrees to meet Jana at the academy. When Jana arrives at the academy, Janet and Margaret are already there. When Janet told Margaret where she was going, she insisted on coming with. They go to Nancy's office and she asks them to sit. She is a bit annoyed that Jana brought her two friends along, but decides to carry on with her plan anyway. 'If I may ask, why are you looking for Eva?'

'I think you know that she challenged my mother to a death match.'

'Yes, off course I do, but last I heard you hated your mother and you broke off your relationship with Eva. Why does a fight between them concern you?'

'I have a good relationship with my mother now and Eva will definitely kill her if they fight. I need you to cancel this fight, or to tell me where Eva is so that I can convince her to withdraw her challenge.'

'I cannot cancel the fight as I have a contractual liability to host it. The only people who can cancel it are Eva and your mother and I doubt whether either of them will cancel it. If your mother would, you would not be here and the whole reason Eva joined the academy and insisted to be your roommate was so that she can revenge her mother's death.'

Janet picks up on what Nancy just said. 'What do you mean she insisted on being Jana's roommate?'

Nancy looks at Margaret for a while before she gives a deep sigh, pretending that she is contemplating whether or not to share the information with them. She looks at Jana and starts to tell the story to her. 'The day Eva arrived here she failed her interview with Helga. However, when Helga went back to the training grounds, she came into my office unannounced. I told her to leave, but she told me that she had information that would allow me to launch my television show. At that stage only a hand full of people knew about my plans and I was surprised that she was aware of it. She told me that she hired a private investigator to find you and when she reported back that you were training at the Combat Sport Academy, Eva asked her to gather more information on the academy. The investigator bugged my phone and overheard a discussion between me and my business partner. Eva told me who you were. I knew this already of course, but she also told me who she was and about her plan to revenge her mother's death. She told me that if I allowed her to join the academy and if I organised that she shares a townhouse with you, she would fight your mother on my show. I asked her why she wanted to share a townhouse with you and she told me that she needed you to convince your mother to fight her. She told me that you were the only reason why she chose this academy for her training. I know it was wrong of me to accept her offer, but I knew that you hated your mother and I also knew that a revenge match between her and your mother would be a perfect way to launch my show. I am sorry, but I am a businesswoman and I have to take money making opportunities when they come my way.'

'How did she want to use me to convince my mother to fight her?'

'She asked me to arrange a death match between you and her. Killing you would convince your mother to fight her. I agreed to this, but only if you showed interest in death matches and if you agreed to such a fight. I asked Olga to train you in death match techniques and to report back to me whether you showed any interest in fighting in these kinds of matches. When she reported that you were not interested, I told Eva that I will not be able to arrange a match between the two of you. She then decided to shame your mother on live television into accepting her challenge.'

Margaret gets to her feet, places her hands on Nancy's desk and in measured way tells Nancy. 'I don't belief you. Eva would not use Jana and would definitely not want to fight Jana in a death match. She loves Jana.'

'I'm afraid that she played you all. If you don't belief me, read for yourself.' Nancy opens her safe and produces the agreement Eva signed the day she joined. She knew then that an emotional Eva would not read through the agreement before signing it and she included stipulations backing what she just told the three friends. Margaret grabs the agreement and reads through it. After a while she sits down again and drops the agreement on Nancy's desk. She cannot belief that Eva was so devious. Jana picks up the agreement and starts to read it. Soon she is convinced that Eva was using her the whole time. It now makes sense why Eva avoided answering her when she asked her why Nancy went against Helga's decision not to accept her. It makes sense that she cheated on Jana soon after Jana moved to her mother's place and why she was so cold with her the last time they saw each other. Jana even starts to wonder whether Eva somehow manipulated her and Lea to fight each other in the octagon when she took them to the biker bar. She also remembers that Lea told her that Eva joined the academy for the purpose of preparing for a death match. This also fits in with what Nancy just told her. She struggles to think straight and her only consistent thought is that Eva used her and never had any real feelings for her. She hands Nancy the agreement. 'Where is Eva now?'

'I really don't know. Olga prefers to have her training camps in total isolation. All I know is that she is training for her next death match in four weeks time.'

'Does she have another fight before she fights my mother? Who is she fighting?'

'We are not sure yet. The opponent we have lined up will not be a match for Eva and we have not been able to find somebody who may really challenge her in a death match.'

'Let me fight her.'

Janet and Margaret shout 'No' together.

'I have to. If I don't stop her, she will kill my mother.'

Both her friends know that she is right, but both don't want Jana and Eva to fight to the death. However, both keep quiet as they now know that the Eva they thought they knew, was just a role she played in order to use Jana. Nancy waits a few moments before she speaks again. 'I will only allow this if you go on a training camp to prepare for this fight. Eva has been honing her skills and you will not be able to beat her without proper preparation. I know a death match trainer who owes me a few favours. Will you be willing to go to camp tomorrow morning?'

'Yes.'

'Ok, I will draw up the challenge contract tonight and give it to Olga tomorrow. I will make it a condition that she fights you before she is allowed to fight your mother. If she declines, I will have grounds to cancel the fight between her and your mother as the agreement she signed when she joined, stipulates that she will fight two death matches for me before the match against your mother.'

Janet insists on going to the camp with Jana, but Margaret does not want to be that close to this. She knows that she will not be able to handle this, no matter which one of the two loses the match. She hates Eva for using Jana in this way, but deep down she still loves her and she still has some doubts about what they just heard and read. Nancy agrees to Janet's request to join the training camp and advises Jana not to share the news of the fight with her mother. Jana agrees to this, as her mother would never allow her to fight Eva in order to save her from facing Eva. She tells her mother that she has to go away for a few fights, and that she may not be able to contact her mother regularly, but that her mother has nothing to be concerned about. After signing the challenge contract, Jana and Janet leaves for the training camp early the next morning.

Nancy is very pleased with herself. Her plan is almost in place, except for one more detail. She doubts very much that Eva will agree to fight Jana. She knows that Eva still loves Jana and that there are a lot to do in order to convince her to agree to the fight.

As she has been doing for many years, Eva's aunt attends a church service at nine on the Sunday morning. Afterwards she goes to her usual street cafÈ for brunch and then returns home for a lazy Sunday afternoon. As she approaches her home, a large van is parked in front of her driveway. Two women seems to be looking at its engine, so Eva's aunt parks behind them and walks over to see whether she can assist them. As she gets next to the van, two more women open the back door and jumps out. Before Eva's aunt realises what is happening, she is bundled into the back of the van and one of the women holds a cloth over her mouth and nose. She tries to fight them, but she soon loses consciousness. When she wakes up, she is in a dark room, bound to a chair and gagged. Soon the light in the room is switched on and a woman with a video camera walks in and starts to film her without saying anything.

On the first Sunday of training camp, Eva and Lea are having lunch together after their morning training session which consisted of a number of nude wrestling matches against each other. The nudity does not bother either of them anymore and their wrestling matches are intense and hard fought. They both enjoy the rivalry between them, even in practice matches and they both use every opportunity to get the better of the other. They are discussing one of their matches of the morning and Eva is sure that she won it, but Lea remembers the opposite. They continue having a light hearted go at each other when the psychologist walks in and joins them at the table. She tells Lea that she needs to speak with Eva in private. Lea gets up and gives Eva a concerned look as it is unusual for the psychologist to be here on a Sunday. The psychologist waits until they are alone. 'We received a challenge for your next fight this morning. It turns out that Emily Theron is Jana's mother.'

'What? That cannot be.'
'It is. Jana confirmed that to Nancy this morning and challenged you to a death match to stop you from taking your revenge on her mother.'
'I cannot fight Jana, I still love her.'
'She realised who you were the day you joined the academy and kept you close to her in order to manipulate you. She knew the day would come when you would challenge her mother and she bided her time, knowing all along that she would fight you in a death match to try to kill you before you could kill her mother. She even got Olga to train her in death match techniques, pretending that she merely wanted these skills for self defence,'
'I cannot fight her.'
'Will you be able to live with yourself if you fail to revenge your mother's murder? Emily Theron is using her daughter's pretend friendship with you to escape justice again.'
'I don't know, I do not want to fight Jana though.'
'Don't make rash decisions now. Take the rest of the day off to think about this. Be careful not to fall in the trap of letting emotions cloud your judgement. You know that Jana has manipulated you over the years and that her only intention was to make sure that you will not keep your promise to your mother. I will discuss this further with you tomorrow, go rest now and think about what I shared with you today.'

Eva looks for Lea, but Olga tells her that Lea had to go with the psychologist as it is important that Eva considers the facts without undue influence. She assures Eva that Lea will be back the next day. The psychologist convinces Lea that Jana was only using Eva and that her only aim was to stop Eva from taking revenge. She further convinces Lea that Eva will regret it for the rest of her life if she does not keep her promise to her mother and that this will probably kill her. She points out that Olga mentioned to her that Eva is the best fighter she has ever trained and that she does not foresee any difficulties for Eva to beat Jana. Lea has to agree that Eva's fighting form is much better than Jana's was when she last faced Jana. She is still shocked that Jana was only using Eva to stop her from fighting her mother, but Jana's challenge clearly shows that this was indeed the case.

Eva lies awake all night, trying to sort through the turmoil in her brain. Even if Jana recognised me, how would she know that I wanted to fight her mother in a death match? Perhaps Helga told Jana before she told her to collect me from the reception area. Is this why Jana did not want to introduce me to her mother? She always told me that she wanted to fix her relationship with her mother first, before she introduced her to me. Why would she challenge me to a death match, why not first let me know that Emily Theron is her mother? Why not come and talk to me about it?

Lea comes into Eva's room early the next morning and after she gives her a long hug and asks her whether she is ok, she tells her that Nancy and the psychologist want to see her. Eva hugs Lea again. 'I don't know what to do. I think Jana just used me, but I still love her. Why would she challenge me to a death match, I thought she loved me too?'
'I am as surprised as you are. I really though that she loved you. I understand that she does

not want you to kill her mother, but why would she challenge you to a death match without even talking to you about your challenge to her mother first?'

Eva wipes the tears from her eyes before she goes to see Nancy and the psychologist. They both look up when she enters the room and Nancy motions to a chair. 'Please sit Eva. Have you made a decision yet?
'I don't know yet. I am very confused by all of this.'
'So am I. I trusted Jana, but I guess she was playing all of us. I don't want to upset you any further, but I have something to show you.' She switches on the television and Eva sees her aunt bound to a chair and gagged. There is fear in her eyes. A script appears at the bottom of the screen reading: 'Accept the challenge or your aunt will die.' Eva is devastated. 'Who has my aunt? Who gave you this?'
'There was a knock on my door last night and I found this when I opened the door. The police are looking for her and a detective will come to talk to you a bit later today. I believe that Jana and her mother are behind this, but I do not have any proof. The police will interview them and they assured me that they will do whatever they can to find her before your fight with Jana. In the mean time, I think you should accept the challenge and prepare as best you can for a fight against Jana.'
Eva takes the contract, which Nancy put in front of her earlier and signs it. The psychologist spends the rest of the day with Eva, making sure that her fear and confusion are turned into hatred for Jana. She reinforces the story they sold to Eva that Jana has been using her and that she is the only one who will gain from kidnapping Eva's aunt. During the morning a woman who introduces herself as a police investigator visits Eva. She tells her that based on her experience, Jana and her mother are behind the kidnapping, but that they do not have any evidence against them at this stage. She assures Eva that she will do her utmost to find her aunt.

Any doubts that Jana had regarding whether Eva was using her the whole time are gone when Nancy informs her that Eva signed the challenge contract without any delay. Jana still had some hope that the challenge would convince Eva to withdraw her challenge against her mother, or at least that Eva would contact her to discuss the issue. She now has to focus on her training to ensure that she kills Eva before Eva kills her mother. Janet supports her friend mentally and with her training.

Eva is very concerned for her aunt, but forces these thoughts from her mind in order to concentrate on her training. The fight against Jana will be very tough and she needs to be at her best to beat her former friend and lover. Lea's body is bruised after every training session, but she does not complain at all. This is a small price to pay to ensure that her friend will be ready to face Jana in a death match.

Chapter 29 – To Kill a Friend

With only a few hours left before her fight against Jana, Eva receives feedback from the woman who she believes is a police investigator working on her aunt's kidnapping case. She tells Eva that she found an informant who saw her aunt alive earlier in the day. According to the witness, two women brought her out of a building and forced her into the back of a van. Police combed the building, but could not find any evidence. They believe that the kidnappers are moving her to a location from where it will be easier for them to release her after the fight. Eva asks her whether she thinks her aunt will be killed anyway if she kills Jana in the fight. She tells Eva that the video would have instructed her to lose the fight, if that is what the kidnappers wanted and that she should do her best to kill Jana so that her aunt can be reunited with her after the fight. After the woman leaves, Lea begs Eva not to throw the match. She says to her that if she beats Jana and the kidnappers still don't release her aunt, they will keep her alive to try and convince Eva not to fight Emily Theron. This makes sense to Eva and any thoughts of throwing the match and dying to ensure that her aunt is not harmed, soon disappears from her thoughts. All her focus is on winning this match.

With only minutes to go before their fight, both Eva and Jana are naked and covered in oil. They are waiting with their seconds, Lea and Janet for the signal to enter the lifts. Nancy has arranged that Lea and Janet will watch the fight from the couch next to the host. She hopes that this will create some tension between them and that she may be able to use this in future. She thinks that a death match between them will increase the ratings as it will have a nice background story. The two seconds of ex-lovers who fought in the pit, facing each other in the same pit, will surely make the headline news. The lights go green and the two fighters leave their change rooms and enter the lifts. When the doors close, Lea and Janet make their way down to the couch. They meet up just outside the area where the host sits. They glare at each other, both believing that the other is backing the person who has used her friend and who caused this death match. An assistant quickly gets between them and escorts them onto the set. They sit down next to each other on the couch and both are very uncomfortable with this. Nancy instructs the producer to focus on them on a regular basis and to save footage of them for later use.

The lift doors open and the two naked fighters get out on either side of the divider. The former best friends and lovers see each other for the first time in two months and both can see the hatred and focus in the other's eyes. The divider starts to move down into the floor slowly and both fighters wait until it is locked before they slowly move towards each other. Jana lands two stiff left jabs and Eva can taste blood on the inside of her bottom lip. She avoids a straight right from Jana by moving her head to the right and answers with an overhead right landing on Jana's cheek and a left to Jana's ribs. Jana steps back to get some distance between them and then moves straight forward and lands a hard right kick to Eva's left thigh. Eva had most of her weight on her left leg as she was about to kick with her right as well, so the kick numbs her thigh muscle. She does not want to show any weakness and tries not to show the pain, but Jana knows that she hurt her and launches another kick to Eva's left thigh. Eva anticipates the kick and moves back enough for Jana's kick to miss her. Jana comes forward again and tries a front kick, which only brushes Eva's tummy on its way down as Eva moves back. Jana resets her balance and kicks again with her right leg, this time connecting with Eva's ribs. She follows this up with a left punch to Eva's jaw and Eva has to take a couple of steps back to remain on her feet. Jana shoots in and tackles Eva to the floor, but Eva manages to twist her body as she goes down and lands on top of Jana She is not balanced though and Jana quickly shoves her off of her. Eva scrambles back to her feet and as Jana is getting to her feet, Eva lands a hard kick to Jana's chest sending her back down to the floor. She tries to jump on top of Jana, but Jana keeps her at bay with her legs. Eva feints to the left and as Jana moves her legs in that direction she moves to her right past Jana's legs and dives on top of her. Eva's upper body pins Jana's upper body and Eva pins Jana's right arm with both her arms, while Jana's left arm is trapped under Eva's body. Jana pulls her left arm free and starts to punch Eva on the side of her body and head. The punches do not have a lot of power behind them, but they are still hurting Eva so she releases the grip on Jana's right arm with her own right hand and uses it to grab hold of Jana's left arm. She is now pinning both Jana's arms and she tries to move her left leg over Jana's body to gain full mount. Jana defends this well and traps Eva's left leg between her thighs. Eva moves her body towards Jana's head to try and release her left leg, but Jana counters this by moving her own body backwards, all the time making sure that she maintains her hold on Eva's left leg. Eva is frustrated by this and tries to headbutt Jana, but she is not high enough and only manages to hit Jana's chest. She realises that they are close to the wall and moves her body up again and Jana counters again, but the moment Jana's shoulders are pressed up against the wall, she is no longer able to counter and Eva manages to move her body upwards until her head is level with Jana's head. Jana knows what Eva is planning and she tries to push her head into Eva's chest to ensure that there is not enough space for a headbutt. When Eva pulls her upper body away, Jana twists hers to the right and they roll over ending up facing each other on their sides. Eva still holds on to Jana's wrists and her left leg is no longer trapped by Jana. She pulls her legs in and quickly gets to her knees and pushes Jana back onto her back before she swings her right leg over Jana's body. She has full mount at last and she has control over Jana's arms. Jana brings up a knee and hits Eva in the back. She repeats this twice more before Eva moves forward and uses her knees to pin Jana's arms. She starts to punch Jana in the face and Jana is only able to move her head about to try and avoid some of the punches. She also tries to hit Eva with her knees, but Eva's body is too far forward for her to do any damage. She tries to twist her body to dislodge Eva, but Eva's balance is good and she does not budge. Eva keeps landing punches and Jana knows that she is in trouble. She is almost out of options and the damage to her face is getting worse with every punch Eva lands. She has cuts above her left eye and on her right cheek, her left eye is almost swollen closed and she thinks her nose is broken and it is bleeding freely. She has to defend herself or Eva will be able to knock her out and kill her at her leisure. She puts all her concentration into freeing her left arm and with all her power she manages to pull it from under Eva's knee. She covers her face with her free arm, but it is not enough to block all the punches. Then she sees her only chance to get out of this predicament. She grabs hold of Eva's clit and pulls and twists at the same time. Eva's body reacts to this before she can think about it. She pulls back and Jana is able to free her right arm as well. She tries to grab Eva's clit again and Eva moves back even further, allowing Jana to hit her with a knee. Eva falls forward and Jana grabs her around the neck and rolls her off of her. Eva rolls away from Jana and gets back to her feet. This time Jana makes it back to her feet before Eva is in a position to kick her again. Jana is unstable on her feet and she is losing a lot of blood from her broken nose. She knows that she will have to do something soon, or she will definitely lose the match. She moves forward and throws a straight right, but the punch is slow and Eva avoids it and lands a right elbow to the bridge of Jana's nose. Jana stumbles back and a hard right kick to her solar plexus sends her crashing backwards, her head hitting the wall and she slumps to the floor, unconscious from the impact on the back of her head. Janet is beside herself and only the reactions of one of the assistants stop her from jumping into the pit. Eva walks over to Jana and lifts her upper body upright. She folds her legs around Jana's middle and locks her ankles, before she puts her left arm across Jana's throat and locks it with her right arm. However, she does not apply any pressure on Jana's throat. Instead, she waits until Jana regains consciousness before she applies some pressure. With her mouth next to Jana's ear, she whispers. 'Where is my aunt?'

Jana turns her head towards Eva's face and they look each other in the eye. Eva can see the confusion in Jana's face and asks her again. 'Where is my aunt?'

Jana still looks puzzled. 'I don't know, why are you looking for your aunt?'

'Did you have her kidnapped?'

'No.'

Eva realises that Jana knows nothing about her aunt's kidnapping. She hears Janet calling her name and she looks up and sees the devastation in Janet's face. She releases Jana and steps away from her. She looks up at the host. 'I am the clear winner and I choose not to kill my opponent.'

Everybody is silent, except Jana. She is barely audible. 'I am not done yet.'

She is back on her feet and is barely able to stand, but she takes a few steps towards Eva, who gently wrestles her down to the floor. 'Stop it, I do not want to kill you.'

'No, I will not stop until you promise me that you will not fight my mother.'

Eva is conflicted between her absolute desire to revenge her mother's death and her love for Jana. Her head is clear now and she knows that Jana had nothing to do with her aunt's kidnapping. Maybe Jana played her all along to stop her from killing her mother, but can she blame her for that. She would do the same if she was in Jana's shoes. She would do anything to protect her mother. She looks up at a crying Janet and then at Lea, who shakes her head. 'Don't do it Eva, don't kill your friend.'

Eva still wants to kill Emily Theron, but she cannot kill Jana. She looks back at Jana. 'I promise you that I won't kill your mother.'

Jana tries to smile at her, but passes out again. Eva gets up and waits for the doctor to enter the pit, but she does not move. Nancy has instructed the host not to allow any help for Jana and the doctor is following these instructions. However, one of the medical staff ignores this and jumps into the pit. She starts to examine Jana and shouts to the doctor that Jana needs to get to a hospital without delay. The doctor reacts to this and she and the rest of the medical staff also jump into the pit. However, the lifts are not lowered. Lea grabs Janet by the arm and they run off the set and upstairs to the control unit. They are followed by two women, who Eva later finds out are off duty police officers. A few moments later the lifts both come down and the medical staff loads Jana in one lift and rushes her to the nearest hospital where doctors are able to stabilise her. She has lost a lot of blood from her busted nose and has a serious concussion. Although her condition is stable, it is still critical.

As Eva gets in the other lift, she realises for the first time that the whole studio audience are on their feet applauding the fighters. They did not get the death they were anticipating, but they saw one of the most brutal and hard fought matches any of them have witnessed. The drama at the end also captured their imaginations and they all have a feeling of euphoria. After all this excitement, they can only hope that the final of the second tournament is half as good as the celebrity match.

Chapter 30 – Rebuilding

Eva gets dressed as fast as she can. She wants to go to the hospital to see whether Jana is ok, but she cannot as she needs to find her aunt. She is not sure whether the people who have her will harm her because she did not kill Jana. She goes to the nearest police station and explains her concerns to the officer who assists her. The officer looks on the system, but finds no kidnapping case involving Eva's aunt. They also have no record of the police officer who was supposedly investigating the case. The officer takes all the detail and promises to get as many officers as possible on the case. When one of them visits Nancy to view the tape, she tells them that she is not aware of any tape and that she never had any discussions with Eva about her aunt being kidnapped. The psychologist confirms this and mentions to the investigators that Eva has been under a lot of stress due to her participation in the death matches.

The police finds Eva's aunt's body in an ally behind a bar early the next morning. The bar owner tells them that she has been drinking heavily the previous night and that she has been involved in a few scuffles during the night. She cannot remember what time she left exactly, but it was after midnight. The crime lab confirms the high alcohol levels and finds that she was stabbed in the heart. She does not have any jewellery on or any handbag with her. Her car is parked half a block away and the police conclude that she got drunk and was robbed on her way back to her car. They cannot find any evidence to collaborate Eva's story. Eva tries to confront Nancy, but she is unable to get hold of her. Olga also tells her that because of her failure to kill Jana and her withdrawal of her challenge to fight Emily Theron, Nancy has kicked her out of the academy. She gives her an hour to gather her stuff. Confused and heartbroken by her aunt's murder, Eva calls a taxi and goes to the biker bar. She has nowhere to stay as she does not want to move into her aunt's home and she struggles to cope with the guilt of getting her aunt killed and of almost killing Jana. Helga agrees to put her up for a few nights until she can find her own place.

Two days later Eva buries her aunt and the only friend of Eva's to turn up in order to support her is Lea. She is sad about her aunt's death and sad that she lost most of her closest friends and she decides to go to the nearest pub after the funeral. Lea wants to go with her, but Eva tells her that she needs to be alone. She stumbles out of the pub at about four in the morning and when she eventually manages to find a taxi, she cannot remember where she stays. They drive around for a while until she recognises the biker bar. When the taxi leaves, she realises that the bar is closed and that there are nobody there anymore. She is too tired too worry about it and she falls asleep resting her head against the bar's door. The police pick her up about thirty minutes later and take her to the holding cells for her own protection and to sleep it off. When Eva wakes up she is totally confused. She shares a prison cell with another woman, who is still sleeping. She cannot remember how she got here, or what she has done in order to be arrested. Did Jana die? Was she arrested because

Jana died? It cannot be, it was a legal fight and she did not kill Jana, even though she could have. She calls out and after a while a burly guard appears. She looks at Eva with disdain.
'What do you want?'
'Why am I here? What have I done?'
'You were drunk and sleeping on the street.'
Eva is relieved to hear that she wasn't arrested for something serious. 'I buried my aunt yesterday and I tried to drown my sorrows. How long do I have to stay here?'
The guard's expression softens. 'You can leave as soon as you feel up to it. You are only here for your own protection. I will get the paperwork ready and you can leave after we signed you out and returned your belongings.'
Eva follows the guard to the front desk where the guard hands her a sealed envelope with her things in it. She opens it and quickly realises that the stuff inside are not hers, but then she sees her aunt's necklace. She will recognise the pendant anywhere as she had it custom made for her aunt. She opens the pendant and the photo of her and her mother inside confirms what she already knew. 'This is my aunt's necklace.' The guard only gives her a sympathetic smile. 'No, you don't understand, you gave me the wrong envelope and my aunt's necklace is in it. She was murdered a few days ago and all her jewellery was taken. Now her necklace is in this envelope. Her murderer must be here.'
The guard calls one of the investigators and she interviews Eva's cellmate, but she does not remember much, only that a handbag was thrown from a passing car and that she went through the handbag and sold everything inside, except for this necklace. She saw the photo inside and thought that she might get more for it from the owner, than from a pawnshop. She takes police to where she left the empty handbag and also to the pawn shops where she sold the rest of the jewellery. Police recover the jewellery, but do not find any further clues. Their investigation soon goes cold again.

That evening Eva finally musters the courage to go visit Jana in hospital. She still does not know what to say to Jana when she enters her room, but she has to try to make things right between them. Jana is asleep, but a woman sitting next to her bed begs Eva to come in. 'She will be out for a while as they gave her sleeping pills about twenty minutes ago. You must be Eva. I am Jana's mother, Emily Theron.'
Eva is totally taken by surprise and just stares at Emily. She has no words and does not know how to react.
'I know this is awkward, but can we put our differences apart for now until Jana has recovered. She needs all of us and especially you. She has been asking for you when she was fighting for her life that night after your fight. She now says that she never wants to see you again, but I know she still loves you. It won't be easy, but the two of you have to work this out, don't allow your friendship to be destroyed because you are both too proud to admit that you both made mistakes. Many things happened and I know that there is not a lot of trust at the moment, but I don't believe most of the stuff she thinks you have done. I know that you still have feelings for her as you saved her life. I will be forever indebted to you for that. I also know that I have caused you a lot of pain and I am still willing to pay for that. Please just allow me some time with Jana until she is strong enough to carry on

without me.'

'I promised Jana that I will not fight you and I will keep that promise, but I still hate you for what you have done to my mother. I will come back another day.'

'I understand. I will tell Jana you were here.'

A few days later, while Eva is busy looking at a flat to move into, Jenny phones her. She does not mention the death match at all, but tells Eva that she is very sorry to hear about her aunt's death. The reason she calls is that the hockey teams have asked her to organise another fund raiser, this time they want fights between them and the netball teams and they want a variety of fighting styles. They are prepared to pay Jenny twenty percent of the funds raised if she organises the event and trains the fighters. Jenny wants Eva to help her with this and thinks that if this event is a success, she may turn organising fund raiser fighting events into a business. Eva has decided not to be involved with fights anymore, but this sounds like fun and she needs something to take her mind off everything else that is happening to her, so she agrees to help Jenny.

When Eva moves in to her own place, she invites her friends for a housewarming. However, only Lea, Jenny, Helga and some of the bikers pitch up. Reka and Amelia confirmed, but cancelled shortly before the party started as Amelia was not feeling well. Jana is out of hospital, but she does not want to see Eva. Janet also made it clear that she does not want to see Eva and Margaret told her that she has to give the two of them time and that she will make sure that Eva gets a chance to sit down with Jana and then with Janet so that they can try to clear the air. She also decided not to come to the party as this would put too much strain on her relationship with Jana and Janet. Eva understands this and thanks Margaret for being a good friend. The night of the party Eva has a long discussion with Helga and as a result of what they discussed, she hires a private investigator to find out what happened to her aunt. She is sure Nancy had something to do with her murder, but she needs proof.

Epilogue

Eva has spent a big part of her life planning her revenge on Emily Theron. Her love for Jana has taken this away from her and she feels empty without a cause to live for. She blames herself for the death of her aunt and she needs to get prove of Nancy's involvement in her aunt's murder so that she can make sure that justice is served for her aunt's murder.

She also lost three of her closest friends and although she will fight to get their friendship back, she is not sure that she will be successful. Jana and Janet do not trust Eva as they both believe that she used Jana to ensure that she would be able to fight Jana's mother. Eva needs time and the help of Margaret to win back their trust and respect.

The new venture she is about to start with Jenny excites Eva and it gives her some distraction from all the issues she is facing, but will this stand in the way of a potential reconciliation with Jana.

In book two we follow Eva's journey into adulthood and her quest to not only revenge her aunt's murder, but also to make sure that the women who were actually responsible for her mother's death are punished. Although she does not want to be involved in fights anymore, she may have to get back in the ring in order to finally ensure justice for her mother and aunt

∞

Thank you for reading my first book. If you enjoyed it, won't you please take a moment to leave me a review at your favourite retailer?

Thanks
Joe Smith.

Lightning Source UK Ltd.
Milton Keynes UK
UKHW050214091019
351185UK00008BA/562/P

9 780368 171048